Books by Julieanne Lynch

Single Titles

Unbreak Me

Unbreak Me

ISBN #978-1-78651-345-8

©Copyright Julieanne Lynch 2016

Cover Art by Posh Gosh ©Copyright 2016

Interior text design by Claire Siemaszkiewicz

Totally Bound Publishing

Published in 2016 by Totally Bound Publishing, Newland House, The Point, Weaver Road, Lincoln, LN6 3QN, United Kingdom.

UNBREAK ME

JULIEANNE LYNCH

Dedication

For Gladys

Prologue

"Keep love in your heart. A life without it is like a sunless garden when the flowers are dead."
~ Oscar Wilde

The ache always got her best when she stood by the grave. Emptiness like no other, and she often wondered if she'd ever find something to fill the void, to replace the pain with a life enriched and worth living. Bowing her head, she took in the sight of the wilting petals of last week's flowers blowing as the wind crept up around her feet and she sighed. It was a ritual, one that she promised herself, one that made more sense to her, none to others. But she was determined not to let herself forget the kindness or words of wisdom delivered by the old woman who now lay in eternal sleep six feet below.

Life had been hard for Molly Rice. Not your average kind of hardship, but the kind of upbringing that meant survival was her main priority. Everything else took second place on her agenda. Had it not been for the kindness of Aggie Morella, it would have been Molly lying in that grave.

Bending down, she took out the dead flowers and replaced the small pot with a fresh bouquet of carnations, and she smiled.

"Just the way you like them, Aggie," she said as she kissed her fingertips before laying her hand on the small gray headstone. "Sleep well, my friend."

It was always at this point in her weekly visit when the reality became too much to bear. She knew that going back to the empty apartment left more time for thinking, and thinking was itself a curse.

Taking the long route back to her small apartment in the city, she reveled in the setting sun and smiled as the shadows danced across the bridge. Just every so often she found herself in awe of life, all the beauty that surrounded her, and craved having her own slice of heaven.

Things, of course, never did go the way she planned and on that fateful night in May, she'd never see things the way she once had. The journey that would follow would open up her heart, mind and soul to the true splendor of life.

Not once in her lifetime had she ever imagined that she would be the one stepping up to the plate and intervening.

Sometimes there was no explaining life.

Chapter One

Connor smashed his fist into the steering wheel. He swore as he hyperventilated. There were some things in life that pissed him off more than others. His father being one of them.

"Fuck!" he roared as he slammed his fists down time and time again until he finally stopped, looked up from the wheel and stared out of the windshield. The heavy traffic coming in the opposite direction blurred his vision, the adrenaline still pumping, fresh from his confrontation with the people who tried to control his every move.

He shook his head. He found it hard to see any way out of it. He'd messed up big this time, and his father wasn't going to let him forget any time soon.

His phone rang, pulling him out of his harangue of abuse. He looked down and saw the caller ID flash *Mom* and swore. "Fuck!"

Connor knew there'd be more hell to pay if he ignored her, so he answered and braced himself for whatever the woman felt like delivering.

"Hello, Mother." He sighed as he ran his hand over the back of his head. "Yes, I'm pretty aware… No, he did not… Mom, please, just give me a break. I've already had it from him. I said I was sorry… No, I didn't do it on purpose. God, do you really think I'm that incompetent?" The frustration was beginning to burn deep in his stomach. "You know what, I've got to go."

Connor threw the phone into the back of the car. He let out a long breath before opening the door and getting out. Much to the annoyance of other drivers, who sounded their horns at him, cars swerving trying not to hit his car. People roared and shouted obscenities at him.

He stood on the verge of the road, and jumped over the barrier onto the pedestrian pathway. The wind hit him hard, taking his breath away.

He paced up and down the pathway and tried to ignore the anger welling inside him. The disappointment he felt in himself for losing such a big investment and the fact that half the board would be gunning for him and his immediate termination added to his growing trepidation.

"I can't do this anymore," he whispered to himself as he looked out over the bay. The last remaining rays of sunlight began to die, leaving him standing in the twilight of what remained of his day, the numbness kicking in.

He'd been battling the unease for a long while. Pretending to everyone around him that he was fine, but all the while dying a little each day. His job sucked the life out him. It had killed whatever get-up-and-go he once had, and he was done.

It's now or never, he thought as he touched the cool cable, looking down over the metal, into the water below. "I'll never be free," he said as the noise of the traffic became distorted, replaced by the sound of his beating heart. "I just need to sleep."

Connor pulled himself up onto the ledge of the bridge and over to the parapet. He held the cable as he looked down, feeling a wave of relief wash over him.

"I can't do this anymore," he muttered to himself as a tear slipped down over his cheek and he let go of the cable.

He closed his eyes, as he stood with his hands by his side. Warmth replaced the cold trembling sensation that had overtaken him mere moments before. He felt at ease with his decision to end his life, and there was no going back, not at that point.

"Seriously," a voice came from behind him. "You, in your flashy suit and fancy car, are going to jump?"

Connor opened his eyes and reached for the cable. Cocking

his head to the side, he saw a pretty brunette leaning over the cold metal, looking at him as if he were nuts.

"Please leave me alone," he replied, clearly annoyed by her interference.

"Sorry, mister, but no can do," she said as she looked at him with pity in her eyes.

He didn't want her pity, and he sure as hell didn't need it. None of what he had planned was about gaining any sympathy. He was the one who had fucked up, and he was the one who'd planned months ago how he wanted to end it all.

"Please, just leave me alone."

"I don't think so. Nothing can be that bad that you're going to jump. Do you have any idea how the water alone will break your bones, possibly killing you before you get a chance to drown. Like seriously, it's not a painless way to go."

"I don't need the specifics. I just need you to go," Connor replied, refusing her attempts at stopping him from taking his life.

"Well, I'm sorry but you're stuck with me until the police get here," she said, smiling at him as he gave her a horrified look.

"Oh my God, seriously? You called the authorities?"

"Of course, nothing is that bad in life that you have to end it all. Do you want me to call anyone? A relative? A friend?"

"There's no one," Connor muttered as his stomach twisted itself into knots.

"There has got be someone."

"Afraid not."

"Then talk to me. I can be a good shoulder," the girl said. "I'm Molly, and I stood where you once stand. Well, not the exact spot, but I was desperate, too, once upon a time ago." She was sincere as she spoke.

Connor wasn't interested in swapping stories. He just wanted to do what he intended to do, but Molly wasn't having any of it.

"So…what happened? What pushed you over the edge — no pun intended?" she asked as she rested her arms on the steel of the bridge.

Connor stared at the water seventy meters below and closed his eyes. How could he tell a stranger his deepest, darkest feelings? The things that kept him up at night, the stuff that no one knew. How could he possibly let a stranger in on the real reason behind his breakdown?

"You wouldn't understand," he whispered as he lost himself for a moment.

He swayed from side to side and felt the urge to jump. A sensation that drowned out the noise from the wailing sirens of the police cars, a helicopter hovering from above and the reasoning coming from Molly.

"Hey… C'mon now, don't do this," Molly shouted, trying to get his attention. "Besides, do you really want this all over the news? I mean, take a look. You're getting a lot of attention — the wrong kind, I might add."

Before Molly got the chance to continue her 'talking him down' routine, an officer approached her. "Excuse me, miss, can you please step aside."

Molly obliged and retreated back to where the other bystanders stood, gasping, their cameras flashing.

Connor knew some of the footage would end up on YouTube, or flying around other social networks. It was a casualty of the times.

Connor wasn't impressed with the influx of attention. In fact, he intended on finding the girl who had stepped in, stealing his thunder and turning his world upside down.

How he was going to explain this to his parents was beyond anything he'd planned for. No doubt things were going to be a lot uglier, especially since he was the reason for Ellison Enterprises losing their multimillion merger deal with Lanscorp.

"Why can't life be fucking simple?" he muttered to himself as officers helped him across the parapet. The flashes of cameras, lights from oncoming traffic and the look of sympathy from everyone who met his gaze made his head ache.

A gun to the head would have been a better option, he decided as he was led to the back of a waiting ambulance and rushed off to the hospital.

All in a day's work.

Chapter Two

Molly was determined to find out if the mysterious stranger was okay. She wouldn't have been able to sleep a wink knowing that he was so close to ending it all. This was typical of Molly. She could never walk away from someone else's plight. That was something she'd learned from spending time with Aggie. In a sense, she was carrying on Aggie's missionary work, and although she enjoyed it, she found it draining.

Molly jumped into her small car and followed the ambulance, trying her best to look inconspicuous and not at all like a loon, or a journalist desperate for a story.

The Golden Gate Bridge was notorious for jumpers and for some reason each one always made headline news, and this pissed her off more than anything. Even with the call box that led straight to the suicide hotline, there was always a jumper or two who was determined to end their lives. All the attention gave suicide this glamorized image, and there was nothing glamorous about taking one's own life.

She parked a block away from St. Francis Memorial and walked the remainder of the way. Blending in well with the other vagabonds in her beat-up jeans, checked shirt and messy hair made her feel invisible, and she preferred it this way. She didn't have to impress anyone and remained completely at ease with her anonymity.

Molly slipped into the ER unnoticed. It was easy. She knew the place well and had spent a bit of time here in her younger days, but preferred to not revisit those times. They were now bad memories, locked away, never to be spoken of.

Molly followed two police officers she recognized from the bridge and continued to blend in with the local surroundings as she eavesdropped outside a side ward.

The two officers walked back out after taking a statement and were followed by a doctor and nurse, both lost in hushed conversation. Peering in through the crack of the door, she saw the man sitting up on the bed, staring down at his hands, as though life had just beaten the crap out of him.

Molly swallowed hard as she pushed the door open and walked in.

"Hey," she said, twisting her hands in awkward movement.

He glanced up and didn't seem at all pleased that she was there.

"You!" he muttered. "Thanks for destroying everything."

"Oh gee, you're welcome—not," Molly replied with a tone of sarcasm. Walking over to the bed, she looked at the well-dressed man, taking in his demeanor and the fact that he looked as if he were going to burst into tears at any given moment. "I'm sorry," she said. "I had to call them. I mean, if you had died on my watch, I'd have never forgiven myself."

"You don't even know me."

"Nope, I don't, but that doesn't mean I don't value life," she replied as she reached out her hand to him. "I'm Molly Rice, nice to meet you."

Connor stared at her, raising his eyebrows. He took her hand and replied, "I'm Connor."

"See, that wasn't so hard, was it?"

Molly smiled and popped her hands into the pockets of her jeans and felt a little bit odd standing there in front of Connor, who was now looking up at her, observing her every movement.

"So, do you make it a daily thing, saving guys from jumping?"

"Erm, no, but I try to make sure that if I see someone in

need, I can help them in some way or another. You just happened to be in my sights tonight."

"You're a modern-day good Samaritan, huh?"

"I wouldn't go as far as saying that, but there was a time when I needed the help of another. Take it from me, there are still some decent people in this world." Molly smiled. "Anyway, I just came by to make sure you were okay. So, I guess, good luck, and talk—for the love of God, try to talk about whatever is going on."

Without saying another word, Molly left the room and disappeared. She was content knowing that Connor was in good hands. Her conscience was at ease, which was a huge plus considering her stress levels had been pretty toxic before seeing the handsome guy so willing to jump.

* * * *

Molly stood under the water for a good twenty minutes and washed the day's events from her. She looked forward to her cup of cocoa and the latest Nicholas Sparks novel. There was something so simple, yet luxurious, about losing herself in a good book and daydreaming. She'd come a long way from the illiterate, scrawny, starving girl Aggie had saved.

As she sat down on her couch, she topped her hot chocolate with a little extra cream and savored the first sip. Closing her eyes, emptiness washing over her, she began to cry. Why? She had no idea, but sometimes, every so often, Molly allowed herself to absorb too much. And given the evening's events, one would hazard a guess and assume that saving Connor from a rather nasty death had gotten under her skin.

Molly had never intended on being anyone's savior. In fact, she was so hell-bent on just shuffling through life, remaining invisible to all those around her, that any attention she got made her feel quite disjointed. Aggie had placed much blame on Molly's parents, who'd failed miserably at raising their only child, leaving her to fend for herself. Of course, Aggie's opinions weren't meant to come across as mean, but every so often, being reminded of her damaged roots hurt Molly in more ways than Aggie realized.

Molly let out a long sigh, closed the book and sat in silence, rubbing the tears from her eyes.

"You stupid dork," she muttered to herself as she tried hard to control the sobs choking her, not wanting to awaken Regina, Aggie's longtime life partner and now Molly's main source of support. She hated how emotional she became. She felt like an alien lost in her feelings and despised the fact that she just couldn't rid herself of her demons, those nasty little picture-perfect nightmares that had scarred her for life.

Life in the Rice household had been far from ideal. By the time she was two years old, Molly had already been admitted into hospital more than seven times. All at the hands of her abusive father who took pleasure in burning his little girl's scalp with cigarette butts. Social workers had placed her in temporary foster care, only for the courts to grant access to her parents, who in turn continued their tirade of abuse and neglect. Until finally at thirteen years old, she'd run away, taking refuge on the streets.

The way Molly saw it, anything was better than being beaten, made to take drugs just for her father to take advantage of her young body, not to mention her mother, who refused to feed her, often accusing her own child of seducing a grown man.

It was an upbringing that made her recoil from the advances of men. It wasn't that she was a prude, but trust was something she didn't give easily. But who could blame her? She had been lost for nearly ten years before Aggie had found her lying unconscious, malnourished and on the brink of death.

Being taken in by a complete stranger and nursed back to health was something Molly would be forever thankful for.

It restored her faith in mankind and made her hopeful for her future. Now she was intent on fulfilling her dream—moving from the city and setting up roots somewhere new.

The phone rang and she jolted up straight. "Who in hell?" she complained as she reached for the phone, picking up the receiver.

"Hello?" she said as she sat back on her couch, pulling her blanket around her shoulders. "Oh, yeah, sorry about that, I got tied up... No, everything is good... Jenna, I'm fine. Yeah, I can do that... Ten a.m., on the plaza! Okay, thank you. Goodnight."

As Molly rested her head back on the cushions, she was thankful to have someone like Jenna in her life. Having a sponsor who cared enough to keep her on the straight and narrow was enough for Molly to accept that there were more good people in the world than bad.

Molly looked over at the picture frame on the side table and smiled. Her, Aggie and Regina together, a huge cake in front of the old white-haired women and pure joy on their faces. That had been taken before the cancer had robbed the woman of her gusto. But Molly smiled. It was a good memory and one she'd take with her wherever she would settle down. "You done good, Aggie," she mumbled as her eyes locked on the face of her savior, and before she knew it, she had drifted off to sleep. That beautiful secure place where none of her demons could touch her.

Peace.

Chapter Three

"What kind of stunt were you trying to pull?" John Ellison stormed at his son, who sat at the large dining table, staring into his cold coffee, defeated by life. "What were you trying to prove? Surely you have something to offer me? Life can't be that bad that you felt it necessary to even consider such an act. Did it ever occur to you that we'd be devastated?" His father's eyes glazed over, but clearing his throat, he looked away.

"How could you drag our good name into such a scandal?" Connor's mother, Eleanor, said as she looked at her son with disgust. "We need Patrick to smooth this over with the press," she said to her husband, who was refilling his glass with Scotch. "Not to mention the damage already done with the failure of closure on the Lanscorp deal. Have you any idea what your childish attention seeking has done? Did you ever think of anyone other than yourself?"

It was bubbling beneath the surface. Anger ready to burst through his seams and he didn't care. He had had enough. How could he continue living under their rule, having them control every inch of his life? He hated everything his family name represented, and was done.

"I guess I'm done," Connor replied.

"You're done?" John scowled at his son. "That makes it okay because you're done."

"Yeah, done, as in fuck you, and fuck her," Connor said as he stood, scraping the chair from behind him as he turned his back on his parents. His outburst was directed at his mother, but he despised his father's refusal to step up and tell her to pipe down. It had always been this way, his mother being the dominant one, his father the one with a noose around his neck.

"You're done when we say so, and until then, you'd do well to remember how we'd cut you off in a split second. You've got it good, boy, don't be a fool." John met his son with a cold glare.

"How can you be so selfish?" Eleanor interrupted John.

"How can either of you call yourself parents?" Connor asked as he shook his head. "Sometimes I wonder why I even bother sticking around."

"Get your ass back here now, Connor Ellison," Eleanor shouted.

Connor walked away from the confrontation, slamming the front door behind him, and never looked back once as he made his way to his car.

Connor had been raised in prosperous Pacific Heights, but he hated everything his wealth represented. There were more skeletons lurking in his father's closest. He had seen firsthand the depths to which his parents would go to make sure the press never caught on to any of the scandals. Especially when some of his father's mistresses had promised revenge for their brief dalliances.

Connor didn't want any of it. He knew from the first day he was introduced into his family's billion-dollar corporation that he couldn't cut it. He wasn't ruthless enough or spoiled enough to do the dirty deeds that were required of him. Tearing other companies down and destroying dreams wasn't his kind of game at all, but it was expected of him. After all, he was an Ellison, and business and blood were cut from the same cloth.

Connor was thirty-one years of age and anyone would have thought he'd have grown a backbone by now, but just like his brother—a whole other level of fucked up—everything in his prominent world was controlled.

Connor switched on the stereo, turned the music up loud and drowned out his thoughts as he drove away from the place that reminded him of everything that turned his stomach.

With his shades on, he drove in the early morning sun, trying his best to pretend he was someone other than who he was.

He failed miserably.

* * * *

Connor walked into his apartment, threw his keys onto the side dresser and headed straight for the refrigerator for a beer. It wasn't even nine a.m., but he had come not to give a damn. He knew he was in a bad place. The pile of paperwork stacked on his home office desk was a telltale sign that things were getting on top of him. Finding the motivation to do the simplest of tasks was now beginning to feel as if he were climbing a mountain. He just wanted to sleep, let the whole pain die. And if he was lucky enough, he'd slip off without anyone noticing.

Connor was frustrated by his parents' refusal to accept that there was something wrong with him. To make matters worse, he was pissed with himself for not doing something about it sooner. It was a recipe for disaster. But now things had changed drastically. The ball was in his court, and there was, of course, the silver lining in all the mess — Molly.

Connor couldn't get her out of his head. No one had ever taken the time to see if he was all right. Not once in his life had anyone shown him the kind of warmth and gentleness that she portrayed in the short moment she was in his company. She was different. She had saved him from his pitiful attempt at suicide and there it was, the little ray of hope.

As he gulped down a mouthful of beer, he knew he had to find her. Even if it was just to thank her, he had to lay to rest that part of their brief encounter and apologize for being a prize dick.

He picked up his cell, dialed a familiar number and waited for his contact at the local police department to answer.

"Hey, can you do me a solid?" he asked as he rubbed his thumb along the neck of his bottle of beer.

"Sure, what's the deal?" a deep male voice asked.

"The girl that made the call, can you trace her?"

"Jeez, man, talk about putting a guy on the spot."

"Eric, it's important." Connor's desperation was evident as he clenched his fists a few times.

"Okay, can you give me a few minutes? I need to make a call or two," Eric said.

"Yeah, I can wait." Connor set the phone on the table, drinking the rest of his beer, wondering about Molly, how things looked from her point of view, then the phone rang.

"Hey," he answered.

"Listen, man, you didn't get this from me, okay?"

"You know this won't get any further. I just want to thank her personally," Connor said as he picked up a pen in anticipation.

"Okay!" Eric replied then gave Connor the cell number.

Connor scribbled down the digits and smiled. "Thanks, Eric."

"Yeah, yeah, you owe me." Then the line went dead.

Connor's stomach began to swarm as he looked at the number. Nervous about making contact with her, he was unsure if it was the right thing to do, but he owed her an apology. In his mind, doing it in person was an honorable move on his behalf.

He swallowed hard, then he dialed the number and waited a few seconds, almost hanging up, when the voice he remembered from the hospital answered.

"Hello!" Molly said.

"Err, hello, Molly, it's Connor," he said, sounding more nervous than he planned.

"Connor?"

"Yeah, the guy from the bridge."

"Yeah, I remember. What can I do for you?"

Connor paused for a second and became lightheaded. "I just wanted to thank you for what you did last night."

"Oh, it was nothing. Honestly. I'd have done it for anyone. I'm just glad you didn't...you know, jump."

"Yeah, about that... I'm sorry for putting you in that position." He ran his hand over his face, feeling worse than he had before he called her.

"There's no need for an apology. Life's a bitch."

"You got that right."

Connor sat back on his couch. He looked up at the ceiling as he listened to the lovely lilt in her voice. He didn't remember her sounding so musical before, but now he was mesmerized.

"I don't mean to be rude, but I've really got to go. I've got a meeting in less than an hour, so—" Molly said, sounding pretty apologetic.

"Oh, of course, absolutely. I just wanted to thank you, that's all," Connor said as his cheeks went a little pink.

"No worries."

"Hey, before you go, would there be any chance of meeting in person?"

There it was. He'd asked.

A little silence followed his question before she replied, "Err, I don't know."

"I promise I'm not a weirdo. I would just like to meet you, maybe get a bite to eat, nothing serious," he said as he sat upright, resting his elbow on his knee.

"I don't know." Molly sounded nervous.

"If it's a problem, I understand. No pressure."

"Okay," Molly replied, sounding a little shy. "When?"

"Today?"

"Well, I... I have a meeting at ten, but we could do lunch?" Molly suggested.

Connor's heart pounded hard as he jumped to his feet. The butterflies began multiplying. "Sounds good. Do you know Chouquet's on Washington Street?"

"I do," Molly replied.

"Midday?"

"Okay. I'll see you then," Molly said before hanging up.

Connor slid the phone into his pocket and went into the bathroom. He looked in the mirror. He was excited about the prospect of seeing Molly, but cringed at the thought of how he'd come across as a complete asshole in the hospital. But at the moment, he knew it was the chance meeting of a lifetime and he didn't want to risk anything.

He had to prove to himself that there was more to life than the façade he'd been living.

Chapter Four

Molly raced to her closet and rummaged through the not so fancy attire that left a lot to be desired. Biting on her bottom lip, she cringed as she tried to choose something that would make her look a little bit decent, especially since she had never set foot in Chouquet's — it wasn't the kind of place her meager salary allowed her to dine — but she was still intent on looking presentable. She was still in shock from the phone call, but it was a lovely surprise, and one she welcomed.

She settled on a little floral dress she'd picked up in a thrift store, applied a little gloss and wore her hair loose. She wasn't much for plastering her face with makeup and preferred her flat shoes to heels, but she smiled as she saw her reflection.

"That'll do," she remarked as she grabbed her bag and keys, and made her way to her meeting with Jenna.

Union Square plaza was buzzing with people shopping at the market, while others took in the sights of the historic statues. Then there were those sitting on the benches, playing board games — checkers being a firm favorite.

Jenna sat at their usual place, hunched over a paper. Her right hand held on to the paper coffee cup from a local Starbucks, and there was another coffee cup waiting for Molly.

"Anything interesting?" Molly asked as she sat down across from the fine-looking woman.

Jenna looked up from her paper and smiled. "Not if you call local rich kid suicide attempt news."

Molly grinned, but didn't bother filling her on the details

that she was the one to stop the local rich kid from killing himself.

"And that there is the reason why I don't do tabloids or newspapers of any sort. Silly speculation," she complained, then asked, "How've you been?"

"Ah, I've been good. But more to the point, how have you been? You missed our last meeting." Jenna made it a point of letting her know that her absence had been noted.

"Well, I haven't fallen off the bandwagon if that's what you're worried about." Molly lifted the coffee and sipped at the vanilla latte.

"Just had to make sure," Jenna said, raising her eyebrows as she looked at her. "How's work?"

"Work is good. Tiresome, but good."

"By the way, you look great today. Any plans?"

Molly tried not to smile too much, so she bit down on her bottom lip and shrugged. "Just having lunch with someone."

That got Jenna's attention. "Oh, really?"

"Nah, not telling you." Molly laughed. "Besides, it's nothing, just lunch."

"That's what I said when Barry asked me out nineteen years ago," Jenna joked. Her warm smile was infectious, and Molly never felt more at ease.

Jenna Saunders had been Molly's sponsor for the past two years. She'd been sober for the best part of those two years, with only a temporary setback when Aggie died, which in essence meant her sober time had started all over again. It had been tough for her, but Jenna and her husband Barry had proved their worth in gold and stepped up when they were needed.

Molly had thought going cold turkey was something she'd never live through, but just like had Jenna promised, she had made it to the other side and come out a little stronger. Still broken, but able to cope with the loss of the woman who'd restored her faith in mankind.

"So who is he?" Jenna asked.

"What's to say it isn't a she?"

"Well, you're wearing a dress. I've never seen you in a dress, so I'm guessing you want to make a good impression, right?"

"Maybe, maybe not," Molly teased.

Molly sipped a little more coffee and observed a couple standing near one of the small stalls, holding hands, kissing each other every so often. She felt a pang of jealousy. It was odd because she had never envied lovers in the past, but this meeting with Connor was opening up her mind to the potential, and while it excited her, she felt nervous.

Molly looked away from them and saw that Jenna had been watching her.

"What?" she asked in defense.

"Just make sure you look after yourself."

"It's only lunch, not a marriage proposal," she was quick to respond.

"Ah, so it is a man." Jenna winked at her.

"Very funny, dork." Molly smiled, rolling her eyes at the comment.

"You know I'm only messing, but I did promise Aggie I'd be looking out for you, so I guess you're stuck with my interfering ways," Jenna said. Her warm manner always eased her anxiety.

"I know," Molly replied. "I really miss her."

"I know you do, sweetie."

Molly fought back the tears and cleared her throat, inhaling deeply before looking up at Jenna, who knew all too well the effect Aggie's death had had on her.

"It's just hard sometimes. There are constant reminders in the apartment. I can't bear to go into her room. I feel like it will be the death of me. Poor Regina looks so lost, and it reminds me of the void that we both have."

"Then don't go in. Leave it. It's still early days, and the last thing you and Regina need is dealing with packing up her belongings, reopening those wounds and crashing," Jenna said as she reached out across the table. "And we both know Aggie would be pissed if she thought you were torturing yourself. Besides, Regina needs you probably more than you need her."

Molly nodded. She straightened her back and sat upright. Looking at her watch, she saw the time and that's when the little sensation began to build in her stomach.

"Nervous?" Jenna asked.

"Slightly."

"Just breathe and you will be fine."

"Easier said than done, Jenna."

"Listen, you're a beautiful woman, Molly. You deserve a little happiness in your life. You've come through a lot, survived things most people haven't. Learn to be happy, honey." Jenna was sincere.

Giving her friend a smile, Molly stood and held on to her bag. "I'll call you if I need you."

"Go have some fun."

* * * *

Chouquet's was busy when Molly walked inside the French bistro. A waitress approached her. Her cheeks reddened as she tried her best not to look awkward.

"Table for one?" the waitress asked.

Run, just leave before you're noticed, she thought to herself, as she tried to concentrate on what the waitress had asked.

Before Molly had the chance to answer, Connor appeared from behind the waitress and smiled. God, he was gorgeous. Molly could feel the flush in her cheeks burn. She looked down at her hands and contemplated fleeing the bistro, forgetting she'd ever laid eyes on him.

"It's okay, she's with me," Connor said and held out his hand to Molly.

"Thank you," Molly replied, all shy and timid as she followed him to their table right in the center of the café.

Connor helped Molly as she sat down and waited until she was comfortable before taking a seat across from her.

Oh my God, what am I doing? she asked herself as she watched him nervously lift the napkin and place it on his lap.

"I was worried you weren't going to come," he said.

His face was beaming, but his own flush had added to his striking looks. Molly couldn't help but stare at him. Radiant and perfect, his skin glowed like the sun gleaming. His tan blended with his dark hair with loose strands perfectly framing his oval face. Wide green eyes brought out his natural beauty, complementing his fine features, and Molly wondered what would cause him to think his life wasn't worth living.

"I was surprised to get your call. How did you get my number?"

Gazing at her, Connor swallowed and smiled. "I have my contacts."

Molly couldn't help but feel at ease in his company. There was something about him that brought out the simpering girl she thought she'd never be.

"This is a gorgeous place." She changed the subject. "How did you get a table? Aren't they normally booked out?"

"Again I have my contacts," Connor replied, trying his best not to sound too cocksure.

"A man of means, I take it?"

"Sort of, but that's a whole other story." He looked down at the menu before sneaking a look over at Molly.

"What made you think you could just jump?" Molly asked. "Sorry, I had to ask."

"I screwed up."

"We all screw up. That doesn't mean your life is invaluable."

"That's true," Connor agreed. "So, why did you stop?"

"Because, like I said, there was a time and place when I was close to death, and I know what it's like to feel desperate."

"Then I guess the two of us could share a tale or two," Connor remarked as he stared at her.

"I bet we could." Molly smiled as she watched the look

of relief spread across Connor's face. She knew then and there that she had made the right decision. Lunch with the gorgeous stranger was what she'd needed.

It was what Aggie had told her to do all those years ago. Never let go of a chance for happiness.

Chapter Five

Connor couldn't believe his luck. He found it hard not to stare at her. She was unlike any of the women he'd dated in the past. She was a cool breeze on a hot summer's day and had an instant impact on his life.

"Can I just say I am so sorry for acting like a total jackass last night," Connor said. "I was pretty lost and didn't appreciate you coming along and stepping in. Not that I don't appreciate it now…"

"It's okay, like I said, I understand."

The waitress walked over to their table, interrupting their conversation to take their order.

"What would you like?" Connor asked Molly.

Looking through the menu, Molly bit her lip. "Can I have the *soupe du jour*?"

"What would you like as your main?" the waitress asked.

"Oh, erm, the *poulet rôti*, please," Molly said as she closed the menu.

"And you, sir?"

"Yeah, I'll have the *salade Lyonnaise* and the *saumon à la Parisienne*, thank you," Connor said. "Would you like some wine?"

"No. No wine, water is fine for me," Molly replied.

"Sure, just water please," Connor said to the waitress as she took the menus and walked away. "The food is really good in here."

"This is my first time here, so I'll let you know." Molly smiled as she lifted the napkin and set it across her lap.

"So what's your story, Molly?"

"Mine?" She laughed. "Have you got all night?"

"You have my undivided attention."

That earned him a bashful look. He couldn't help but stare at her as she spoke. He was bewildered by her soft voice, the way she bit down on her bottom lip when shy, to the way she brushed her hair behind her ear when it fell over her face.

"I had a troublesome upbringing," she said, shrugging her shoulders. "But I suppose most people aren't raised in ideal homes, right?"

"That is very true."

"I had a lot of issues growing up, which led to many bad decisions...and things that nearly destroyed me," Molly said.

"I'm sorry if talking about your past bothers you."

"No, not at all," Molly said, smiling gently. "I mean, I've nothing to hide. I am what I am. What you see is what you get."

"I wish I could say the same."

"Why's that?"

"My parents have this incessant need to control everything in my life. From the suits I wear, to the woman they expect me to marry. Basically, they're control freaks. More so my mother."

"Ouch!" Molly replied, shaking her head. "Are they the reason you wanted to, you know, kill yourself?"

"No beating about the bush with you, huh?" He laughed. "Well, yeah, basically, plus the fact that I lost my father a merger deal worth a lot of money."

"Oh, that bad, huh?" Molly said. "Is your father pissed with you?"

Connor shook his head. Sitting forward, he really looked at her hard. He loved how her eyes glistened and how he had her attention. No one else mattered at that moment.

"Yes, they all are. But if I'm being honest, this has been coming on for a long time. The pressures, the constant phone calls, the late-night meetings—the whole shebang, it's destroyed me in a sense."

Molly sat forward, reached across the table and touched his wrist. "Never feel like taking your own life is the only way out. You are the master of your own destiny. Don't allow anyone else to control that."

In that very moment, Connor knew there was a glint of hope. Something finally worth living for. The burdens of the past twenty-four hours began to lift and he was thankful for Molly's interference. She had redeemed him.

Lunch went smoothly, both of them relaxing to the point that they forgot all their woes until it came time for them to part.

As they stood outside the bistro, Connor stood a good two inches above Molly as he contemplated asking her out on a proper date.

"So, that was lovely. Thank you so much," Molly said as she held on to her bag with both hands.

"No, you deserve way better than this, but it's a start," he said and cringed at the line. He didn't want to appear as if he were coming on to her.

"Nah, this kind of fancy does me just fine. Besides, I don't do this kind of thing often, so count yourself lucky that I said yes." She laughed. "That was a joke by the way."

Connor chuckled and stepped in close to her, bent down and kissed her on her cheek. "Thank you for saving my life."

Molly stood there, fidgeting, and remained silent, only smiling as she turned her back on him and walked away. She looked around once and waved goodbye before stepping off the curb, crossing the road and making her way to wherever she was going.

Connor watched as Molly disappeared among the pedestrians and soon lost sight of her. The swarming in his stomach intensified to the point that he thought he'd faint, but was happy in knowing he'd be seeing her again. He was now on a mission.

* * * *

"Where've you been hiding?" a voice said from the door to his office. "It's near four."

Not looking up from his desk, Connor continued typing. Pretending he was doing something important, anything to avoid the conversation with Bruce, his partner in assets.

"Lying low," Connor remarked.

"Your father has been on my back the entire day. He said you're not returning his calls."

"Yeah, it seems that I'm no longer the golden child."

"Connor, it's all over the news. Have you seen the papers?"

"We both know I'm not into the whole rumor thing," Connor refuted his comments.

"Connor, you tried jumping off the Golden Gate Bridge. I mean, that's fucked up, man," Bruce whispered.

"Technically speaking, I didn't attempt anything, I just climbed over onto the parapet to take in the view," Connor replied.

"Your father is doing a lot of damage control."

"Unfortunate, isn't it?"

"Is that all you're going to say?" Bruce asked, looking pissed.

"For now, yes," Connor replied before beginning typing again. "Close the door on your way out."

"I don't know what's going on with you, but you'd better straighten yourself out. It's both our heads on that failed merger. I have a wife and kids. You've your daddy's bank balance," Bruce vexed as he pulled the door closed behind.

As the door closed, Connor sat with his head in his hands and felt as if he were going to burst. The anger was something that was beginning to control every inch of his life. He was losing it fast and didn't know what to do.

If Molly saw me now, she'd run, he thought to himself as he stood from his desk and walked to the window. The view from the multistory building was spectacular. The view itself made him feel as if he were up among the clouds, but the nagging pain in his chest brought out the inner torment and he didn't realize what he was doing until it was too late.

Connor lifted the computer monitor from his desk and smashed it against the wall. The noise alone was enough to make his PA run into the office, gasping as she saw him flip the desk, demolishing everything in sight.

"Someone call security!" his PA, Anita, shouted as she ran from the room. Glass shattered into the corridor as Connor threw his chair through the transparent wall, causing fellow colleagues to hide under their desks, some even running for the emergency stairwell.

This was it, the moment Connor broke—and from the looks on everyone's faces, there was no way he'd be back any time soon.

Chapter Six

Molly had just finished filling out the last of the paperwork when her phone rang. It was close to midnight and she was tired, certainly not in the mood for any prank callers or late-night telemarketing. She put the phone on silent and continued filing the paperwork then turned off the light to the small office in the shelter for the homeless.

Grabbing her bag from the staff room, she called down the corridor to a small woman. "That's me done, Regina. I'll see you tomorrow evening."

"Okay, sweetie, you get yourself on home and get lost in one of those love books of yours. I'll not be too much longer."

Molly giggled, knowing her little secret was out there for all to hear. "Yeah, I'll do that, while you flirt with Al." Molly winked at Regina as she left the shelter and walked outside into the blissful breeze of the spring night.

The phone vibrated in her bag and she rolled her eyes as she lifted it out. No caller ID flashed and she contemplated ignoring the call, but something changed her mind.

"Hello!" she answered.

"Molly, it's Connor."

"Oh!"

"I know it's late, it's just… I messed up."

"What's wrong?"

"I don't know what's happening to me… I feel so confused."

"Connor, where are you?" she asked, her voice demanding and hard. This wasn't a time for being sweet and gentle.

"Lands End."

"Jesus, what the hell are you doing there?"

"I don't know."

"Okay, just stay there. Can you do that? I'm on my way," she said as she ran to her car. "Promise me you will just stay there… Connor?"

"Yeah… I'll stay."

Molly drove fast, breaking a few traffic rules along the way. It took her less than fifteen minutes to get there, and as she pulled into the lot, she scoured the area for Connor. Turning off the ignition, she was overcome by nerves. It was dark, and she didn't do well with being out in the dark, alone and completely at the mercy of a man she'd just met.

Locking her door, she sat in the car as she dialed the last number. As it rang, she saw someone through the windshield, sitting on the ground next to a tree. Peering out through the glass, she saw the movement of the person, the light flashing on his phone, and knew instantly that it was Connor.

Getting out of the car, she ran up the small path toward him. "Connor!" she yelled as she knelt down on the ground where he sat. "What's wrong, Connor?"

"I fucked up…"

He'd been crying. He wasn't the confident man she'd met earlier that day. The man she saw now was broken, completely torn, and she didn't know if it was in her best interest to intervene again. But if she were to ignore him, it would have gone against everything she stood for.

"Come on, I'm taking you home."

"I can't go back there. I know they'll be there waiting for me, probably some court order to have me sectioned. I don't know what to do," he muttered as he held his head in his hands.

"You're coming home with me, okay?" Molly coaxed him to his feet. "I promise you there won't be any surprises when you get there. It might not be up to the standards you're accustomed to, but it's home to me."

Connor stood and avoided looking at her. His face was

red. His cheeks were wet from his tears. He was a shadow of the man Molly had seen in the restaurant.

"Why do you care?" he asked.

"Because if I don't, who will?"

Connor gazed at her. He didn't ask any more and allowed Molly to take over. Molly never thought she'd be any good in a crisis, but right at the moment, she realized how much she was willing to do to help the handsome stranger from the bridge.

* * * *

Molly finished stirring the milk in the pan as Connor walked into the small kitchen. He'd showered and wore some clothes that Molly had found stored away in the hall closet — old clothes belonging to Aggie's nephew, whom she helped raise when her sister had passed away.

"A little more presentable, huh?" Connor joked as Molly handed him a cup of hot chocolate.

"You scrub up just fine," she replied, not realizing how silly she sounded.

"That's what they all say," he tried a joke, but it fell flat.

"So, what happened?" she asked as she saw the marks on the backs of his hands.

"I flipped out today."

"I can see that. But why?"

"I suppose you've seen all the press coverage," he remarked, assuming Molly was like everyone else.

"Nope. I don't do papers, magazines or social networking of any kind. It's not my thing, so I am quite out of the loop."

"Wow, well, you're probably the only one in the Bay Area who hasn't a clue about who or what I am," Connor said, looking timid and tired.

"Connor, I don't care who or what you are. I am not here to pass judgment on you," Molly said.

"Then you are the first person to not give a shit."

Molly slid in the seat next to him at the small table. She

rested her chin on the backs of her hands as she stared at him. "You know, if you were to spend less time caring what others thought of you, and more time on the amazing person you are, then you'd be a whole lot happier."

"You think I'm amazing?"

Molly's cheeks blushed and she tried to look away, but it was impossible to deny the now-burning attraction between them. For the first time in as long as she could remember, a feeling she'd never experienced before ignited in the pit of her stomach. A whole new sensation that made her want the handsome stranger.

"Well, yeah. I mean, you're lovely." She blushed as the words came out.

Connor smiled. The attraction between them was mutual and Molly couldn't help but take a sharp intake of breath when he reached out his hand and touched the small of her back.

"I think you are pretty amazing too," he whispered as he moved his hand up her back and touched the side of her face.

Molly turned toward him, saying, "I don't usually do this. I mean… I'm not that kind of girl."

"Do what?" he asked, his lips inches from touching hers.

Breathless, Molly found it hard to resist him. "This… Letting my guard down."

Before she had the chance to resist any longer, or play emphasis on her excuses, Connor brushed his lips against hers. At first it was gentle, soft and perfect, as if he were afraid of hurting her. But as soon as she began kissing him back, he responded by pulling her against him.

Connor kissed her with so much passion that Molly saw stars as her head spun from the dizziness. She couldn't believe how much she wanted him. This wasn't her. This wasn't who she was, but she was relishing every last second of it.

Connor ran his tongue across her bottom lip, looking into her eyes as she opened her mouth to let their tongues explore and taste each other. Running his fingers through her hair, he pulled her in closer, kissing her as if he were afraid of never feeling that way again. Molly, willing and hungry for his touch, held on to him, responding to every kiss and touch with light murmurs.

The butterflies fluttered hard in her stomach. It had been a long time since she had been last intimate with anyone, but that didn't stop her letting her hair down and just going with the flow.

Molly broke the kiss and pulled the shirt over his head. She glanced at his chest, then her eyes rose and met his. Taking him by the hand, she turned and led him toward her bedroom. Connor's fingers lightly brushed against her shoulders as he slipped her dress over her head. Goosebumps prickled her skin. The touch of his hands sent a sensation that was new and thrilling, running through her.

They stood at the foot of her bed and Molly began trembling as she stood facing him. Bending down, he kissed the tip of her nose as she held her breath, eagerly waiting for his lips on hers again. Falling into his arms, she kissed him passionately. He returned her kisses, her mouth opening wider with each caress of his lips. His tongue explored her mouth as he slipped his hands behind her and unhooked her bra, revealing her breasts. Connor cupped her breasts and pinched her nipples as her back arched and she pushed her breasts into his palm.

"God, you're so beautiful," he whispered as he ran a finger along the lace of her panties. Sliding his fingers inside the material, he touched the throbbing spot between her legs, gently stroking her.

Letting out a moan, Molly trembled from his touch.

Connor moved Molly against the bed and gently pushed her down onto her back and pulled her panties off, throwing them to the floor. Kneeling between her legs, Connor lifted her feet to his shoulders as he began kissing, nibbling and licking at her very core.

Molly let out a deep moan, writhing under Connor's greedy mouth as she arched her back. The hot sensation built fast as she was about to explode. The orgasm took a hold of her, making her cry out.

Not giving her a second to breathe, Connor slipped one finger, then two inside her as he used his thumb to rub her clit in small circles, allowing the orgasm to begin to build again. Moaning, she rode his hand and held him there as her insides clenched around his fingers. She was lost in his touch. The way he handled her lit her body on fire.

Then she came again.

Finally, they couldn't wait any longer.

"I want to be in you now," Connor panted as Molly lay back, spreading her legs, inviting him in. Reaching for his jeans, he pulled a condom from his wallet.

"It's okay," Molly whispered. "I'm on the pill."

Smiling, Connor shook his head and put on the condom. "Just to be sure."

He rubbed his hand along his shaft and entered her. Connor bent his face down over Molly's and they kissed. Connor began making love to her as she wrapped her legs around his waist. Molly tensed her inner muscles, squeezing him as he thrust in hard, making her moan with each force, sending pulsing waves of heat through her belly. They were completely lost within each other. His eyes found hers as he started moving in her again and she tried hard to keep eye contact. His thrusts grew faster and she found it impossible not to close her eyes as she lost herself in the pleasure.

Molly's breath came in quick gasps as the orgasm grew little by little this time, slowly moving through her, working itself up from the inside. Intense pleasure had every nerve of her body standing on edge.

Molly gazed up at Connor as he reached his peak. She smiled as he bit down on his lip before letting a series of soft moans escape. The warmth of his touch sent her climax through the roof.

Connor slipped a hand behind her head before he kissed

her again and rolled onto his side, pulling her with him as he kissed her slowly. That single kiss was full of meaning. Their breath danced together. Finally, he pulled away and looked into her eyes, satisfied.

"You are amazing."

Not saying anything, Molly rested her head against him and fell asleep, their bodies fitting together perfectly.

Chapter Seven

Connor stared at Molly as she slept and couldn't believe that the pretty girl from the bridge had saved him for a second time. But now she was more than just a passerby who'd done a good deed, she was someone he knew he was falling for fast, and there was no way in the world he wanted to risk losing her.

With everything that was going on with him, Connor needed something to live for and Molly was it. She was good, she had a heart of gold. She didn't try to be something she wasn't. Above all else, she saw him, saw past the money, the hijinks, and accepted him, his flaws and all.

Connor smiled as he brushed her hair from her face and looked at her, observing the small line of freckles that were speckled across the bridge of her pretty little nose and the way her lips pouted as she slept.

"God, you're beautiful," he whispered as tears filled his eyes.

No matter how much joy Molly had brought to his life, there was still the relentless pain from the depression that refused to leave him be.

Stirring from her sleep, Molly groaned as she began to awaken and looked over at him before pulling her sheet and hiding under it.

"Oh my God, I'm...dying," she mumbled.

"Well, I certainly hope not," Connor replied. "Don't be shy, though it's cute. I don't think you've anything to be embarrassed about."

Molly peeped out from under the covers and her eyes lit up as Connor bent forward to kiss her. "I...haven't been with a guy in nearly three years," she confessed. "I know, I was practically a born-again virgin."

Connor pulled her into his arms and wrestled the sheet from her grip. "Well, I don't care. Because from here, you're damn perfect."

"You do know that perfection is just something created by the media to corrupt young minds?"

"Really?"

"Nah, but still, no one is perfect. It's not real. I am just me, little Molly Rice. Dreamer, thinker, good Samaritan or whatever tag is suitable."

"Girlfriend?" Connor said, making Molly pause, her look saying it all.

"Girlfriend?"

"That's what I just said." Connor smiled. "You could be the perfect girlfriend."

"I didn't realize I was girlfriend material."

"Why ever not?"

"You have no idea what skeletons I have in my closest, Connor," she said as she got out of the bed, tying her robe around her waist.

"Molly, did I say something wrong?"

"I think you should go," she said.

"Molly?" Connor could sense her resentment.

"Connor, please... Just go. I can't do this. Not now. I'm sorry."

Connor, not being one to ask twice, grabbed his stuff and hightailed it out of the small apartment. He felt terrible. How something so wonderful turned ugly in a split second annoyed him. He didn't understand what he'd done wrong. From the way they had made love, to the way she had awoken next to him, he'd never imagined her getting angry and rejecting him like that.

Miserable and pissed, he hailed a cab and went back to his apartment, and to the waiting entourage.

* * * *

"Where have you been all night?" his mother asked as she lifted her head from reading the morning paper.

"Nice to see you made yourself at home," Connor replied, ignoring her as he marched through to the kitchen and poured himself a cup of coffee.

"Connor, this behavior is something I'd expect from a fourteen-year-old, not a grown man."

"Then go home, Mother. Go back to Dad and fill him in on all the gory details."

"What's going on with you?" she finally asked. "Is it drugs? Money? Are you in some kind of trouble?"

"Jesus Christ, Mom, it always comes down to those things, right?" he shouted. "Fuck, I'm not James. I don't need coke or prostitutes to make it through the day."

"Then what in hell's name is wrong?"

"I'm depressed, Mom. I've been depressed for the best part of the past year and the merger deal pushed me over the edge." His voice faltered. "I wanted to die... I still want to, but..."

Eleanor looked uncomfortable at the revelation. "I don't understand. You have no reason to be feeling like this."

"No reason, huh? I've just spilled my guts to you, but you still don't get it," Connor shouted.

"There is no need to be rude," his mother quipped. "We will get you a therapist. This is something that is easily fixed."

Frustrated, and let down by his mother's refusal to accept the truth, Connor walked away from the lounge. He couldn't stand looking at her a second longer. She just brushed his feelings and pain under the carpet and wouldn't offer him something that told him she loved him. Eleanor was as cold as ice and there was no way in hell that Connor could trust her.

Connor switched on the shower and the steam began to build. He looked at his reflection.

"What did I do wrong?" he muttered to himself as the influx of anxiety began to build again. His walls began caving in, suffocating him as he tried to breathe — there had to be a way out of the hell he was in, but he didn't want to lose Molly, not now — not when he'd had a glimpse of what true happiness could feel like.

Kneeling on the tiles in his bathroom, he controlled his breathing, laying his focus on the small design in the tile. "Get a fucking grip," he stormed to himself.

Pushing himself back onto his feet, he stumbled into the shower and stood under the steaming water, letting the heat penetrate his skin, making him feel again. He wanted to experience the pain, have the numbness gone completely. The horrid emptiness that plagued his core. He needed to live again.

A knock on the bathroom door sobered him up. "Connor?" his mother called.

"What?"

"Someone is here to see you," she said.

Connor grabbed a towel and dried himself before throwing on a fresh pair of slacks and shirt. He wasn't in the mood for more interference, and certainly not another lecture from his mother.

He walked out barefoot into the small hallway and heard hushed voices in the sitting room. As he stepped in, he was surprised to see Mark, his friend. "I'll leave you two to it," Eleanor said as she lifted her purse from the side table and left the apartment.

"Want to tell me what's been going on?" Mark said as he undid the buttons on his jacket before sitting on the couch.

"I suppose she filled you in."

Mark sat forward, rubbing his hands together. "On the contrary, the press are having a field day out there."

Shaking his head, Connor threw himself down on the couch, letting out a sigh before resting his hands behind his head.

"Of course they are," he muttered. "The whole Lanscorp shit has done enough damage."

"Man, you've got to give me more than this bullshit," Mark

said. He clenched his jaw and let out a long exasperated breath. "Why didn't you tell me?"

"What's to tell? I fucked up. I've lost all hope of salvaging that part of me. I'm done with it all."

"Connor, you can't just walk away from this. You, of all people, know that your parents would never allow it. You are part of a huge empire. And let me be blunt, you will never be free from this," Mark said as he observed his friend.

"The sad thing about it all is that I feel so guilty. The guilt alone is destroying me. I should never have walked into the boardroom." Connor's voice broke. "My heart wasn't in it… It hasn't been for a long while now."

"Then tell me what's happened. Something must have set this off."

"That's the thing, I've no idea what's happened. I'm just so…lost. I don't know how to explain it. That day on the bridge, I was actually relieved. Like I was free. It was the best feeling in the world, then she walked into my life."

"She?" Mark asked, raising an eyebrow.

"Molly. The girl who called it in."

"Ah, a girl."

Connor stared at Mark and he nodded. "Yup!"

"So tell me about this Molly," Mark said, sitting back on the huge cushions, staring at his friend as if he was looking at a stranger.

"She's just amazing," Connor gushed. "I spent last night with her. It wasn't planned… She saved me again, and I don't know… I think I've fallen for her, and that is just crazy, right? I mean, I barely know her, yet I am being pulled toward her."

"Listen to me. It's natural that you're going to cling on to the first piece of skirt that comes along." Mark was cold. "You've had a rough time. She served a purpose, and it's nothing serious."

"How can you sit there and say that?"

"Connor, you know that Marissa won't wait forever,

but she is the one you need to focus on. She's the kind of woman you need, not some girl who happened to walk into your life. It was a chance meeting, but it's not real." Mark stood, walked over to the bar and poured himself a drink. "By all means, fuck her as much as you want if it helps get whatever this is out of your system, then do what you have to do. But you need to get some perspective. Besides, your family would never allow an outsider to come along and destroy all their plans — you know that."

Connor looked at his friend, completely dumbfounded. "We both know that's not how I function."

"Then you need to re-evaluate your choices. Is this *Molly* Ellison material? Would she cut it in the world we live in?"

"I told you, I'm done with it all," Connor shouted. "Why can't you just listen to me, Mark, instead of judging her, writing her off before she's even had a chance?"

"Because if this girl means anything to you, you will spare her any pain. You and I both know Eleanor would eat her up and spit her out. Could you live with that?"

Connor knew Mark was right. His mother would never allow any kind of relationship to flourish, especially if it had not been orchestrated by her. She had chosen exactly whom her children would marry and would stop at nothing to make sure the family's bloodline was strong and not tainted with the likes of Molly.

"I'm willing to risk anything to be with her," Connor muttered as he stood looking out of his bay window. "If you're my friend, Mark, you will help me. Don't judge me, okay?"

"Man, I've never judged you in my life. How long have we been friends? In all that time, have I ever treated you like your opinion didn't matter?" Mark sounded hurt. "You were there for me through some pretty shitty times — I don't forget — but you need to be sure that you know what you're doing."

"I need to know if there is something worth fighting for with her. If she doesn't want me, then I'll walk away, but I can't not try."

"Then you've got my support. But you need to fix this thing with your folks soon, because the press isn't going to leave you alone." Mark walked over beside Connor and looked at his friend. "Connor, as your friend and attorney, you need to prepare a statement, take some control of the situation before it blows up."

Connor sighed and ran a hand down over his face. "I guess I'd better do a little damage control of my own."

Chapter Eight

Molly cried as she sat on the bathroom floor. She felt weak, stupid and dirty. She couldn't get over the fact that she had allowed herself to fall for him so quickly. It wasn't meant to be this way. Not for her. Things had moved too fast and it didn't bode well with her insecurities.

She rubbed her eyes and sat in silence for a moment before deciding on facing the day ahead. It was at times like this when she craved a drink the most. She wanted to kill the pain, numb the feelings and eradicate the sense of filth running through her. Everything she'd thought she had control of was lost in a single moment with Connor.

Who am I kidding? she tormented herself.

She had nothing to offer a relationship. Everything she touched died or was destroyed. She couldn't face the prospect of letting down her guard, only to have her heart broken. She'd been hurt and humiliated too many times in her life, and she wasn't about to let someone like Connor come along and turn everything she had built for herself upside down.

She composed herself and tied up her hair, avoiding having to look at herself in the mirror. There were days that she hated her reflection and today was one of them.

Molly closed the door behind her, walked into the kitchen and scrolled through her phone until she found Connor's number, blocking and deleting him. As much as it hurt doing that, she knew it was for the best.

Just as she put the phone back on the counter, she saw the two cups of unfinished hot chocolate and her heart sank.

"Stupid moron," she scolded herself as she lifted the cups,

pouring the contents down the drain and aching inside as the memory of their intimate encounter flashed through her mind.

A knock on the door startled her and she jolted, dropping one of the cups in the sink, smashing it. "For crying out loud."

The knock came again.

Molly ran to the door and opened it. In front of her was a delivery man with a huge bouquet of flowers.

"Delivery for Molly Rice." He handed the flowers to her and left the foyer.

Molly closed the door and smelled the fresh arrangement as she saw a small gold envelope sealed on to the side of the organza bow. Setting the flowers down on the counter, she opened the envelope, taking out the small card inside.

I'm sorry.
Connor XO

Molly's heart sank as she read the words. Was he purposely trying to destroy her? Angry and vexed, she lifted the flowers, grabbed her keys and left her home.

The scent alone was beautiful. There was no denying that Connor had taste. But how many times would she have to reject him before he got the message? She wasn't ready for what he wanted and she needed to make sure he understood.

Molly drove for the best part of an hour, but didn't know where she was going or what she was doing. Not until she realized she was sitting at a bar, looking into the full glass of wine, contemplating that first sip.

She sat there, frozen, just watching the red claret teasing her, willing her to drink it.

"It's not gonna bite," a voice said from behind the bar.

Looking up, Molly felt drained. She wasn't in the mood for idle conversation. "I don't know what I'm doing here." She trembled, holding on to the stool to stop from losing her balance.

"It's the perfect place to drown your sorrows," the blonde bartender said as she filled a shot glass with vodka and downed it straight. "And I'm guessing you have some serious shit to drown."

"No, not really," Molly muttered as the thirst burned in the back of her throat. "This was a mistake." She panicked as she grabbed her bag and fled the bar. Outside, she leaned against the wall of a nearby pawn shop and cried. "You stupid fool," she whispered to herself as she caught the glares of a few passersby, looking at her as though she were insane.

With shaking hands, she lifted out her phone from her purse and called the only one who knew how much she was struggling. "Jenna..." she cried. "I think I need that pep talk." She crouched down on the ground, resting her head on her hand as she tried to control her breathing.

"Where are you?" Jenna asked.

"It's okay. I didn't touch the liquor...but I think I'm gonna break."

"Are you able to stop by my place?"

Molly wiped her eyes and gazed up at the blue sky, squinting from the radiant light of the sun, and the familiar pang of guilt swept through her. "Yeah, I'll be there soon."

The short drive to Jenna and Barry's comfortable home was one mixed with apprehension and growing anxiety. Not once had she thought about the implications of taking that drink. How she'd have set herself back months, and not to mention the disappointment she'd cause Jenna and everyone else in her AA group.

Molly parked outside the two-story home. She sat in silence, gathering her thoughts before walking up to the front door, leaving herself open for scrutiny and indignation.

Barry answered, welcoming her with a hug. "It's okay, sweetie." He held on to her tightly as she cried. So much relief from a single embrace. The caring nature was enough to calm the mental strain that had overtaken her.

"Come on in, I've fixed you two something to devour in the den," he said as he ushered her in through the front door.

"I'm so sorry about this."

"What have I told you before? If ever in doubt, you call us, otherwise Jenna would be failing in her role as sponsor and friend."

"I know," Molly whispered. "I just... I don't know. I allowed him to get under my skin."

"Hey," Jenna called as she walked up to Molly. Gazing at Molly, Jenna placed her hands on either side of her shoulders and gave a gentle squeeze. "You did the right thing calling me."

Jenna closed the door to the den and sat on her favorite chair while Molly threw herself on the couch, lifting a cushion and holding it under her chin.

"What happened?"

"I don't know. I just flipped. The poor guy never stood a chance with me."

Jenna poured the coffee into the cups then lifted hers and gestured for Molly to help herself.

"I take it that things progressed?" Jenna inquired, trying not to pry too much.

Shrugging, Molly shook her head. "I was such a fool."

"How?"

"I don't know... I let my guard down."

"Molly, look at me," Jenna said. "You deserve to be happy. You don't need to keep punishing yourself for what has happened in the past. You have paid the ultimate price for what your father did to you. Don't you think it's time to allow nature to take its course and allow someone into your heart?"

"But that would mean revealing all the dirty, sordid details about my past and I'm not sure he'd want me after that."

"You are a silly girl, but I understand completely," Jenna sympathized. "Listen, do you like this guy?"

"Well, yeah."

"Then why not give him a chance?"

"Because he's the guy everyone is talking about... The guy from the bridge the other night. That's why I missed the meeting. I was the one who called it in and stayed with him until the cops came."

Jenna's eyebrows raised as her mouth opened, unsure of what to say. Then a smile spread across her face. "And you've been beating yourself up over this?"

"No," Molly replied. "I'm afraid that if we fall too deep, we're heading straight for disaster."

"But you won't know unless you try."

"It's pretty obvious that we're both fucked up. I mean, he's got issues, and let's not even begin to scratch at my problems. It couldn't possibly work out."

"What would Aggie say if she were here?"

That made Molly sit up straight and she knew she was right. There would be no way Aggie would sit back and allow her to wallow in so much self-doubt and deprecation. Aggie would have encouraged the thought of a blossoming relationship.

"We both know what she'd say," Molly responded as she looked down into the coffee swirling around in the cup. "But she's not here."

"Don't be such a defeatist. Look at it from this angle — if you had never stepped in, stopped him taking his own life, you'd have never faced the opportunity of finding that someone who could complete you." Jenna made a fair point.

"So, you suggest I give him a chance?"

"I do. Otherwise you are going to beat yourself up over this in many months or years to come. Don't let the chance pass you by, honey."

"And ignore the fact that I nearly had a drink today?"

Getting up from her seat, Jenna walked around the small coffee table and sat down beside Molly. "No, we don't ignore that, we address that."

"I was so close to taking that drink," Molly cried.

"But you didn't. You left, and you called me, which tells me you're stronger than you give yourself credit for," Jenna said as she touched her shoulder. "I'm not saying it's going to be easy, but sobriety is a lifelong commitment. To allow your addiction to stop you from moving on, and living your life, would be unfair to you."

"So you're saying to take a chance?"

"Absolutely. I am living proof there is life after addiction. You just have to work at it," Jenna said, her smile warm and genuine.

"Then I guess I should apologize to him."

"That, my dear, would be a start."

Chapter Nine

The gym was quiet, which meant less chance of having to make idle conversation with any of the patrons eager to poke their noses in his business. Not that he had much chance of avoiding it. The local press coverage meant that it was slightly impossible to hide, so he began to slip back into his old routine, only altering the times he went to the gym, or out for his morning paper. Simple things that eased the burden of facing the same questions time after time.

Mark had made sure that his statement went out simultaneously as the news broke about the fall of the Lanscorp merger. He watched the stock fluctuate on the markets and knew that his father would have been spitting fire. Avoiding the ridicule of his parents was one thing, but to hear the hushed conversations between his siblings was harder to stomach.

Running fast on the treadmill, Connor didn't hear the door to the gym open. He was too focused on ridding his body from the tension and mind from all the clutter.

Connor's heart pounded hard. His breathing was fast and sharp as he concentrated on the last few miles, only to have a hand touch the handrail, making him stop.

"So this is where you've been skulking?"

"Marissa!"

Lifting the towel, he rubbed the sweat from his brow as he took a swig of water from his bottle, glancing at her from the corner of his eye.

"You've been ignoring my calls, Connor, why's that?" Running her long red fingernails along the bar of the treadmill, she tilted her head to the side, waiting for an answer.

"I've been keeping a low profile."

"Is there something you need to get off your chest, darling?" Marissa was far from concerned. She was more worried about saving face and not being associated with someone who had a delicate constitution.

"Nope," Connor replied as he stepped down from the treadmill, walked over to the water fountain and refilled his sports bottle. "Besides, shouldn't you be sunning yourself in the Bahamas?"

"Well, yes, I was, but once Daddy called, filling me in on the events, I had to come home," she remarked as she followed him. "And what kind of girlfriend would I be if I weren't here for you in your hour of need?"

"Marissa, we've discussed this before—we're not in a relationship." Connor rolled his eyes before looking at her, watching the scowl appear on her perfectly made-up face.

"You are such a pig, Connor Ellison."

Letting out a laugh, Connor shook his head. "I've been called much worse."

Marissa Rivers—spoiled, arrogant, beautiful, controlling, delusional—everything he didn't want in a partner, had been pushed in his direction when he had been selected to escort her to her debutante ball. There was no mutual attraction. It was more her obsessing over him. Connor had expressed on many occasions how she wasn't right for him, but his mother was insistent that he gave her a chance. Little did his mother know that the more she pushed, the more distant he became.

"Connor, don't be so rude!"

"Marissa, what do you want?"

"I just wanted to make sure that you're okay. Is that so wrong?"

"No, but if it were genuine, I'd stomach your words a little easier. Has my mother put you up to this?"

Walking up beside him, she touched his arm. Her warm hands were like silk against his sweaty skin. "She may have mentioned that you were a little jaded."

"Typical, you women can't leave it alone."

"Connor!" she screeched.

"What? You think coming here, offering to, what—blow me, fuck the bad feelings out of me or maybe try to coax me into agreeing to do something I'd never want under normal circumstances—all to aid your mission of nailing me? I might be a little fucked up right now, but I still have my faculties attached," he shouted. "Get the fuck out of here. I'm not interested."

Marissa stared at him. She was at a loss for words, which was heaven for Connor as he smirked before sauntering out of the gym, leaving Marissa looking every inch the prize ass he'd always wanted her to be.

Taking a quick shower, he vacated the premises out through the back door and sped home, where he knew he wouldn't be disturbed. He intended on getting wasted. There was nothing else for it. He wanted to forget the rejection from Molly. Her name alone made him close his eyes, mourning something he had never been able to have. But he was intent on not giving up on her just yet. There was a fire that burned between them. It wasn't a fleeting moment or a one-night stand. It was something more, and he needed to show her that he could be someone she could trust.

* * * *

Connor sat back on the couch and ate a few slices of pizza as he drank his eleventh beer. Scrolling through the channels, he felt irritated. Nothing caught his attention long enough that he could forget the way Molly looked when she slept.

Every time he closed his eyes, he could hear her, see her and taste her.

Rolling onto the floor, he picked up his cell from the rug and dialed her number.

Nothing.

The called failed.

"What the—?" he muttered as he dialed the number again.

Again, nothing.

"Fuck!"

Tightening his grip around the phone, he held it to his chin as he thought long and hard.

Dialing the number again, he prayed. This time it rang. His heart began to pound.

"Hello," a groggy voice answered.

"Molly, don't hang up," he pleaded.

"Connor?"

"I know it's late."

"It's two in the morning."

"I really had to talk to you… I'm sorry."

"Connor, I…don't know what you want from me."

Connor slid onto his back as he stared at his ceiling, listening to her voice.

"Connor, are you there?" Molly asked.

"I'm still here," he replied as he tried to focus on not sounding any drunker than he was. "I feel so bad about how we left things the other morning."

"I can't do this now."

"Then when?" he asked, sounding a little angry. "You just blew me off, like I didn't matter. Do you know how that made me feel?"

"I'm not doing this. Not over the phone, and certainly not when you're smashed."

"Then can I see you?"

Silence.

"Molly?" he asked.

"I don't know."

"Please."

Another pause.

"Saturday," she replied. "That's when I am free next."

Connor jumped up, rubbed his eyes and smiled. "Saturday

is good for me. I'll pick you up, say noon?"

"Okay, I'll see you then," Molly said. "Goodnight, and Connor?"

"What?"

"No booze."

"Okay."

The phone went silent, then the dialing tone buzzed. Lying back down, Connor smiled as he held the phone in his hand and drifted off into a drunken sleep. One that wasn't exactly peaceful, but it was sleep, and boy, did he need it.

Chapter Ten

Molly made sure her days were full as Saturday got closer. She couldn't believe she had agreed to meet him, never mind talking to him on the phone, especially since he was clearly inebriated. She took on two extra shifts at the shelter, helping Regina make up the beds and check inventory.

"You seem lost, sweetie," Regina remarked as they counted sheets.

"I'm good, Gina."

"You sure, honey? Because from over here, you look like a girl who has the weight of the world on her shoulders."

Molly stopped what she was doing, looked over at the elderly woman and sighed. "Guy trouble."

"Then why in hell didn't you say so? I could tell you a tale or two." Regina laughed. Her presence was infectious. "Now, tell me what he has done."

"It's not that he's done anything to me." Molly sounded down. "It was me who kind of rejected him after, you know, spending the night with him."

"Uh-oh, he didn't take it well?"

"Nope."

"Do you like him?"

"Well, yeah, I mean, I've agreed to see him tomorrow. But, I don't know, it's all happening too fast."

Regina walked over to where Molly stood and wrapped her arm across her shoulders. "Sometimes you've got to take risks, otherwise life will pass you by and you'll wake up one morning an old woman with no family, no happy memories — life will have just been one long, wet, miserable day."

"I know… I'm being stupid."

"Nope, you're not stupid, honey, but you're just a little too hard on yourself. It's quite obvious that this young man has gotten under your skin."

"I hate it when everyone is right." Molly smiled.

"Oh, me too. Nothing like a know-it-all, huh?" Regina winked at Molly before going back to the closet and checking off bed linen from her inventory list.

Sometimes Molly was thankful for those who played her conscience. She needed sound counseling every once in a while, and if it made her sit up and take stock, then she graciously accepted the advice — even if it went against her better nature.

* * * *

Saturday morning came faster than she expected. It was odd, because although she was nervous, a little part of her was excited about seeing him again. It was as though she was on a roller coaster, fighting with her demons, trying to get off and just be normal.

She sighed and sipped her coffee as she looked out of her window, taking in the beauty of the sun shining down on the little cluster of crystal chimes Aggie had placed outside the kitchen window. The luminous colors of the rainbow danced in through the window, making everything pretty and radiant. Another piece of Aggie firmly attached to the small apartment.

Regina was busy stacking books on a shelf, smiling over at Molly. "You okay, honey?"

"Yes," Molly replied.

Molly finished off her coffee and set the cup down before she began writing in her journal. It was a coping mechanism that Aggie had encouraged from the first day she had begun her long road to recovery.

Molly had written in several over the past six years, but not once did she ever read through them. She firmly believed that if she read anything she'd penned, then it would be like opening up a can of worms, and Molly didn't like worms – or snakes, or spiders, or anything that reminded her of the pain from her past.

She sat at the kitchen table, biting on the tip of the pen before she closed her eyes. It was another ritual – silent prayer before she unleashed her thoughts onto paper.

Saving someone's life comes with a whole other level of responsibility. I had to stop, I mean, it was only natural to step in, but I didn't realize I'd be seeing him again, or sleeping with him for that matter. Connor is everything I thought I'd never like, or want, or need. I know that sounds cold and harsh, as though I am judging him, but can two people – two very different people – truly find each other like we did and be happy?

The way he made me feel, that is something I've never experienced in my entire life. Not when I was a child, and certainly not when I was a teen. He made me feel beautiful, but that also made me feel vulnerable. If I am to allow my heart to let him in, I am leaving myself in danger of being hurt, and I don't know if I can handle being damaged – not like that.

But everyone is right. If I don't at least try, then what kind of life am I really going to have? I want to settle down. I want to have children – I want a home. Could Connor really be the one? Could he truly be that person who can salvage everything that I've lost?

Dear God, if it's him, please give me the strength to trust and believe. I could really use your guidance and love.

Molly

Closing the journal, Molly picked it up, placed it at the top of her bookshelf, deciding on a long soak in the tub before embarking on whatever would happen that afternoon.

* * * *

Dressed in a white fitted shirt and cutoff jeans, Molly

slipped her feet into her silver flats as she brushed her hair.

"Way too much," she said, staring at her reflection. She decided on no makeup. She didn't want to pretend to be something she wasn't. So she settled for the less is more look.

The slight knock at the front door caused a swarm of butterflies to begin their dance. She was nervous but knew it was only natural, considering how she practically threw him out earlier in the week.

"I'll get it," she shouted to Regina, who peeped out from the kitchen.

Pausing before she opened the door, she trembled as she inhaled deeply. *You got this*, she thought to herself as she reached for the handle and opened slowly.

Connor's face lit up when he saw her. "Hey."

"Hey there, yourself."

Moving out of the way, she let him in. As she closed the door, the familiar feeling of wanting to be lost in his arms scratched the surface, but she did well as she quashed the desire, replacing it with a more composed manner.

"You look lovely," Connor remarked as he stood with his hands in his pockets, looking more afraid than ever before.

"Thank you. Not sure I scrub up as well as you, but this is me."

"Well, I think you're beautiful," he said as he gazed at her. "I figured a day at the beach would be a nice place to start."

Smiling, Molly looked at him, surprised. His gorgeous green eyes glistened as he watched her move over to where her purse sat "I'd really like that. It's been a while."

"You ready?"

"Sure... Should I make us up some food or something?"

"Already taken care of." He winked at her.

As they were about to leave, Regina appeared, her dark eyes inspecting Connor.

"Connor, this is Regina. She's kinda like my surrogate mother," Molly said. "Gina, this is Connor, my friend."

Regina walked down and shook his hand. "Good to meet you, Connor. Have you something nice planned today?"

"A day at the beach," he replied.

"Molly sure loves the ocean," she said, smiling. "Go have a wonderful time."

As they walked out of the door, Molly looked back, seeing Regina giving her the thumbs-up, winking at her. Giggling, Molly closed the door.

Connor was already on course to woo her. Molly knew he was going to go all out for her, but never expected the things he had planned.

Chapter Eleven

With a heart that refused to stop galloping, Connor opened the passenger side of his black BMW convertible and smiled as he waited for Molly to get comfortable. God, she smelled good. A light floral scent swept through him, enticing him, tempting him to break his own promise and kiss her hard. Shaking the thought out of his head, he closed the door and walked around to his side.

"Nice car," she said as he slipped behind the steering wheel.

"I like nice things," he replied then instantly regretted sounding so materialistic. "Sorry, I meant—"

Molly laughed and touched the back of his hand. "You're so silly. I knew what you meant."

Letting out a sigh of relief, Connor started the ignition and drove. Soft music played from the stereo as they traveled down the 101, passing Bair Island and Redwood City on the way.

The conversation was flowing and their awkwardness had been replaced by a newfound confidence.

"I was such a dork at school. I swear, my mother made me stand out like a sore thumb—and the braces didn't help."

"And there was me thinking you were the school hottie." Molly giggled.

"Are you serious?" Connor laughed. "I was a complete moron. God, I was this awful little shit. I had this complex about entitlement."

Molly gave him a curious glare.

"I kid you not. Until I was fifteen, I was a complete ass. I'm the baby of the family, so, in a way, I was ruined from a young age. It wasn't until I started dating, moving away from the circle of friends I associated with, that I realized that there was no way I could go through life walking on people, expecting others to pick my shit up after me."

Connor wanted to be honest. But he didn't want to ruin the day by bringing up too much of the past. Bad memories were bad omens.

"So what changed? I mean, your family is a big deal, right?" Molly asked.

"Yes, they are." He sighed. "Don't get me wrong, I've had a privileged upbringing, but that meant love, or the kind of love a parent showers their child with, was missing. Instead of a kiss or hug, it was a new gadget or toy, or trip abroad. I missed out on a lot of things."

"That makes two of us," Molly mused.

Connor could tell from the way she had said that that there was a deeper understanding of how hard childhood could be. But he didn't want to rock the boat too much and scare her off, or, even worse, be rejected again.

"When I have kids, I'm gonna tell them every day how much I love them," he said, his face lighting up at the prospect of being a father. "They'll be sick of hearing it, but they'll have felt love."

"You will make a great father one day."

Connor's cheeks burned at hearing Molly's compliment. As he glanced over at her, she smiled, just a little grin at first, but as it grew, it pressed her blushing cheeks upward. When the smile reached her eyes, they sparkled, causing them to crease at the corners. It was at that moment she became everything he had ever hoped for. Molly was all he needed. "Why, thank you." His own smile said it all.

"Don't mention it."

After a smooth ninety-minute drive, they reached Capitola, and Molly's eyes lit up when she saw the ocean. They could see it from a mile away, looking like a giant azure mass. It was a rising enormity that seemed to obscure the horizon, which was lost in the shimmer of the far reaches of it. It was a sight that both Molly and Connor appreciated.

"It's been forever since I stood in the sand," Molly remarked. She stared at the beauty ahead of her and glanced at Connor, smiling. "I feel like a child on Christmas morning."

Connor was content knowing that he'd made the right choice.

"Ah, but this isn't quite it." He winked at her.

"Connor, what have you done?"

"You'll see."

A nervous smile and arched brows told Connor that Molly wasn't the type to take surprises very well. But he knew that she'd appreciate what he had in store for her. "Don't look so worried. I've got this covered."

"O-kay." Molly held her hands together tight, swallowing hard as she looked out of the window.

Connor turned the car onto a small, steep slope, driving toward a private gated lane.

"I thought we were going to the beach?" Molly asked, her eyes scanning the area.

"We are."

The gate opened slowly, allowing Connor access to the well-maintained driveway. The garden was bursting with life with trees, flowers and a small fountain. Molly's jaw dropped.

"Are you sure?" she asked as she turned to face him.

"Honestly, don't worry about this," Connor replied as he parked the car in the driveway, close to a two-story villa. "This is just private access, that's all."

"To what?"

"Follow me."

Getting out of the car, Connor stood by the hood and waited for an anxious Molly, who held on to her purse for dear life as she walked slowly over to him.

Holding out his hand, he waited for her to take it before gesturing to continue his little mission. "Shall we?"

"Do I have a choice?"

"Molly, you always have a choice."

Molly squeezed his hand tight. She didn't reply. Instead, they walked around to the side of the property, which led to a huge terraced garden. The view was impressive and the scent from the flowers and fruit trees was unbelievable.

"Is this your house?"

"Would it be a problem if it was?"

"Well, no, but… It's gorgeous."

Giving her hand a gentle tug, he pulled her in a little closer to him. "You're gorgeous."

"You're a dork."

They both laughed as Connor led her to some steps that took them down to a beach—a private beach that was beautiful, perfect and peaceful. Molly slipped off her shoes as she walked onto the warm sand and looked over at Connor who stood gazing at her, smiling.

"We won't be disturbed here," Connor started. "And lunch has been taken care of."

"What have I done to deserve this, huh?" Molly winked at him playfully. "I'm joking. This is just lovely, thank you."

Molly turned to face him. She stood on her toes and kissed his cheek. Her warm smile mirrored his happiness. "You are most welcome," he whispered. "Now come on, time to chill and soak up the sun."

Connor lifted Molly over his shoulder. She squealed, giggling as he marched across the sand, setting her down on a blanket that had been laid out especially for them.

Connor wanted to make the right impression, and at that precise moment, he knew that Molly wasn't the kind of woman to be bought, and he didn't want that. There was more to her. She had an air of something about her that made him want to strip back the layers, healing any of the pain that still haunted her.

"I could get used to this," she whispered.

"That could be arranged."

"Behave, you dork." She hit him playfully. "But seriously, this is just heaven." Cocking her head to the side, she looked over at Connor, who lay beside her, staring back at her. "Just don't break my heart."

Molly ran her fingers over his cheek. Connor leaned in, kissing her softly. "I could say the same thing."

Chapter Twelve

Molly couldn't believe it. There wasn't another soul on the beach, just the two of them, the sun kissing their skin and the sound of the waves lapping as they walked along the shoreline, talking, hugging and falling for each other.

Walking hand in hand, Molly and Connor were lost in deep conversation. A gentle breeze blew Molly's hair as she talked a little about herself. "I like giving back to the community. It helps me sleep a little better at night."

"But aren't you be afraid of being alone with…them?"

"Them?" Molly asked, raising her eyebrows. Molly had a thing about getting on the defensive when people dared to look down their noses on the weak and vulnerable.

"The homeless… Not that I mean anything bad by saying that."

Molly stood still and sighed. Looking up at Connor, she could see that he was genuinely interested. "They pose no risk to me," she said. "I've never felt exposed when in their company. They are no different than you or me. You wouldn't believe some of the stories. Businessmen, kids, military veterans — they all lost something and ended up alone, solely depending on the grace of man." She turned her face away, gazing out at the endless sea. "I was in their shoes once."

Connor's expression said it all. He was stunned by her revelation. Molly defended her job by highlighting her own experience — it was proof that no one should be judged.

"Wow… I wouldn't have guessed." Connor shook his head.

"But how would you?" she asked. "You really don't know

anything about me, or what I've been through. Only what I've allowed you to see."

"Molly, I'm not about to let you disappear from my life because of your past. Remember, it was you who saved me more than once… You're too special." Pulling her by the arm, he gently coaxed her against his chest, embracing her in his warm arms. "You can tell me anything and I'll still be standing here, falling for you."

"Are you sure about that? Because my story is dark."

Connor kissed her on the head and brushed his nose against her forehead. Molly could feel him inhale deeply.

"You have my word."

Connor swept the hair back from her face and held on to her cheeks as he bent, kissing her gently at first. Their lips moved lightly together as they breathed in each other's souls. Hard, yet soft. Heated with raw passion. A moment in their lives, lost in a memory that would last forever. In that one moment, there would be no going back, and it made their newfound feelings grow into something they had never believed possible.

They stood still, holding on to each other. There was an explosion of total peace and tranquility, which besieged them both. Their worlds had come crashing together in the most unlikely of circumstances, and though a week had passed, they had come to understand the true meaning of life. The desire for love — to be loved. Knowing that for both of them, this may be the one time in their lives to prove that they were entitled to the freedom of falling in love, they grabbed it with both hands and refused to let it slip away.

"I think I'm falling for you in a big way," Connor whispered as he rubbed the tip of his nose against Molly's.

Molly gazed up into his green eyes, melting into him. How could she not? Connor had fast become the only man to ever get in under her skin. To see the vulnerable, yet strong woman hiding under those layers. She had exposed her very core to him and there was no turning back now.

Molly took a quick glance around and smirked as she

broke from their embrace. Lifting the white shirt over her head, she threw it aside before taking off her jeans, standing in front of Connor in her underwear.

Molly knew Connor couldn't hide his arousal. She loved taking control. Unhooking her bra, Molly dangled it midair before she threw it at him, laughing as he caught it mid-air, only for him to drop it onto the sand before pulling off his shirt, revealing his toned chest.

Molly stood almost naked in front of him and enjoyed the risk of exposure, which was beginning to turn her on more than she thought it would.

Connor dropped his slacks onto the sand, with only his briefs shielding his now-evident excitement. Molly smiled when she saw the desire burning in his eyes. Finally, after a little hesitation, she removed her panties, gazing over at him looking coy, yet sexy.

"What are you doing to me?" Connor muttered as he too removed the last remaining piece of clothing. Both of them were naked, standing mere inches apart, staring as if they were only seeing each other for the first time. But before Connor could touch her, Molly turned her back on him and ran into the water, diving down into the warm crispness of the sea.

Connor followed her in but stood waist high in the water, waiting for her to resurface. A smile spread across his face as her hand brushed against his thigh. His eyes glistened as she emerged from below the surface, her gaze intense. Grabbing him, Molly kissed him. She threaded her wet fingers through his hair, pressing her breasts against his chest.

Connor didn't waste any time in responding. Connor squeezed her breasts hard. Molly let out a little moan before gently biting into his shoulder, her breath ragged against him as her nipples hardened under his touch. Moving her hand down to cup his erection, she kissed him, sliding her tongue inside his mouth, letting him taste her desire. Connor moaned into her mouth as she began stroking him, making his hips jerk forward from the touch of her hand.

Molly ached for him with a need she couldn't quite get her head around. She let all her inhibitions go when she wrapped a leg around his waist, never breaking the momentum between strokes as Connor cupped her buttocks, supporting her.

Hard and rigid, Connor's cock twitched in her hand. His gasps made her throb for him. "I want you in me," she muttered as her own arousal became too much to contain.

Using her hand, she guided him inside her as he pushed down on her ass, steadying her as she let out a soft moan in his ear.

Molly was confident that if anyone had been watching, they would look like an embracing couple, but beneath the water Connor's hips slowly began to thrust in and out of Molly. Their breathing was heavy with every penetrating thrust as Molly rode his shaft.

The heat began to build deep inside her as the first wave of the orgasm began to take over. Feverish, Molly cried out as Connor pounded her, tilting her head back as the climax shot through her body, leaving her gasping. The spasms gripped tight around Connor's cock.

The sweet combination of their building orgasms merged together. The surge began to increase, bubbling, tingling, until finally neither could hold back anymore. Wild like beasts, they gazed at each other. Eyes hungry and craving what was about to happen.

"Fuck!" he moaned as he fucked her hard and fast. Then with one last almighty breathless gasp, he came, shooting his seed deep inside her.

Quivering, Connor held on to Molly as he waded in from the water. He gently set her down on the blanket and grabbed two towels from the chairs that had been carefully arranged under a blue pergola, the voiles lighting moving in the warm breeze.

Molly took the towel from Connor and dried her hair before wrapping the towel around herself. Kneeling on the soft material, she watched Connor as he brazenly sauntered naked around the small table, pouring two glasses of juice.

"You are full of surprises," he said as he walked back over to Molly, handing her the glass.

Giggling, Molly's cheeks flushed. "Well, just sometimes I surprise myself too."

"You hungry?"

"Famished."

"Then let's eat."

As Connor held out his hand to her, Molly took it and let him help her to her feet.

Just sometimes, Molly did shock herself, but this time, it felt right.

Chapter Thirteen

Connor loved the way Molly sipped at her juice. She was so delicate looking, yet he knew how strong she could be. There was no denying the surprise he felt from their passionate encounter in the water, and he certainly wasn't going to complain. It had been a long time since a woman had been able to seduce him like that. It being Molly only added to the thrill of the experience.

"It's so gorgeous out here," Molly said as she looked out. Sailboats dotted the horizon, barely visible, bobbing in the water. "How could you ever want to leave?"

Cutting into his cheese, Connor put a few bits on a dry cracker, popping the whole thing into his mouth, smiling at her. "Because my job requires my presence and...soul."

"Sounds ominous."

"Oh, it is." He raised his eyebrows. "My father, King Dick, he likes his empire run a particular way, and unfortunately, I, his lowly minion, am not cutthroat enough for him."

"Is that the reason you've been feeling the way you have?"

Taking a mouthful of juice, Connor looked over the rim at the glass. Molly stared at him, waiting for his reply. "Can I be honest with you?"

"Absolutely," Molly replied, lifting her feet up from the sand and resting them across Connor's lap.

"I've not been feeling well for a while." He looked at Molly as he ran his hand over her feet. "I think the catalyst was the loss of millions last week. I was treated like a child in front of our entire board, held accountable and left to clean up a mess that was started long before I ever took over the contract."

"Wow, I'm sorry."

"Yup! And when I finally try to talk to someone, I'm told to stop being a pussy and fix things. That was it. I wanted out." Connor was sincere as he spoke.

"What about your mother?"

"My mother cares more about saving face than saving her son."

Connor became uncomfortable from the sheer mention of his mother. If ever there was someone who made him feel ill and uneasy in their company, it was her.

"Well, I'm here, you can talk to me. I told you that before." Molly lifted her feet off him, got up and sat on his lap, wrapping her arms around his neck. "I know that this is all new, and totally crazy, but if you need to talk, then talk to me. Don't bottle it up because believe me, doing that will destroy you from the inside out."

Running a finger up and down her back, Connor kissed her arm. "Is that something you've learned from experience?"

"Yes!"

"What happened?"

It was the one question Connor had tried to avoid asking, but he knew that to understand the real Molly, he had to get beneath the surface. Even if it meant bringing up painful memories. "Long story short?" she said as a frown creased her forehead.

"If it's too painful—"

"No, I want to… It's just… I guess I'm afraid."

"Don't be. Not with me."

Molly sighed and fidgeted awkwardly before getting herself comfortable in his arms.

"I ran away from home the day after my thirteenth birthday," she said as she looked at her hands, her voice trembling as she spoke. "Up until then, I had spent much of my younger days being moved back and forth between foster homes and the places my parents would set up what they constituted as a home. My father did things to me, stuff no daddy should do to his little girl, and my mother

beat the shit out of me, blaming me for leading my dad on."
A tear ran down her cheek and, sniffing, she worked hard
not to break down. "I took to the streets, trying to survive.
I mean, anything was better than being force-fed meth and
vodka—right? But the problem was I got addicted to the
taste of liquor, how it numbed the pain, the ugliness that
I felt within me. I spent much of my teens in a drunken
haze."

"My God, Molly. I'm so sorry," Connor said as he listened
to her.

"I was convinced I'd die on those streets. I was starving to
death and stealing to get my hands on booze. Those shelters
I work at, those places saved me. Not that I knew it then,
but, if it hadn't been for Aggie, I'd be dead right now." She
looked at Connor as the tears began falling. "I was barely
alive when they found me that morning. Normally you have
to vacate the premises by seven a.m., eight by the latest—I
was still in the bunk when Aggie shook me. I'd OD'd on
Benzos and cheap vodka. I was in respiratory arrest and I
was in a bad way."

"I don't know what to say," Connor whispered as he
wiped the tears from her cheeks.

"What can you say? I was a train wreck."

"But look at you now." Connor touched her face. "You've
come out the other side stronger."

"Maybe, but some things are hard to forget and live
without, you know what I mean?" She paused. "I'm an
alcoholic, Connor. Is that something you can deal with?"

Connor was stunned by her revelation. He had only
half expected her to have issues with alcohol because she
didn't like the stuff. Not once did he imagine her having an
addiction. "Is it still…a problem?"

"It will always be a problem, but do I still drink? No, I've
been clean for over two years. My only setback was when
Aggie passed away earlier this year."

"I'm sorry. I can't begin to imagine how hard life has been
for you. My problems seem so mediocre compared to what

you've been through," Connor said, overcome with guilt about his own selfish depression.

"Don't you dare," Molly said as she stood. "Don't give me your pity. I don't want it, okay?"

"Molly, I didn't mean—"

Molly turned her back on him and walked away, gazing out at the sea as tears flooded her eyes. Connor felt so bad. He hadn't wanted to upset her, not like this. He was just floored by how hard her life had been. Not wanting be a complete jackass, he pulled on his pants before walking over to her. He had to let her know it was okay to be open and honest with him.

Standing behind her, Connor placed his hands on her shoulders, kissing down on the top of her head.

"Then let me love you." The words had come out before he had realized what he was saying.

Molly froze.

Connor was stunned and rendered speechless. He couldn't believe he'd said them. Words he was convinced he'd never say. Slightly giddy, he laughed nervously, but as he tried to think of something to do or say to help them move past the awkwardness, Molly turned around.

"Okay," she said as she met his gaze.

Connor stared at her, his heart dropped hard into the pit of his stomach and the old familiar feeling of butterflies began swarming inside. Her beautiful eyes, fresh from crying, looked up at him, and all he wanted to do was wrap his arms around her, protect her from ever being hurt again.

"Are we crazy?" he asked her as he took her hands in his.

"Probably, but what have we got to lose?" Molly shrugged.

"I could think of a few people who could compile a list," he joked.

Kicking a little sand at his feet, Molly moved in close to him, wrapping her arms around his waist. The warmth of his chest next to her skin calmed her down. "Then let's not think of anyone else."

The way her lips connected with Connor's felt right.

Somehow, among all of the dizziness and confusion from everything that had happened in the past week, Molly had become a lifeline to him. Something had changed inside him and he was content to have his breath come and go with hers.

Connor couldn't believe what they were doing, but it had never felt more right.

Chapter Fourteen

Molly couldn't quite get her head around the fact that she had done a complete U-turn and was now embarking on something that had no rhyme or reason, other than the fact that it felt like the most natural thing in the world.

Being with Connor was so easy. He accepted her for what she was, all her flaws and insecurities along with it. For someone who didn't trust so easily, she found herself falling headfirst for the guy from the bridge and knew there'd be no way back—not unless he broke her heart. That was a risk worth taking, for he'd opened up her heart and soul to everything she thought she didn't deserve.

The setting sun—warm with fiery colors—slowly moved aside, allowing the beauty of the awaiting moonlit canvas to open up, leaving the night air sweet and fragrant.

Molly stood on the shoreline, loving the sensation of her feet in the tide coming in. The calmness that took over was second to none. If this was heaven, she didn't want to leave.

"Let's go up to the house," Connor said from behind her as he wrapped his arms around her waist, pulling her in close to his chest.

"Hmm, just two minutes more," she replied as she looked up at the star-studded heavens, the twinkling skyline a breathtaking sight.

Connor kissed her on the side of her face. He smiled as he followed her gaze, and lovingly stood there, taking in the wonder of the night.

* * * *

Hot steam immediately enveloped their bodies as Connor guided Molly into the custom shower. There was a narrow walkway lined with beautiful crisp white and bronze stacked stone walls. He smiled as his hands explored her body and moved in for a kiss.

The multiple rainfall showerheads sprinkled hot water over them from every angle, their bodies glistening from the moisture and steam, washing away the salty remnants of sea water.

"I never want to leave your side," Connor gushed as he ran his hands over Molly's lower back, his fingers moving down, resting on her well-rounded ass.

Molly didn't say anything. She looked up at him, mesmerized by the way he touched her, the way he leaned down, groaning into her neck, his light kisses tingling her — the desire burning deep inside. Molly lowered her hand and ran her fingers around his growing hardness, rolling his balls in the palm of her hand. She loved how she made him hard, which in turn made her horny.

Without saying anything, Molly dropped to her knees, gripping the base of his cock as she licked the underside of him before taking him into her mouth.

Connor's hips jerked forward as he let out a groan. "Fuck!"

Smiling, Molly began working him in her hand before taking him in her mouth, sucking and teasing, making the hardness swell as she moaned.

She'd never given a man oral sex before and was quite impressed with how quickly she learned. Connor held on to the back of her head as he pushed himself farther into her mouth, making her look up at him, her eyes blazing with the same hunger that burned in his.

Connor was unbelievably sexy. His well-ripped abs were glistening from the water droplets running down his chest. The muscles on his arms were clenched tight as his body tensed up from the way Molly pleasured him.

"Ah, baby!" he moaned as she teased him, taking him down her throat, then back out again. "If you keep doing that I'm gonna come."

Lifting her chin with his hand, he pulled out of her mouth, helping her to his feet. Connor cupped a breast and kissed her as Molly ran her fingers through his hair, enjoying the taste of his tongue. His hardness rested against her pelvis, twitching with arousal the harder their kisses became.

Connor growled with a primal urge. He turned her around, pushed himself up behind her, pressing her hands against the tiles. One hand rested on her hips as the other guided himself inside her, thrusting up hard, making Molly cry out in surprise.

Slow at first, Connor moved in and out of Molly, letting the wave of pleasure submerge her completely. Molly was so overwhelmed by the way Connor made love to her. Her heart pounded hard in her ears. Leaning over, Connor tweaked at her nipple, massaging her breast, intensifying the building orgasm that was beginning to swell deep in her womb.

Molly cried out as the orgasm shook her body. The power behind the climax left her dizzy, her spasms clamping around Connor's cock, sending him into a frenzy.

Grabbing her hips, he dug his fingers deep into her flesh as he buried himself inside her. Her ass against his hips, her feet tiptoeing on the floor as he leaned back, grinding her hard onto him. Gritting his teeth, Connor screamed as his own orgasm left him breathless.

Minutes ticked by before Connor released his grip of her. Molly stood up straight, letting the water fall onto her face, the heat refreshing against her. Turning to face him, she fell into his arms as they embraced, holding on to the other, clinging on to the moment, savoring the passion and love beginning to consume them both.

* * * *

Molly had just finished getting dressed when she heard Connor talking. Drying her hair as she walked down the steps that led to the open-plan living area, she saw Connor staring out of the patio doors, holding the back of his head.

"I said I will be back on Monday." He sounded exasperated. "God damn it, Bruce, can you not give me a break?"

Molly stood in silence as she listened. She knew that the pressure was getting to him and worried that any more annoyance would send him over the edge. Connor saw her silhouette in the reflection of the glass. Turning around to face her, he rolled his eyes as he pointed to his phone and mouthed the word *moron*, making her smile.

But he wasn't fooling her, she could see the stress on his face.

"Bruce, I'm going. I'm busy. Why don't you go and enjoy that family of yours before you lose sight of your priorities." Throwing the phone, Connor walked over, greeting Molly with a soft peck on the lips.

"Trouble?"

"Nothing that needs my attention until Monday," Connor replied as he walked over to the refrigerator, taking out two steaks. "You hungry?"

"Well, I'll not say no to steak," Molly said as she watched him taking control, treating her like a princess, tending to her every need. "Do you want any help?"

"Nope, you just sit yourself down, let me sort this."

Molly didn't argue with him. She sat on one of the stools next to the white island, resting her hands as Connor set a pan on the burner, waiting for it to heat up before placing the sirloins inside.

Sitting contentedly, Molly took in her surroundings. Everything looked opulent from the gleaming wood floors covered in stylish throw rugs to the sheer curtains that billowed like mist as a breeze blew in from the open glass sliding door. The furnishings were modern, yet soft, and suited Connor well.

"How do you like yours?" he asked, pulling her attention right back to him.

"Medium — not too bloody."

Connor winked at her and got to frying their steaks. With ease, he grabbed two plates from a cupboard behind him, giving them a wipe before setting them on two place settings at the other end of the isle.

"Want to make up some salad?" he asked Molly, who was more than happy to help out. She felt quite redundant sitting there, doing nothing.

"Sure!"

The two of them worked together as if they had been partners for a lifetime. Smiling and chatting as they each helped the other, it was hard to believe it had only been a week since they'd met.

The weekend had been a huge success, and one Molly never thought would be so relaxing. They explored each other, made love and fell into the kind of love that she'd only read about in one of her Nicholas Sparks novels. It was truly an amazing time and she hated having to say goodbye on Monday morning, but was excited at the prospect of seeing him later that week.

Some things in life were worth waiting for, and Molly was happy knowing that Connor was her silver lining.

Chapter Fifteen

The stress was clear on Connor's face as he walked into the boardroom. Several heads turned to face him as he sat down in his usual spot, trying his best not to make eye contact with anyone. Bruce cleared his throat as he tugged at his tie. He was clearly on edge.

"Relax, man!" Connor whispered, trying his best to control the tight knot in his chest. The pressure from the anxiety was toxic as he tried to breathe through it. He could feel the sweat bubble, the uncontrollable sound of his heart vibrating in his head. If this was the start of a heart attack, he was convinced he'd die then and there.

The doors opened at the other end of the long room as his father entered, dressed in a gray tailored suit, his face emotionless—cold as ice. His brown eyes found Connor, who kept his own eyes locked on his father, bold enough to show him that he wasn't intimidated. But deep inside, he felt the urge to run from the room, quit while he was ahead, but who was he kidding. As long as his name was associated with the fall of the Lanscorp deal, he'd never get hired anywhere else.

"Gentlemen," John Ellison greeted his staff, scanning the room. Each person sat around the board table nodded, a few murmurs were made and the lights were dimmed.

Richard Chase, the vice president and John's right-hand man, took center stage as the large screen came down—the Ellison logo flashed across it.

"We have all read the transcripts, and most of us are up to speed on the loss of the Lanscorp merger," he began. "To those new to this, there is a lot of speculation surrounding the legality of the deal. Hearsay and gossip are on the tips of the tongues of those who were opposed to the decision in breaking Lanscorp down and selling it off bit by bit—assetless sales with bigger turnover. Sixty-five million dollars later and we are doing damage control. If the deal had been successful, we would have seen a profit of more than one hundred forty-five million—big money to lose. Which leads us to Connor and Bruce who were heading up the deal."

Connor shuffled uneasily in his chair as Bruce twitched his leg up and down. Both their fates hung in the balance. John Ellison cocked his head to the side, narrowing his eyebrows as he watched his flesh and blood squirm in the hot seat.

"It was unfortunate," Connor began, his voice shaky at first. "We didn't anticipate a proxy contest. The dissident shareholders successfully obtained enough votes to gain control of the board of directors, overthrowing our bid to take charge."

"How do you suppose these dissidents obtained such power?" John asked his son.

"Honestly, I don't know—" Connor began only to be interrupted by Bruce.

"It's come to our attention that crucial information was breached and the details of the contract were leaked."

Connor glared at Bruce, giving him a peculiar look as if to say, 'What the fuck did you just say?'

"You mean there was a tip-off?" Richard asked, folding his arms as he stared at Bruce.

The room was still as the silence floated through the air, the question on the tips of everyone's tongues.

"What Bruce means to say," Connor interrupted, the unease clear by the way his hand trembled. "We are unsure, but there may have been some files leaked."

That did it. That caused the influx of raised voices, pens stabbing down on files, eyes blazing in all directions.

"Are you insinuating that someone in Ellison Enterprises

had access to such classified information? Passing sensitive data to the Lanscorp shareholders?" Richard asked as the lights came on.

Bruce piped in, this time with a newfound confidence. "Yes."

Connor lifted the file and held it under his arm, as his chair scratched on the floor. He stood and glared at the faces of all those he'd let down. He needed air, and he needed it fast. Not wasting another moment in the boardroom, Connor aimed for the door. He slammed it shut behind him as he ran for the elevator.

Pressing the call button a dozen times, he swore as staff looked on, raising eyebrows, talking in hushed tones — judging him.

"Fuck it!" he mumbled as the sweat began dripping down his forehead. He had to get out of there. The air was tight as he tried to swallow. Dizziness nearly consumed him as he burst through the fire exit and down the stairs.

Not realizing how many flights he cleared before running past reception and security, he practically fell out through the revolving door, gasping as his head spun.

Loosening his tie, he opened the top button of his shirt, squinting as he looked up at the sky, sucking in as much oxygen as possible. Panting, he knelt on the ground for a good three minutes, blocking the way of pedestrians moving to and fro from the building. But he didn't give a shit. He was relieved.

"Are you okay, sir?" a familiar voice asked as he felt a hand on his shoulder.

Turning his head, he saw Martin, his father's chauffeur, looking down on him sympathetically. "Yes, I am fine, thank you."

"Would you like me to call for medical assistance?"

A crowd had formed. Nosy fools more interested in the fact that the rich 'almost jumper' was now having a breakdown in public.

"Sir, I think it would be best if I were to drive you

somewhere."

"Agreed."

Standing, he ignored the flashing lights of camera phones, the chitter chatter, the gossip brewing, and followed Martin to his father's personal car.

Martin closed the door behind him and quickly drove away from the very place that brought out the simpering child inside.

* * * *

Mark poured two glasses of whiskey and handed one to Connor as he sat across from his friend. He wasn't a man of many words, and certainly wasn't on course to judge his best friend. It wasn't his style. He was concerned for his friend. He was worried about how the growing attention was going to affect him. Another public meltdown was something Connor didn't need.

"The press are having the time of their lives with his, huh?" Connor said as he stared into his glass. The scent of the golden liquid rippled up his nostrils, tantalizing his taste buds.

"They will find some other poor bastard. You'll be yesterday's news soon enough."

"Fuck!" Connor shouted before he drank the liquor down in one gulp.

"I think between the loss of the contract, the pressure from your parents and this thing with the new girl—it's all catching up with you. Maybe we need a guy's weekend away. Take a break from the scene, unwind a little," Mark suggested.

"I couldn't think of a worse thing to do."

Letting out a loud, exasperated sigh, Mark sat forward. "Then are you going to continue moping around? Having panic attacks? Losing sleep over something we both know you had nothing to do with?"

"I don't know what the fuck I'm going to do." Connor

closed his eyes. "I have so much to do. Leaving town would be insane and not to mention totally admitting defeat to my father. He'd love nothing more than to see me crumble before his eyes."

He ran his hands through his hair and didn't move when the door to the room opened.

"Honey, I'm just going over to help Victoria with the decorations. I'll see you for dinner tonight." Cassandra smiled at Mark, winking at him as she blew him a kiss.

Cassandra's eyes lit up like a Christmas tree as Mark winked back at her. "See you later, sweetheart."

Cassandra closed the door, her footsteps clicking as she walked down the hall and out of the front door.

"I take it Victoria is still insisting on being there when Cassie gives birth," Connor said, changing the subject.

"Man, you haven't a clue about the stuff I've had to look at. Birthing magazines, perineum oil—fucking nipple cream."

Connor laughed. "Well, it's all good practice. You guys are going to need to be in the know."

"Can I be honest with you?"

"Sure."

"I'm scared shitless," Mark said as he got up, fetching the decanter, filling up their glasses. "I worry that she'll be in pain. She was so sick for nearly sixteen weeks. The thought of her suffering any more scares me."

"All you can do is be there for her, make sure she's okay, and I'm pretty sure that you both will come out the other side pretty damn happy." Connor tried his best to ease his friend's burden.

"Impending fatherhood is scary shit."

"You're just afraid of all the diapers she'll make you change." Connor laughed. "But at least you get to rub some of that nipple cream in."

"Are you kidding me? They are a no-go zone right now. Mind you, they've grown and just look like they need devouring." Mark beamed.

Connor smiled at his friend. It warmed his heart to see him so happy. He wanted that happily ever after too, then his mind drifted to Molly — sweet, beautiful, sexy Molly.

"What's on your mind?" Mark asked, noticing the immediate change in Connor.

"Ah, man, she's amazing. I mean, literally amazing. I know that if we are given half a chance, we could be something solid," Connor said as his face relaxed. "She totally gets me."

"Marissa will be pissed."

"Fuck Marissa."

"That's what she's hoping for," Mark joked.

"We did it once. I was drunk and I can't remember a thing."

Mark poured them another drink. "Have you ever thought about what your mother is going to do when she finds out that you have no intention of ever popping the question to Marissa and have moved on to pastures new?"

"That, my friend, is a good question, but right now I honestly don't give a fuck."

"That's good, because you need to prepare yourself for this weekend," Mark warned.

"Why?"

"Because your mother has gone all out for the gala."

"Well, that's just great," Connor complained. "Nothing like Mummy dearest playing cupid."

Connor was right. There was nothing Eleanor wouldn't do to make sure they remained royalty in their dynasty. Fuck those who got in the way.

Chapter Sixteen

Three times she filled out the same form, and three times she messed up. Regina looked at her, pursing her lips, contemplating what to say. She could clearly see how the young woman was off somewhere else. She had been singing, engaging more with the residents — finally coming out of her shell.

"If this is what love does to you, long may it last," she said.

Molly looked up from her failing attempt at filling in her timesheet and blushed.

"What?"

"You can't hide the look of love, honey, it's pouring outta you like it's the Fourth of July."

Molly didn't respond. Instead, she kept quiet, got back to putting in her hours, and smiling as she felt Regina's eyes on her.

"Deny it all you want, baby girl, but let me tell you something — when love comes along, you hold on to it, don't let it go," Regina said as she held her hand over her chest. "And make love like there's no tomorrow." Winking, Regina walked away from the small office, laughing and breaking out into song.

Once Regina was out of sight, Molly dropped the pen, picked up her phone, checking for messages or missed calls from Connor.

Nothing.

Her heart threw a little tantrum, but she knew that he'd be in touch, and she really didn't want to be the one to make the first move. Then she smiled, remembering how she had most definitely been the one in control once or twice over the past weekend.

The bell on the counter pinged. Molly looked up.

"Hey, Eugene, what can I do for you?"

"We need more bleach," the man said as he chewed on a toothpick, before sniffing and playing with his nose ring.

"Sure, let me just grab the keys and I'll get you a few bottles from the store."

Eugene stood, by the front desk as Molly got up. Molly could feel his eyes on her as she lifted the keys from the drawer. She hated how he rested his tongue on his lower lip, breathing heavily. Molly left the small office and began walking down the narrow corridor, passing the dorms. Unlocking the door to the basement, she hummed to herself as she stepped down the stairs, opening to the store door.

Molly didn't hear the door click behind her.

Grabbing two bottles of bleach, Molly put them under her arm. As she turned around, she came face to face with Eugene.

"Jesus Christ, Eugene, you scared the crap out of me." She nervously laughed.

Eugene didn't say anything. He licked his lips as his hand began moving. Molly looked down and could clearly see his penis in his hand, jerking off in front of her.

"What the fuck!" she shouted.

Molly dropped the bleach and pushed him, trying to move him out of her way. But before she got the chance to run up the stairs, Eugene pulled her by her hair, swinging her back, slamming her into the wall.

Molly screamed. The reality of the situation came crashing around her. She tried to get up from the ground but her head spun as she fought to regain her balance.

A hand came down hard, slapping her across the face.

"Please... You don't want to do this, Eugene," she begged.

"Fuck you," he stormed. "I'll be the best you'll ever have."

Hitting back, Molly threw her weight behind a closed fist, punching his face, only for it to make him more violent.

With one hand, he pulled at the waist of her jeans, using the weight of his other arm across her chest, restricting her breathing.

He was repulsive. His breath stank of stale nicotine. Everything about him had alarmed her from the first time he'd shown up to do his community service, and she'd expressed her concerns to Regina, only to be told the usual — everyone deserves a second chance.

She tried her best to pry his arm from her and cried. His fingers slid in under the waistline, his clammy flesh making her stomach heave.

"You make me so hard, baby," he said as he brushed his cock against the crotch of her jeans. "I know you want it. I can smell your pussy juice from here."

"Someone, help!" she screamed. "No... No—" She fought back in a failing attempt of breaking free.

Desperate, she looked to her left, eyeing a toolbox on a nearby shelf. Grunting, she reached out her arm, trying her best to touch the box. Eugene licked the side of her face as he dropped his pants to the floor.

"I want to come in your sweet ass," he mumbled as he stroked himself a little more, loosening the pressure on her chest at the same time. Only for him to see what she was trying. "Bad girl."

Smash!

His fist made contact with her mouth, splitting it open. The taste of her own blood was metallic on her tongue. Molly cried out as tears fell down her cheeks, knowing that she'd never forgive herself if she let another man take what he wanted from her. Closing her fist tight, she made contact with the side of Eugene's head, the pain burning up her arm.

"You bitch!" he said, gritting his teeth as he pressed his face against hers. "Just for that, when I'm done I'm gonna rip your insides out."

Not taking any more chances, Molly pushed at him until the two of them lost their balance, falling to the floor hard.

Trying in vain to break free from his grip, Molly desperately moved toward the shelving unit, hitting at boxes as she struggled to reach for the toolbox. Eugene's hands pulled her back by her ankles, but in doing so, she hit at the base of the shelving unit, sending the toolbox crashing to the floor and its contents spilling out.

Eugene's eyes blazed. "You cunt," he shouted as he slapped her again. This time a ringing sounded in her ears.

Sweating and fighting for her life, Molly held her breath as she reached out, stretching her fingers as far as they could go. Desperate as she tried her best to grasp hold of anything that could be used as a weapon.

Eugene pushed her shirt up, revealing her bra, his hand roughly rubbing her breasts. "Pert puppies," he groaned as he ripped open her jeans, pushing his other hand down, desperate to touch her in the one place she didn't want.

Molly was now in autopilot mode, survival instinct kicking in.

The spanner had made contact with his head before she had the chance to comprehend the severity of her actions. Screaming out, she heard footsteps pounding down the stairs.

"Someone help me," she screamed over and over again until her throat felt raw. Her tears stung her eyes.

Ash ran into the basement and saw the nightmare in front of him. Behind him Regina appeared, her face in complete shock.

Running over to where Eugene had Molly pinned down, Ash pulled Molly out from under him, cradling her in his arms as she sobbed, shaking uncontrollably.

"Shush, it's okay, honey, I got you," Ash said as he glanced up at Regina. The exchange of looks between them said it all.

Regina bent down beside the motionless body of Eugene, feeling for a pulse. Sighing, she shook her head. "He's alive, but only just."

Another set of footsteps came down the stairs. Cheryl,

the center manager, appeared. "Jesus Christ," she gasped when she saw the blood and Molly crying. "Let's get Molly upstairs," she instructed Ash, who in turn helped Molly to her feet, turned his face away as she pulled her jeans back up.

Regina and Cheryl talked, their voices low as Molly was taken back to the safety of the small office. Ash wrapped a blanket around her shoulders, looking after her attentively.

It all soon became a disorientating blur. Molly hardly noticed the cops, the paramedics or the faces of pity staring at her. All she wanted to do was go home, lock the door and drink.

Chapter Seventeen

Racing in his car, Connor didn't give a fuck about breaking speed limits. He just needed to get to the hospital and didn't care whether he got there in one piece or not.

Parking the car in the nearest bay, Connor ran into the emergency department, his heart thumping hard. Sweat ran down his face as he approached the information desk.

"Molly Rice?" he asked.

The receptionist looked at him. Her round lips mumbled something.

"What?" Connor asked, his head spinning from agitation.

"And you are?" she asked, her voice penetrating through his skull.

"Her boyfriend."

"She's in triage at the moment. Take a seat and someone will come for you soon," she replied.

"No, I need to see her now."

"Sir, please take a seat and someone will be with you shortly," she insisted.

"Please, I need to see her," he begged.

"Sir, do I need to call security?"

Not saying another word, Connor walked to the seating area and sat down. The anxiety began to get the better of him as his palms became clammy. He couldn't believe it when the call came through. Running his right hand over his fist, he felt sick to his stomach.

Some motherfucker tried to hurt my Molly, he thought over and over, torturing himself with the visuals. Shaking his head, he didn't hear the nurse approach.

"Sir, are you here for Molly Rice?" she asked.

Connor jumped to his feet. His heart began thumping again. This time he could feel the pounding beat in his throat, almost choking him. "Is she okay?"

"Yes, just come with me and I'll take you to her."

The short walk to one of the small cubicles had Connor on edge. His insides twisted in knots as his mouth became dry. He was afraid and angry. Afraid of what the son of a bitch had done to her, and angry that he wasn't there to protect her.

The nurse pulled back the curtain. His eyes filled with tears when he saw her sitting on the gurney. His heart calmed down, but only enough to let him breathe a little.

"Molly!" he said as he raced to her side, taking her in his arms.

Molly cried as she held on to him. Her soft body trembled in his embrace.

"Baby, it's okay, I'm here now," he said, kissing the top of her head.

A voice came from the other side of the bed. A short, older woman, with tight black curls, stood from her chair. "She'd been crying for you. So I insisted on making the call," she said.

Connor could feel the heavy weight on his heart. He was thankful that Regina had called him but so angry that Molly had been subjected to the attack.

"What happened?" he asked.

Molly sat back on the bed, still holding his hands, her eyes puffy from crying.

He saw the sutures in her lip and his face vexed. "I'll kill the —" only for Molly to cut him off.

"What's the point?"

"Molly —"

"No, Connor. You can't think that you can suddenly fight all my battles for me."

Regina stepped in. Her face was warm and calm, but her voice firm. "I think Connor has every right to express his anger, honey. We're all shocked and angry."

Molly looked at Connor as her eyes filled with tears. "I really thought he was going to... I didn't mean to hurt him, but..." She cried. "I didn't want it. I begged him... He just wouldn't stop."

"Baby, I'm so sorry." Connor felt terrible. "I can't believe this has happened."

Regina stepped up next to the bed, touching the side of Molly's face. "I'm going to step out for a while, sweetie. You and Connor need some time, and the officers want to ask me some questions, but if you need me, just call, okay?"

Molly nodded, giving a halfhearted smile as Regina closed the curtain, leaving them alone.

"I really want to go home."

"I know...but we've got to make sure you're okay," Connor said as he touched her face. "You're coming home with me either way."

"Why?"

"So I can look after you."

"I'm not a baby, Connor," Molly said.

"I know you're not." Connor's hand rested on the bed as he leaned his head against hers. "But I'm here to protect you, and you're not leaving my sight."

Sighing, Molly shrugged.

Connor could sense she didn't have the energy to fight. He knew that deep down inside, she needed him — his love, his protection — his heart.

Connor never knew how much he had to live for, not until Molly walked into his life. And now she was there, he couldn't imagine his life without her. It was crazy, it was unpredictable, but it was everything he wanted and needed.

When he had gotten the call from Regina, and the details had emerged about the attack, he had never felt rage like that. In all the times he'd read about attempted rape, or seen news coverage highlighting such subjects, Connor had never batted an eyelash. He'd never come face to face with anything like it before, and though he knew that he had to be strong for Molly, the sheer thought of another man abusing her like that made his skin crawl.

"As soon as you're given the all clear, we'll escape the city for a few days."

Molly gazed at him, her face pale. Connor noticed how she fidgeted on the edge of the blanket, running her thumb over the coarse material. He wanted to protect her more than ever.

The officers who took Molly's statement were decent. They were aware of how sensitive she was and didn't press her for too much detail. It was Connor who had a hard time listening to the woman he loved giving an account of what happened.

Every time she mentioned Eugene's name, Connor's stomach recoiled in disgust. The very thought of the creep touching his girl sent a shock wave of adrenaline pumping through his veins. He had to stop short of going up to ICU and smothering the motherfucker to death.

"Mr. Ellison," the officer pulled him out of his reverie.

"Yes."

"Miss Rice will be staying with you?"

"Yes, absolutely."

The officer wrote on his pad. "Can we have your number just in case we need to make contact?"

"Sure," Connor replied, giving him two different numbers.

"We'll be in touch, Miss Rice, please try to get some rest," the officer said.

"Thank you," Molly muttered.

"Thank you," Connor followed with a gentle smile. "You ready to leave this place?" he asked Molly, who was in the middle of getting off the bed.

"Yes, please."

A nurse came in with a discharge letter. "Here you go, honey. Now don't hesitate to come back, okay?"

"Don't worry," Connor said. "Any sign that she's not well, I'll bring her in myself."

The nurse smiled at them both and gently touched Molly

before she left the cubicle, giving Molly the privacy to get dressed.

"As soon as we get to your house, can we burn these?" she asked as her face paled, touching her clothes.

"You bet."

* * * *

They'd stopped by Molly's place to gather a few of her belongings before taking the road trip to the beach house in Capitola. Molly welcomed the escape. She needed to be away from everything that reminded her of the attack. She needed to feel safe again.

Molly rested her head against the seat rest, listening to the wind as it blew her hair wildly over her face. Connor took it easy. In his eyes, she was precious cargo and he wouldn't risk hurting a hair on her head.

Once they arrived at the beach house Connor ordered in Chinese after running Molly a bath.

"Go soak for a while, I'll sort the food out when it gets here," he said as he lit the candles around the huge tub. "Call me if you need anything."

Molly nodded. "Connor!" she called after him. "Thank you."

"That's what I'm here for."

Closing the door, he left Molly to relax. He had this primeval need to protect her. It was an all-consuming feeling that resulted in him removing all traces of liquor from the house. He didn't want the temptation sitting in front of her. To keep her safe, he had to make small changes, and if that meant making sacrifices of his own, then so be it.

Molly was more important to him than a glass of wine. She was the real deal, and there wasn't a thing in the world that was going to change that. Promising himself that if someone dared touch her again, he'd walk to the ends of the earth to kill them.

That was a fact. She was now his, fuck the rest of it.

Chapter Eighteen

The hollow ache inside made it impossible to sleep. Twisting and turning, she was afraid of disturbing Connor, who was now fast asleep. Staring at him, she observed his unshaven face, the dark stubble that made him deliciously irresistible, the full lips that knew how to kiss her and the way his eyes moved as he dreamed.

It was hard to believe that for two people who were only getting to know each other, they had fallen quickly into the kind of love that was only ever seen in the movies.

Guilt washed over Molly. She felt dirty. She believed that she didn't deserve Connor.

"Stupid idiot," she muttered to herself as she turned to lie on her back, staring at the ceiling as the tears fell down the side of her face.

Just knowing that she had dragged Connor into her nightmare, the more the shame consumed her. All of a sudden there was an aura of gray around her. It was a mist that refused to lift. A state of despair that she couldn't see herself through.

Her mouth ached and the sutures were tight as they knitted her wound together. Not able to lie still another minute, Molly sat up, resting her hands on either side. Her heart was heavy, like it was being pulled down into an empty pit of darkness, giving her the impression that she would never recover from the ordeal. She knew the same old gloom was creeping in and she wasn't sure if she had the resolve to resist it.

Molly began to cry when she glanced over at Connor.

He stirred from his sleep and reached out for her. "Hey!"

Gazing at him, Molly felt the weight of the world on her shoulders. She could no longer see the light at the end of the tunnel, and the scariest thing of all was knowing that the craving for booze was beginning to take hold of her.

"I…don't think I can do this."

Sitting up on the bed, Connor moved over to her. Touching the small of her back, he kissed her shoulder. "I'm here for you no matter what."

"The road may get a little bumpy," Molly replied, her tears leaving their streaks on her face.

"I'm not afraid of a challenge."

Connor pulled Molly back into his arms. They lay down together, gazing at each other. "Two weeks ago I'd never have believed it if someone had told me that I would have met a beautiful woman who would save my life, enriching me in a way I never thought possible."

Nuzzling her head in under his chin, Molly wrapped her arm around his waist, holding on for dear life.

"What happened today proved to me how much you mean to me," Connor whispered as he closed his eyes. "I love you, Molly Rice."

Molly felt like she was floating on air. Her heart fluttered. She was dizzy from hearing the words. Yes, they'd both been feeling it, but wow, he'd said it.

Not waiting a second longer, Molly shifted her head back so she could look at him. His beautiful, sleepy green eyes gazed at her, absorbing her, allowing her to become his. "I love you too."

The words slipped off her tongue, sounding like sweet music to Connor. The two of them gazed at each other in silence, realizing how far they'd come in a short period of time.

"Are we nuts?" Molly asked as she held on to him tight.

"If we are, at least we're in it together."

"I'm sorry."

"For what?"

"For waking you."

Running a finger under her chin, Connor placed soft kisses on her lips, being careful not to hurt her. "You are silly sometimes."

"Really?" She sounded surprised.

"Yup, but it only makes me fall deeper."

"You're adorable."

"I'm glad you noticed." He winked at her.

All of a sudden, the pain from mere moments ago began to evaporate. Being with Connor seemed to make all the bad things disappear, and if he was the kind of medicine she needed to have in order to recover, she was happy to indulge.

"You're a dork."

"Yup. Now get some sleep."

Smiling, Molly sank into his arms, listening to the tender beating of his heart. Right then, at that moment, Connor and his strong arms washed away all the pain from the attack and her insecurities. In its place came something more — hope.

* * * *

Molly stood on the sand, a hot cup of coffee in her hand, the noise from the sea refreshing. Connor ran in the distance, looking like a black dot, moving closer to her with each stride.

The morning sun, warm with a rosy glow, was amazing against her skin. She felt almost renewed standing under its magnificence. There, in that moment as she watched the man she loved run toward her, her heart skipped a beat, and the ash from the day before scattered away, leaving enough room for her to ingest the new phase of her life.

Hot and sweaty, Connor ran up to her, planting a kiss on her cheek.

"Aren't you a sight for sore eyes," he breathlessly greeted her.

"Yeah, yeah, you old charmer."

"Less of the old," he said as he took the cup of coffee from her and sipped the creamy contents.

The two of them began walking back toward the steps that led to the beach house. There was no denying the love between them. It was new, radiant and inspiring.

Breakfast consisted of crispy bacon, waffles, eggs and coffee. The smell in the house was divine and Molly enjoyed every last mouthful, sitting back, feeling full and content. Connor was more than happy to wait on her hand and foot, but Molly wasn't having any of it.

"Oi, let me help," she insisted.

"If you wish, but we have plans today."

Winking at her, he carried the two plates to the sink, knowing she was curious as she followed him with their coffee cups.

"What kind of plans?"

"It's a surprise."

There it was again, that deliriously enticing smile of his. The smile that melted her insides, making her crave him.

"Surprises and me don't go well together," she pouted.

"Tough luck. Go put on something that'll keep those knees warm, we leave in forty minutes."

"Connor...what have you done?"

Holding his hand on his chest, he smiled at her. "I promise, it's nothing bad, or one that requires us doing anything naughty—not unless you want to of course." He winked at her again. "But this little excursion is for the soul, nothing more."

"And by keeping my knees warm, you mean?" she queried, raising her eyebrows.

"Something comfortable."

Molly's stomach did a somersault. She knew he was up to something, but what, she couldn't quite put her finger on. But one thing was for sure, she knew that whatever he had planned, she'd love it regardless.

* * * *

Connor was full of mischief as he drove them along the coastal route to God knows where. Molly kept asking for clues, but Connor was pretty tight lipped. He didn't want to ruin the surprise.

"Then is it something I can eat?" Molly asked, determined to break him.

"Nope. But we are going to have a bite to eat on it."

"Oh, c'mon, you've gotta give me more than that."

"Later on, baby." He winked at her, earning himself a jab in the arm.

"You're such a meanie."

Molly pouted, looking every inch the cutest thing he'd ever seen. Even the sutures on her lip and the bruising, which was now developing, couldn't put him off.

"Trust me, you will love it — or at least I hope you do."

Butterflies began to flock inside her stomach. A good nervous sensation, one filled with anticipation and excitement, ran through her. It was like being a kid again, full of the wonder of what was going to happen. The heightened adrenaline was good. It meant that although the attack from the day before flashed its dirty memories once in a while, Connor was doing an amazing job of creating new, fresher memories. Ones filled with love, and that was the kind of therapy she needed.

Chapter Nineteen

Connor found it hard to hide his excitement. He used his powers of persuasion to get him and Molly fitted in at the last minute. Of course, with a name like Ellison behind him, he could get what he wanted any time he felt like it, but rarely used his prominent name to get things his way. Everything in moderation was his motto.

Connor pulled into the lot of Heron's Head Park. He stopped the car, got out and ran around to Molly's side. Being a gentleman, he opened the door.

"Madam, if you will join me," he said, all smooth and confident, as he held out his arm for her to take.

Giggling, Molly gave him a curious look but played along.

Connor wanted Molly to be comfortable around him. His overzealous confidence made it easier for him to open his heart and soul to her.

"What are we doing here?" she asked, looking around.

From the back of his pocket, he took out a black handkerchief, dangling it in front of her face, teasing her. "Not so easy, little lady, you gotta wear this first. I promise it's nothing bad. Do you trust me?"

Molly nodded and swallowed a little anxious breath. "Yes, of course I do."

Walking behind her, Connor gently placed the cloth over her eyes, blinding her for a few moments, just to make sure the surprise was worth the wait. Once he was happy that she couldn't see, he took her by the hand, leading her up a little path to their awaiting ride.

Connor could not hide his happiness. The smile swept across his face, as he carefully led Molly toward the balloon.

"Connor, where are we going?" she asked.

He took her hand and gave her a reassuring squeeze before holding her still. "Are you ready?" he asked, his voice full of mischief.

"Erm, okay!"

"I just need to lift you for a second, okay?"

"O-kay," she muttered, sounding more nervous than he thought she would.

Connor took Molly into his arms with ease and walked the last few feet until he popped her over the side of the basket, then jumped in beside her.

"Can I take this off?" Molly asked, holding on to Connor's arm for dear life.

"Nope, not yet, just a few minutes more," he said, gently holding her close to him. "When you're ready." He nodded his head at the man in the balloon and before they knew it, the *whoosh* of air in the burner made Molly jump.

Connor reached behind her head, untying the fabric.

Molly gasped as the balloon started to lift off the ground. She inspected everything.

The bay was magnificent. The blue of the sky was a welcome sight. And gazing at Connor, she asked, "You did this for me?"

Pulling her into his arms, Connor kissed her before answering, "I'd do anything for you."

And up they went, floating through the sky, in what was a memory neither would forget.

"This is just amazing," Molly gushed as tears formed in her eyes. "You did this for me."

Connor stood behind her and wrapped his lean arms around her waist, resting his head on her shoulders. He'd made the right choice, and he was pleased with himself because he could clearly see from the look on her face how much this meant to her.

"It's so beautiful and calm up here. It's like we're on top of the world," Connor mused as they both took in the wonder of the world below.

The view of the Napa Valley was spectacular. The rolling and lush hills of the surrounding wine country made both of them gasp in admiration. Then there was the Napa Valley castle of Castello di Amorosa, with its roaming fields and generous forestry made for a special moment.

"This is what heaven looks like," Molly said as her fingers touched his.

"I couldn't agree more."

They spent three and a half hours taking in the beauty of the Napa Valley. Connor loved the expressions of surprise and awe on Molly's face as they moved through the sky, each one taking a turn at steering the balloon as the pilot guided them.

Connor with all his money, his high-powered connections—everything that his prestigious world could offer—did not get close to how he was feeling with Molly. Taking stock of it all, his mind accepted that there were changes to be made. He had no choice. Molly took priority over everything, and if that meant eradicating a few habits and connections along the way, then it had to be done.

"How did you decide on this?" Molly asked him, as she held on to the basket, looking down over the swirling water.

"Honestly, it just came to me. I thought what better way to escape the humdrum of reality for a few hours than looking down on the world?"

"Well, it's done the trick." Molly reached out and touched his face. Her blue eyes shimmered as sunbeams trickled in through the lines of the balloon.

"I'm glad," Connor replied as he rested his hand on the small of her back, "because I would do so much just to make you happy. I swear it, Molly. I've never felt like this before. This is a whole new world to me, and one I am thankful to have. It was you who saved me, always remember that."

Molly gazed over at him. Her face was a picture of happiness. It was mirrored in Connor's expression. They were perfect for each other, and Connor couldn't wait until he got the chance to show her off and declare his love to the world.

* * * *

"Oh my God, that was amazing," Molly gushed as they drove back to the beach house.

Connor smiled at his girl. She looked sexy as hell. Her hair all windswept, her cheeks pink and the cute little blue shirt she wore clung in all the right places. He loved how she made him feel. He loved the effect she had on him.

"It's right up there in my top three," he replied, smiling as the words left his mouth.

"Oh, top three, enlighten me."

Clearing his throat, Connor licked his lips and grinned before he spoke. "Well, number one, this car, she's a beauty. Of all the cars a guy could have, this little lady turned my head. She's reliable, gorgeous to look at, and has never let me down." He winked at Molly, who looked at him with a curious glint in her eyes. "Number two, you — the night you walked up to me, scaring me, letting me know how I'd be dead before I hit the water. That was a defining moment in my life and one that I promise we will tell the grandchildren — but maybe leaving out a few little things, we'll whitewash it a little." His grin got broader. "And last but not least, the night we made love for the first time — I've never felt anything like it in my life. You did something to me, woman, and I swear I want to experience it time and time again for the rest of our lives."

Molly's face went a pretty shade of scarlet as she absorbed what he'd just said. Connor loved seeing her cheeks flush. He adored how bashful she became when given a compliment. He treasured every second gazing at her, afraid that he'd miss witnessing something new.

"I don't think I've ever been included in someone's top anything," Molly gushed.

"Well, get used to it because you are on the top of this guy's list."

Connor pulled into the driveway of the beach house. The sun had set, casting a glorious purple hue across the horizon. The day had been a success. A memory created. Something they'd both look back on in their twilight years. A little piece of heaven had been shared and Connor's heart was fit to burst.

If this was perfection, then he'd die a happy man.

Chapter Twenty

Molly nearly dropped her cup of coffee when she heard the sound of her phone ringing. Rushing to her bag, she searched through the contents, pulling out her diary before finding the cell, seeing Barry's name flash across the screen.

"Hey, Barry," she greeted him.

Connor looked at her, mouthing a curious 'who's Barry?'

Putting her finger to her mouth, she gestured for him to keep quiet for a minute.

"I was meaning to call, but Connor took me out of town," she replied. "Yes... I promise I am doing well—" She paused as she listened to Barry. "Friday night? Yeah, I can make that. Can I bring a friend?" she asked, looking over at Connor who sipped at his coffee. "Brilliant, thanks, Barry... Yes, I promise. Okay, bye."

"Barry?" Connor inquired as he set his cup on the large, ornate table.

Molly reached behind her, lifted a cushion and threw it at him. "He's my friend."

"Oh, a friend, what kind of friend?" He winked at her. "I'm only messing."

"His wife, Jenna, is my go-to gal. She's my sponsor. Between them both, they tend to do a lot of picking me up when I feel like drowning my sorrows."

Slipping in close beside Connor, she rested her head on his shoulder as he clasped his fingers around her hand. "He sounds like a dependable guy."

"He's a good man. There have been some dark times in my life, especially my meltdown after Aggie passed. Between Barry and Jenna, they got me back on my feet. It was Jenna who encouraged me to live a little, hence lunch with you."

"Then I am forever in her debt." Connor kissed the top of her head.

"They are good people. You will like them." Molly cocked her head back, smiling up at him. "And, you get to meet them on Friday."

"Friday?"

"Yup, we've been invited to their daughter's fifteenth birthday party. It's just a simple easygoing get-together." Molly gave him her cheesiest grin.

"Well, isn't this interesting?" He grinned at her. "So, this will be like our first formal outing as a couple."

"Yeah, I suppose it will be."

Molly had never been a part of anything before. The feeling that he could be her family was enough to make her cry. But holding back those happy tears, Molly swiftly pulled up her knees and cuddled into Connor instead.

"Cool, because on Saturday night, my family has this annual thing they do and I'd love for you to be my plus one." His eyes met hers.

"Are you sure?" Molly asked, knowing that his thing with his family would be a lot more formal than hot dogs and s'mores in Jenna's yard.

"Absolutely. I can't think of anyone else I'd rather spend the night with, and believe me, you will be a welcome distraction from all the pretentious fools my family loves to surround themselves with. But it's for charity and I like to do my bit," he said.

Molly felt a little nervous at the prospect of meeting his family. She knew by now that they were some kind of a big deal, but she had never anticipated having to meet them. This was going to be something on a whole other level of scary. Panic began to set in.

"What if they hate me?" she panicked.

"They'd be fools if they did," Connor teased. "And besides, it's my opinion that counts the most. I am officially your biggest fan."

There, he did it again, turning her insides into mush. Connor had a way of saying the most beautiful, yet honest things. There was no denying the effect he was having on her.

"You are the best thing to ever happen to me," he said as he pulled her into his arms. "I want to show you off. Let the world know that I love Molly Rice."

"You do know that you're going to make me cry now, don't you?" Molly asked, on the verge of breaking down.

Before Molly got the chance to shed a tear, Connor kissed her softly. A sweet, tender kiss that had so much emotion behind it that Molly felt like tiny little butterflies were brushing against her.

"No more of this, okay?" Connor whispered as he touched the side of her face, kissing the tip of her nose. "No more tears. Just happiness."

Molly couldn't help but believe what he was saying. There had never been an instant in her life when she felt like giving herself to someone so completely. But Connor — gorgeous, kind and generous Connor — had opened up her heart, restoring her confidence, building up the self-esteem she had lacked for much of her life and giving her the reassurance to let herself go.

Outside, the wind picked up pace. Gone was the gentle breeze from earlier in the day, as a storm made its way along the coastline. Molly closed her eyes as she listened to the gentle tapping of the rain hitting the windows. If there was one thing Molly adored, it was the rain. It was therapeutic, always calming her.

Molly loved the feeling of being so close to Connor.

They couldn't get enough of each other. The way they gazed into each other's eyes, their want and desire matched. Both craving the other, unable to hold back. The burning passion radiated from them.

Afraid of letting the moment go, Molly stood and reached out her hand to him. "Make love to me," she whispered as her body trembled. Connor touched her fingers, gently slipping his hand into hers.

Connor stood up, pressing his body against hers. "Are you sure?" he asked. Tipping on her toes, Molly brushed her lips against his, being gentle. "Yes!"

Molly grabbed Connor by the hand and they ran up the stairs together, eager to show each other just how much their love meant to them. Outside the door, Connor turned to her, pressing his body into hers as he pushed her in through the bedroom door. They kept moving backward until Molly forced him to sit on the bed. Standing in front of him, she could see that he was looking her up and down, yearning for the touch of her body against his.

Molly leaned forward, tugging at his shirt, lifting it over his head, revealing his gorgeous, toned chest that made her giddy just from the look of it. Connor didn't waste any time as he squeezed her hips, touching the roundness of her ass, making her giggle. Connor undid the buttons of her blouse then ran his hands over her abdomen. He ran the tips of his fingers up and down in light strokes. The sensation alone aroused her. She hardly noticed that he had unzipped her jeans, pushing them down over her ankles, leaving her standing in front of him in her underwear. Reaching up behind her, Connor unhooked her bra, releasing her breasts, his tongue tracing the contours of her nipples as she ran her fingers through his hair.

Holding on to her waist, Connor gazed up at her. She knew his appetite had been whetted.

Connor pulled her to him, lying back on the bed, guiding her body onto his. With one hand, he ran it up and down her bare back as the other traced the line of her panties.

Her breath was hot against his, as they barely allowed their lips to touch, both wary of her sutures. Their breaths danced together as Molly slipped her hand down, unzipping his jeans and sliding her hand inside.

A smile spread across her face when she felt that he was wearing no underwear. Connor's mischievous grin said it all—*come and get it*. Kneeling, Molly slid his jeans down, throwing them across the room.

Molly eyed his naked body and her heart began to race as she crawled back up over him, pressing her body against his, wanting to feel his growing hardness against her.

Connor flipped Molly over and she let out a squeal. She giggled as Connor ran a finger up her inner thigh, letting it brush against the material of her panties, making her squirm from his touch.

Sliding off her panties, Connor opened her legs wide, revealing her glistening pussy.

Connor kissed her neck. His mouth felt amazing. Molly ran her nails up and down his back. She gasped from the way his tongue set her insides ablaze. Molly knew how hot he was getting. His cock pressed into her pelvis and turned her on in a way she felt as though a fever was consuming her.

Connor tended to her needs with such tenderness that everything became disorientating as he pushed into her, making love to her slowly, wanting to savor the moment. She couldn't take it, the tension almost too much to handle. Arching her back, she pushed her hips up to meet his and felt him move all the way out of her before he thrust back in hard and deep.

The momentum lasted until both of them cried out together, their orgasms consuming them both.

Complete satisfaction.

The night was more than she wished for. With the rain hitting the window, Connor expressing his love for her and the new dizzying heights she found herself on, Molly wouldn't be coming down any time soon.

Molly had finally found her Prince Charming and held on to him with an iron-clad grip.

Chapter Twenty-One

"You do know that I am actually petrified about meeting Jenna and her family," Connor shouted from the bathroom as he shaved. He was right. He was frightened. He was so used to being judged based on his wealth and didn't want to come across as an arrogant motherfucker who had to defend himself.

Molly stepped up to the door, looking pretty in a blue floral mini-dress. Her tan, toned legs were very easy on the eye. Connor couldn't help but smile as she stood there barefoot, looking at him with her arms folded across her chest. The memories of the past few nights making love, having those legs wrapped around his waist, did things to him he had never thought possible.

"It's just a family get-together, nothing to worry about, you dork."

"We'll see." He winked at her. "Besides, I get to show you off tomorrow night. Kind of tit for tat, though I much prefer the tit part myself."

Giggling, Molly threw a towel at him before walking away.

"I know you like the tittie comments, you're just too shy to admit it," he shouted as he finished shaving.

"You are a tit. A prize tit," Molly's voice sounded back.

This was what he loved about her. The fact that she wasn't afraid to be herself around him. She was easy to be with. She had taught him a lot about who he truly was, and that alone was a testament about the woman she was.

Knowing that she was involving him in her life, introducing him to her 'extended family', as she liked to call them, was something Connor found hard to believe. Yes, everything was still new and surreal, but the sense of completion that she gave him, in figuratively speaking terms — she brought out the best version of him, and he loved that.

"You nearly ready?" he said as he got dressed, fixing his watch around his wrist. He observed her painting her toenails. He adored the way her hair fell over her shoulders, little strands resting against her nose as she concentrated.

"Almost… Just a few minutes more."

"Should we bring anything? I mean, I'd feel like an ass turning up at someone's house empty handed," he said as he popped his wallet in his pocket.

Molly looked at her toes and smiled. "Don't be silly. Jenna and Barry aren't like that. They want us there for our company, nothing else."

"Then at least let me pick a gift for their daughter. What's her name?"

"Arianna, and that would be a lovely idea, but, Connor —"

"Yup."

"Nothing flashy, okay?"

"What does one get a fifteen year old?" Connor asked, his expression priceless.

"You are kidding, right?"

"I've never had to, you know, do something like this before."

"We'll get some gift cards, you can never go wrong with gift cards," Molly said as she walked up to him, tipping on her toes, kissing him gently on his cheek. "And besides, I think my hot boyfriend should be enough eye candy for one night."

That earned her a laugh. Connor's face lit up as he gazed at her. It was a cute moment and he loved that they brought out the best in each other.

Connor wrapped his arms around her, embracing her for a moment before they headed up the 101 and back to city life.

It was shortly after three p.m. when they finally returned

to San Francisco. Connor was getting fairly anxious, and who could have blamed the guy? It had almost been two weeks since the episode on the bridge, and in that short period of time, the unlikeliest of things had happened. His life had changed dramatically, and for the first time, he began to contemplate what it all meant to him.

Molly — his sweet, beautiful and gentle Molly, an angel who just so happened to have walked into his life and did something no one else had ever bothered to do — she cared.

There were no half measures, this was the real deal. Molly wanting to introduce him to her close-knit friends gave him a great sense of achievement. He was on cloud nine and couldn't have been happier.

"Stop fidgeting," Molly said as she rested a hand over his. "They aren't going to bite."

Connor pulled at the neck of his shirt. He felt as if he couldn't breathe. "I am no good with these kinds of things."

"Relax, Jenna is going to love you and so will Barry, so be prepared for a bromance." She winked at him, earning herself a playful jab in the arm.

"Now that image is going to play over and over — thanks, babe."

Molly walked in front as they climbed the steps to the front door of the modest two-story house. Music and chatter could be heard. Connor's stomach flipped. He was a little too nervous but knew he had to go with the flow for Molly.

The door opened and a beaming man greeted them both, welcoming them inside.

"Barry," Molly said as she wrapped her arms around Connor's waist. "This is Connor."

Connor reached out and met Barry's hand. They exchanged a nice, firm but sincere handshake.

"Welcome, Connor. Thanks for joining us this evening."

"The pleasure's all mine."

Connor smiled, holding Molly in close for comfort. She reciprocated the attention with a gentle touch of her hand against his chest. Barry smiled.

"So, come on through. The girls are dying to see you, Molly, and of course, Jenna is pretty eager to meet you, Connor," Barry said, winking at the two of them as he led the way to the lovely, cozy back yard.

As they walked out, Jenna jumped up. She and Molly greeted each other with a warm hug. Connor couldn't help but notice how family orientated the get-together was. It felt natural to be a part of it, and he adored seeing Molly interact with Jenna.

"Oh, honey, we were so scared when Gina filled us in. You do know that I am going to give you a hard time about not calling me. But, for now, I'm just thankful you're here," Jenna said as she touched the side of Molly's face.

"I know... I feel so bad for not calling, but Connor whisked me off, giving me a chance to relax. You know what I'm like when I hit a crisis," Molly said.

"Honey, we understand and we're just thankful that you had Connor"—she paused as she made eye contact with Connor—"to take care of you, and from the looks of things, it was a well-earned break."

Connor was beaming. He could feel the warmth from them all. It wasn't what he had been expecting at all.

"So, where's the birthday girl?" Molly called out as she glanced around the small gathering of people.

"Right here!" a squealing Arianna shouted as she ran up to Molly from where she had been sitting with her friends. The two embraced, giggling like silly girls.

Connor loved everything about seeing Molly in her natural surroundings. It was more than he had ever imagined.

"Oh my God, these are perfect," Arianna shouted as she opened her present. "I never get to do my own shopping." She pursed her lips at her mother. "And I know exactly what I'm getting. Thank you so much." She hugged Molly first. She then ran over to Connor, taking him by surprise as she hugged him too.

"You're welcome," he laughed.

Running back to her friends, Arianna showed them the

rather generous gift cards. The small group of girls looked over at where Connor and Molly stood, whispering to each other.

"You guys hungry?" Barry asked.

"Always," Molly replied as she walked over to the patio table and sat down next to Jenna.

"Connor, want to give me a hand?" Barry asked.

"Sure!"

Connor followed Barry to the kitchen. It was a nice, clean and bright space. One that Connor could actually visualize the family sitting in, enjoying meals together, talking, joking and just sharing the kind of love he had missed as a child.

"So, Molly seems to have taken a shine to you," Barry remarked as he took some patties out of the refrigerator, setting them on the counter before lifting out three Tupperware containers. "And by the look on your face, the feeling is mutual."

Connor felt as if he were under the microscope. "She's incredible."

"Don't worry, I'm not about to give you the third degree," Barry said. His reassuring smile eased some of the inner turmoil roaming around inside Connor's head. "Molly's had a rough ride. I'm sure she's filled you in, but I think she may have left a few details out."

Connor's heart stopped beating for a split second. "What kind of things?" he asked, trying his best not to let his voice quaver.

"That girl has had a tough life, and I know she's probably told you about the alcohol and the abuse, but I bet she left out the minor details of how her parents turn up every few months, sometimes it's a year or two, torturing her," he whispered. "They emotionally blackmail her into giving them money for their next hit. Her mother — a nasty piece of work — screws with her, making her feel like she's dirty. Damaged goods that no man will ever want, which as you can imagine makes some of those old wounds bleed."

"Jesus, she never mentioned any of this," Connor said.

"Of course she wouldn't. She's afraid that if she lets you in on the real nasty things, you'll walk away."

"I would never do that."

"Then when they come knocking, which I can guarantee they will, don't hold Molly accountable for any of their crap."

Connor swallowed the information and knew that Molly needed him more now than ever before.

"Absolutely."

"Then let's go fire up the barbecue and eat like we're kings," Barry said, smiling. "Or at least pretend we're kings."

Chapter Twenty-Two

Molly couldn't hide the happiness. It was radiating from her like never before. Hundreds of different emotions twirled around inside her, dancing like leaves spinning in spirals around her head. It was an ethereal feeling and one she never wanted to forget.

Watching how Connor felt at ease interacting with her friends confirmed her love for him. She adored the smile, the crinkling of his eyes as he laughed when Barry made his ridiculous jokes, to the way he helped Jenna with the plates, carrying them back to the kitchen. Being a gentleman and every inch a god in her eyes.

"What are you daydreaming about?" Barry inquired as he sat down beside her.

Molly gave him a gentle dig against his ribs, trying to stifle her giggle. "Nothing."

"Liar," he said as he smiled at her. "I like him. He's a good guy." Then his eyebrows narrowed. "How are you dealing with what happened?"

Molly knew it was going to be asked. She knew what Barry was like and there was no getting away from the subject.

"Honestly, I wasn't dealing with it. In fact, even when Connor took me to the beach house, all I wanted to do was drown my sorrows...but I didn't, because he didn't give me five seconds to sit, wallowing and feeling sorry for myself." Her voice was soft, like a delicate piece of china, ready to break if pushed too hard.

"How's that lip? It looks sore but not as bad as Gina made out—which I am thankful for."

"It hurts, but it's healing," she said as she touched her bottom lip, the swelling beginning to subside. "Has there been any word on Eugene?"

Molly couldn't leave well alone. It was her natural instinct to inquire, to ask the awkward questions others avoided. There was a part to her that others rarely got to see. She kept it well hidden. The little part of her, that if given half the chance, would destroy all those who'd hurt her, spit on their graves, and walk away not blinking an eye. But that was the person she didn't want to be. That was the Molly who was bred on hatred and lies, the kind of stuff that would convince a child that being bad was the right way. She didn't want that and fought hard to push those demons back into their tiny coffins inside her soul.

"Is this something you really need to hear?" Barry asked.

"Yes, we both know I won't leave well alone until I find out."

"He's still under. They've sedated him to help reduce the swelling on the brain."

"Oh, is the prognosis bad?" A sickening sensation began to pulse through her. She hated herself for hitting him. That wasn't the person she wanted to be — a cold-blooded killer — but she knew that it was either be raped or survive. She chose survival.

"It was self-defense. If you hadn't — God knows what would have happened," Barry said as he took her hand in his. "Listen to me, you've got a good thing going with Connor. I know it's new, it's exciting and it's been owed to you for a long time, but here's something you need to keep check of — your mental wellbeing. And by that, I mean don't overanalyze things. I know what you're like, Molly. I can see the cogs turning as we speak. You did nothing wrong. You did what any other rational person would have done, so don't you dare start blaming yourself."

"You know me a little too well, huh?"

Smiling, Barry gave her hand a gentle squeeze. "You're like a part of this family. Fuck it, you are family. We look out for each other, and if that means being blunt, and saying it like it is, then so be it."

"I know I can always count on you," Molly replied, giving her friend a well-earned smile.

Molly kicked back a little, relaxed some more, enjoying the company, the atmosphere — the general feeling of her and Connor being accepted as a couple. It was weird for her even to think that, because only two weeks in, it was as though they'd been lovers forever. It was fast, it was crazy, but it was good.

Connor walked over to where she sat, slipping down beside her, wrapping an arm around her shoulders. "This was a great idea. Thank you for inviting me."

"You're welcome," Molly said as she gazed at him. "I'm glad you said yes."

"These are good people. Jenna is sweet and Barry is hilarious. I can see why you love them," Connor said, looking at her with his gorgeous doe eyes.

"They are the best." Molly beamed. She had never been more proud.

"About tomorrow night," Connor changed the subject.

Molly's stomach did a somersault at the mere mention of the gala. She swallowed hard, the stress beginning to overtake her mind. "I had forgotten about that."

"Are you still okay with attending?"

"Of course I am. I just don't know what to wear," she lied. "I'm not so good with all this formal stuff."

"I'd hate to think that you felt obligated."

Molly took hold of his hand, running her thumb over his knuckles. "That could never happen. I just am a bit nervous, nothing else."

Connor pulled Molly in close for a sweet, gentle kiss. They got the approval of a few eyes watching them.

Molly stared over at Barry and Jenna. They smiled at her. She knew she looked every bit the loved-up girl she was. There was no hiding that she had been renewed. She was content knowing that she had found her soul mate, someone who was willing to put her needs first. Barry and Jenna's blessing was all that Molly needed.

The rest of the evening was spent in such relaxed splendor, Molly was floating when they bade their goodbyes.

* * * *

Shopping was never Molly's favorite pastime. She was more of a pick-something-up-in-a-local-thrift-store girl. She couldn't think of anything worse than standing around super swanky shops, staring at row after row of cocktail dresses and feeling very much out of her comfort zone. But there she was, standing, glaring at rows of dresses, deciding what to purchase.

Only for Connor, she wouldn't never have considered such a high-profile outing. The world he lived in was so different from hers she was afraid of standing out like a sore thumb. She didn't want to be the one to turn heads for the wrong reasons. It was bad enough that no amount of gloss would cover her lip, not to mention that her budget was probably peanuts compared to what his mother spent on clothes.

Sighing, she walked up to a rack to begin her search for something suitable when a voice startled her from behind.

"Can I help you with anything?" the store assistant asked.

Molly turned around sharply, grimacing. "I'm just looking, thank you."

"Well, if you need anything, please don't hesitate to ask."

The assistant walked away, taking a look back at her every few steps. Molly smiled at her and began looking at the dresses.

One pretty navy dress caught her eye. Molly picked up the price tag and bit down into her lip. It was expensive. But the occasion called for something beautiful, and the dress was almost perfect.

Looking around, Molly eyed the assistant, gesturing for her to come over.

Molly took the dress off the rack and said, "I'd like to try this on." The butterflies were already beginning to move inside.

The assistant smiled and led the way to the changing rooms. "It's a beautiful dress."

"Thank you."

Once inside the privacy of the cubicle, Molly began to undress, looking at her reflection in the mirror as she did. There were moments her cheeks blushed, and others when she felt stupid for taking a glance at her shapely figure. But once she had the dress on, she couldn't stop looking. The chiffon of the dress was luxurious against her skin. The A-line princess, one shoulder dress clung in all the right places. It was simple, yet beautiful with the small embroidered beading and appliqué lace. The dark blue complemented her pale features. She looked stunning.

Molly glanced at the price tag again and groaned internally as she contemplated the month's budget. But as she took another peek at her reflection, she smiled. "Screw it," she muttered.

As she walked from the store, her grip was tight on the bag, not wanting to let it go. She had this air of excitement running through her. Yes, there was also a little apprehension thrown into the mix, but for the first time, she truly wanted to look like a princess and the gala was to be her ball.

Chapter Twenty-Three

Connor listened to his mother, but his mind was elsewhere. He really wasn't interested in the formal seating plan, or the order in which he was expected to greet guests. In fact, he wasn't really in the mood.

The gala was a yearly run event organized by Eleanor on behalf of John Ellison Senior — the battleax — for the brain and spine federation. They raised money from some of the most prestigious men and women in the country. Elite people who adored getting the attention for sharing a slice of their fortune for the sick and needy, and of course the real cause at heart — brain stem cell research.

"Connor, do you hear me?" Eleanor called to him from across the table.

"What?" he asked, clearly distant.

"I was just telling your brother the order of the evening," she snapped. "You aren't at all bothered about how important this is."

"Mom, I am here, isn't that enough?"

From beside him, his brother James cleared his throat. "I think we should give the guy a break. After all, he's had a pretty intense two weeks. It can't be easy having your face plastered everywhere."

"Fuck you," Connor snapped.

"He has balls, who knew," James mocked him.

"Oh, would the pair of you act your age. Jesus you aren't toddlers anymore," Eleanor scolded them then got back to her list. "So, Connor, the car will be picking Marissa up at five-fifteen, that gives her enough time to get to the hotel — "

"Marissa?" Connor asked, narrowing his eyebrows, a

knot twisting itself into a tight ball.

"Yes," Eleanor chimed. "Whatever is wrong with you?"

"I am not sitting with Marissa."

Eleanor's eyes widened as she looked up from her list. "What do you mean? You always sit with Marissa. It's how things are done."

"Not anymore."

James snapped his neck to the side to glare at his younger brother. The curious look said it all. "Uh-oh, someone's in for it."

"How old are you, James?" Connor asked. "Jesus Christ, get a grip."

"Connor, you will be seated with Marissa, just like you have in years gone by," his mother insisted.

"I'm afraid not, Mother. I have made alternative arrangements this year."

Well, that did it. That earned him the look of scorn.

The sound of the chair scraping on the floor rang through the room. Silence befell them all as Eleanor's eyes blazed. Her faced turned purple as she became enraged. Her nostrils flared.

Connor looked at his mother, witnessing the way her face contorted when incensed with anger.

"You will do as you are told," she spat. "There will be no room for discussion. Your grandfather is fond of Marissa. Do you really want to disappoint an old man?"

"Fuck!" Connor muttered as his insides began to recoil in disgust.

"*What* did you just say?" Eleanor marched over to where Connor sat, pointing her long, well-groomed finger in his face.

Connor looked up at his mother, rolled his eyes and stood up from his chair. "I am not an impressionable eight year old any longer, Mother. Don't you think it's time you accepted that?"

"Excuse me?" her voice screeched.

"Well, seeing as things are turning sour, I shall bow out of this," James said as he made a quick exit.

"You just never quit, Mother. Always interfering, trying to control a life that you really have no say in. Who I attend tonight's fund-raiser with is really no concern of yours, but if you ask me kindly, I just may introduce you." Smiling, Connor tugged at the cuffs of his shirt, feeling the tension in the air. "And if that is all, I have things to do. I'm sure Father is eager for your report. That's how you two function, right? Giving each other daily reports on how disappointed you are in your offspring. Good day, Mother, I shall see you tonight."

As he walked away from where Eleanor stood, Connor smirked. The more they tried to push him inside the box they wished him to conform to, the more he began to rebel. It may have been twenty years late, but he was now a man who was in charge of his own destiny, and he sure as hell wasn't going to be controlled by the puppeteer any longer. He was now steering toward his own horizon, and for once in his life, he was in charge.

How he loved the power rush.

* * * *

Sitting in the busy bar, Connor hardly heard the noise from the patrons. He was lost in thought, staring into his glass of whiskey, swishing it around every few mouthfuls. He was trapped by his name. His parents and their controlling nature were beginning to tighten like a noose around his neck. For the first time in the two weeks since his dance with death on the bridge, the same old darkness loomed, gripping him tight. Refusing to allow him to think straight.

"Penny for your thoughts," the bartender said as she refilled his glass.

"Have you got all night?"

The pretty redhead smiled at him. Her eyes were sympathetic, but her body was sending out a whole other message as she pushed out her chest, letting her ample cleavage do all the talking.

Connor was used to this. Used to the attention, and for the most part he liked it. It replaced some of the ugliness of everything that reeked from him. Of course, women like the pretty bartender, they were hoping for their own Prince Charming to come along and save them, but he'd already found his Sleeping Beauty.

"I can be a good listener," she said as she gazed at him.

"So can my girlfriend."

"So, it's not woman trouble?

"Nope."

Leaning on the counter, the redhead smiled as she gave him a good angle to view her breasts. "Then what could ever have a nice guy like you all troubled?"

"The parentals."

"Enough said, I got daddy issues too."

Looking up at her, Connor smiled, signaling for her to refill his glass.

The stool beside him got his attention. As it moved, Connor looked to his left and watched as Mark sat down beside him. "So this is where you're hiding?"

"Not really hiding, more like drowning my sorrows."

"Can I have two coffees, please?" Mark asked the redhead, who was more than happy to serve him. "Your mother called. She was pretty pissed."

"Yup, that'd be her." Connor sipped at his whiskey. "Did she send you to talk some sense into me?"

"Of course."

"And are you?"

"No."

"Good, because I'm picking Molly up in a few hours."

"Then you don't need whiskey in your system. You need to get a grip, Connor. If you want to prove a point to your mother, it isn't going to be found at the bottom of a bottle."

Connor knew his friend was right. His mother always found a way to fuck with him. If it wasn't something about his job, then it was about whom she wanted him to be connected with. He was done with it all.

"Then what do you suggest?"

"First of all, drink this." Mark set the coffee in front of him, pushing the whiskey aside. "Then you take Molly to the gala, show her off and prove to them all that you are capable of making decisions on your own."

"Sure, Dad," Connor mocked, which earned him a playful smack on the back of the head.

Throwing down twenty bucks to cover the price of the coffee and a tip, Mark cleared his throat. "Well, Romeo, you going to take the belle to the ball or what?"

The redhead waved goodbye as they left the bar. Once they were outside, Connor's heart skipped a few beats when he thought of Molly and the fact that he had just downed a good few measures of the one thing she found hard to resist. He felt like a fool. A stupid, childish idiot.

"Tonight's going to be a disaster," he mumbled as he got into the passenger side of Mark's Audi. "My mother will eat Molly alive. You know it and I know it."

Defeat wasn't becoming on Connor. In fact, it made him look weak, a glimpse of how self-deprecating he could actually be.

"How the fuck do you know?" Mark snapped as he drove away from the bar, taking Connor back to his apartment. "If you don't try it, you will never know. If you're serious about this girl, then you've got to introduce her to your world at some point. You can't hide who you are or where you come from forever."

"Jesus Christ, Mark, I'm not trying to hide anything. I'm trying to protect her."

"Then why did you invite her and make such a fuss about bringing her?"

"I got caught up in the moment."

"You can be such a dick when you want to be. I swear it. As your friend there are times when I just want to kick your ass and tell you to wise the fuck up," Mark shouted. "This girl, whoever she is, better be worth all the hassle because

Cassie has been itching to meet her—"

"What? You told Cassie?"

Mark laughed as he turned onto Connor's block. "What do you expect? She's my wife. I tell her everything."

Connor's head began to ache as a migraine made its presence known. Holding his fingers against his temple, he closed his eyes. His frame of mind was all over the place. "I think I need to lie down," he said as Mark stopped the car.

Looking at his friend, Mark sighed. "Connor, you know I've got your back, but believe me when I tell you that you need to get your act together. I know things have been bad recently. Hell, I could see that things had changed in you a while ago. But I'm your friend, and I gave you the benefit of the doubt. So for your sake, and Molly's, straighten yourself out. Don't allow your mother, father or Marissa to take something that you so obviously care about away from you."

Connor knew Mark was right. "How come you get to be the grown up all of a sudden?" Connor asked as he looked over at Mark.

"If you hadn't noticed, I am approaching impending fatherhood, so I'm practicing the pep talks on you." Mark grinned and the mischievous glint in his eyes eased some of Connor's burdens. "Now get the fuck outta my car, and go sort yourself out for tonight's festivities."

Connor smirked, said nothing as he got out of the car, only to lean back in. "Hey, when you finally get around to talking sense into your kid, you might need to tone it down a little. The whole expressionless look is kinda off-putting."

Connor walked into his apartment, closed the door behind him, instantly regretting what he was introducing Molly to.

Unbearable, overwhelming dread began to seep through him. He felt as if he were being crushed. If anything happened at the gala, he'd never forgive himself. Not this time.

Chapter Twenty-Four

"Will you please stop fidgeting?" Regina chided Molly as she wrapped the last few strands of hair around the curling iron. "I can't do this if you don't stop moving."

"I can't help it."

"Of course you can."

"Easy for you to say," Molly muttered as she began picking at the skin around her nails.

When anxiety presented itself, Molly was the worst person for pulling herself apart. The unease swirled in her stomach. Her throat burned as she fought the urge to say 'to fuck with it' and run away.

"Honey, you will be fine." Regina tried her best at easing the worry.

"What if I say something stupid? What if I embarrass Connor?"

Letting out a giggle, Regina applied some hairspray to the loose curls she had pinned to the back of Molly's head. "Honey, these are all natural feelings. You're only human. Believe me, being nervous will serve you well. It means you won't be a cocky bitch, which, in my world, is a huge deal."

Sighing, Molly took a sip of her sweet tea. "Do you think I will fit in? I don't want to look cheap."

"Oh, baby girl, when have you ever worried about fitting in? Remember the strong woman you've become. Aggie wouldn't rest well if she thought you were beginning to lose faith in who you are," Regina said as she rested her hands on Molly's shoulders. "Honey, you are so beautiful, inside and out. I wish you could see that."

Molly stared at herself in the mirror. Then she looked up

at Regina's soft face. Her dark eyes sparkled as she gazed at Molly lovingly. Regina had taken over some of the good that Aggie had done. She had stepped up to the plate and made sure that Molly kept her head well above water.

"What would I do without you?" she asked, touching Regina's hand.

"Probably drop off the face of the earth."

Molly would always have a special place in her heart for Regina. Aggie and Regina had been lifelong partners, never to be given a chance by society. Their love had made Molly believe that there was a special person out there for everyone, but because of how hard her own life had been, she had always accepted that love and all the joy it brought wasn't destined for her.

How wrong she had been.

Aggie and Regina, two unlikely souls brought together during the sixties. Their devotion to do-gooding and their mutual taste for standing up for the greater good would always stand the test of time. Molly loved listening to their stories about their wild, younger days. Everything they had made for good memories, and now it was Molly's turn to make the same kind of memories.

Placing all her anxieties to the back of her mind, Molly began getting ready. Deciding on a little makeup, she applied a nice shade of blue that would complement her dress. Red lipstick finished off the look, making her smile at her reflection. Slipping on her dress, she grinned, knowing she had done something Connor would never expect.

Finally, after a good two hours, she was ready.

A knock at the door echoed through to her room. Molly glanced at the clock and her stomach did a double flip as her heart raced.

Regina's voice could be heard talking, and Molly instantly recognized Connor's smooth tone. Not sure of how she wanted to make her entrance, she swallowed hard before grabbing her purse then opened the door and walked down the small hallway that led to the living room.

Regina couldn't hide the tears as Molly waltzed in. Her dark skin glistened as tears left their mark on her cheeks, pride bursting from the seams.

With wide eyes, Connor couldn't help but gaze at her. She was without doubt dazzling. She knew it and could see it in the way he responded.

"My God, you look amazing," his said, his hand shaking as he held it out for her to take.

Regina wiped her eyes with her white handkerchief, her smile a permanent fixture on her face. "I concur, you are stunning."

"Oh, the pair of you are dorks," Molly responded, jokingly brushing off their compliments. She wasn't used to this kind of attention. Granted, it felt good, but it was so very odd.

Molly took Connor's hand, their palms touching as their fingers entwined. Warmth radiated between them and it was clear to see that they were completely one.

"I am the luckiest man alive," Connor whispered.

"You are such a sap." Molly giggled, touching the tip of her nose, trying her best not to be bashful and losing the whole time.

"You two look great together," Regina said. She walked over to them and touched Molly's face. "Go and enjoy yourself. You only get one chance in life, so make the most of it when you can." Winking at Connor, Regina stepped to the door and opened it. "Now get, I have a date with a good book and the Sandman."

Connor led Molly out of the small apartment and down to their waiting car.

"A limo!" Molly all but yelled when she saw the black limousine parked out front of her apartment block.

"Absolutely. Tonight, we travel in style." Connor beamed as the chauffeur opened the door.

Molly's insides began to feel like mush. If Connor was trying to woo her, it was beginning to work. It was as if she were walking on air. A complete transition from her old life. How, in such a short period of time, he had gotten deep under her skin, she'd never know. But the fact that he was there, with eyes only for her, gave her the impression that she was invincible.

* * * *

The Ritz Carlton was lit up as if it were Christmas as the limo pulled outside the main entrance. A red carpet was laid out, ready for the gala patrons to enter the hotel in style. Lavish flowers of lisianthus, hydrangea, gloriosa and saffron crocus were on display on either side of the door — their colors exuded opulence and money.

Walking up the red carpet was a surreal moment. Molly wrapped her arm around Connor's, holding on for dear life.

"Relax," he said, looking down at her. "You will be fine. I promise."

Molly didn't reply. She placed all her focus on walking, trying her best not to stumble, and already her feet were beginning to ache in the heels that she'd never got a chance to break in.

Champagne was on offer as they entered the grand foyer. Molly's first instinct was to run to the bathroom, but she fought through it. If she wanted to survive the evening, then she had to deal with the little devil dancing on her shoulder.

Her finely painted fingernails dug into Connor's arm. Resting his hand on hers, he gave her a gentle smile. "I will look after you."

Molly let the anxiety go, threw caution to the wind and began relaxing.

"Connor Ellison," a gruff voice called.

"Jim Franklin." Connor smiled as he greeted the middle-aged man, shaking his hand firmly. "It's been a while."

"A year," Jim replied as he scanned the foyer. "Where's the old bastard hiding?"

Connor laughed as Molly looked on, curious.

"Probably following an order or two from the old ball and chain," Connor said, making Jim laugh.

"And who's this pretty little lady?"

"How rude of me, Jim, this is my girlfriend, Molly," he introduced Molly. "Molly, this is Jim Franklin, an old family friend. Don't trust him."

Winking at Molly, Jim reached out and took her hand. "I hope you're keeping this crook in check."

Molly laughed nervously.

"He's joking," Connor said as he pulled her in close, wrapping an arm around her waist.

"Don't mind me, sweetheart, I'm an old fool." Jim smiled at her. "Now I'd better go find your father and figure out how much money your mother wants from us all tonight."

"Millions!" Connor said, smiling the whole time.

"That'd be right." Jim walked away, still laughing as he greeted another few people.

"Sorry about that," Connor said as he led Molly toward the grand ballroom.

"He's funny."

"You sure?"

Connor looked at her.

"Yup."

"You ready to meet the parentals?" Connor asked, his voice now a little softer.

Molly, as much as she tried not to show it, became so nervous she thought she'd throw up then and there, but little did she know that was to be the least of her worries.

Chapter Twenty-Five

Holding Molly's hand tight, Connor entered the ballroom. The colors were bright, bold and lavish and it was evident that his mother had not spared any expense. When she did these events, she went all out.

The room was beginning to fill, but his mother still saw him, standing there with Molly, and like a bullet, she went straight for the kill.

"Connor, aren't you going to introduce me to your friend?" She practically slurred the word as her eyes scornfully moved up and down Molly. Inspecting every inch of her.

Connor shifted a little. His posture was becoming rigid, but to prove a point, he refused to allow his mother to feed on his own deep-rooted insecurities.

"Mother, this is Molly, my girlfriend," he said it slow and concise so the words would burrow themselves into her tiny brain.

"Lovely to make your acquaintance, Molly," Eleanor said as she took Molly's hand in hers. "Tell me, where did you get your dress? It's rather fetching."

Connor wanted to shut his mother up. The way she spoke to Molly made the bile in the back of his throat rise. He despised her. Detested how she treated anyone she believed to be beneath her. He pushed his anger to the back of his mind and was about to say something when Molly stepped in.

"Thank you, it's lovely to meet you too," she said, not once breaking Eleanor's steel glare. "The dress I got in Ambience, not sure if you know it," Molly said, then changed the subject. "You have done a fine job of the ballroom. You must be happy."

"Oh, this." Eleanor laughed. "I could do this in my sleep, darling."

"Wow, now that's devotion," Molly said as the irony slipped off her tongue.

Eleanor noticed. Her face crinkled as she glared at Molly. "Connor never mentioned you before now. Are you his dirty little secret?"

"Mother," Connor interrupted.

"Well, the sex has been amazing, but dirty? No."

Connor looked at Molly as she said it. He couldn't believe it. She was actually putting his mother in her place.

"Isn't that lovely? I just hope he knows how to clean up after himself. He wasn't the best as a child when he was finished with his playthings." Eleanor wasn't backing down.

Molly was about to respond, when Connor's father came over to where they stood. He gave Connor that all-knowing look of his as he touched Eleanor's arm.

"Well, hello there." He shook Molly's hand. "Glad you could join us tonight. I'd like to say they're not a rowdy bunch, but their hearts and wallets are always in the right place." Turning to his wife, he smiled at her. "Dear, my father would like to talk to you." John was doing his best to avert any kind of public exhibition.

Nodding in Molly's direction, John pulled Eleanor away, leaving Connor fuming.

"I cannot apologize enough for that," he said as his stomach churned.

"Don't worry about it," Molly lied. "That's nothing compared to what I'm used to."

"You shouldn't have to put up with shit like that. Not from her or anyone."

Connor couldn't believe that his mother never gave Molly a chance. She'd practically written Molly off before she got the opportunity to get to know the wonderful woman she was. He was so incensed in a simmering rage, he wanted nothing more than to drink a few shots and make a fool of them all. But he soon stopped thinking like that. He didn't want to become a monster, a product of his parents' disastrous attempt at procreation.

"Baby, I promise, I am good. Now let's check out the seating chart and find where we sit, or you at least." Molly gave Connor a gentle nudge.

As the evening rolled on, the dinner was served — so much food that Molly swore she'd burst out from her dress. Connor loved watching how she chatted with the other people at the table, engaging, giving them all much room for thought. Molly was not only beautiful but intelligent. He truly had struck gold with her.

"Don't you ever get frightened working late at night? The streets really aren't a place for young women," Claudia Vanderbilt asked. Another lady of luxury, who just so happened to be intrigued by Molly.

"Not at all," Molly responded as she stirred the milk in her coffee. "We face risks every moment of our lives. If the boogeyman is going to get you, it doesn't make a difference if it's day or night."

Murmurs of agreement told Connor that she had more than wooed them. Connor rested his arm on the back of her chair as he observed her demure presence. He'd never seen her so stunning. Yes, she was always stunning to him, but right then, in that moment, talking away to people she'd never met, nor had anything in common with, made him fall deeper in love with her.

"You are an incredible young lady," Claudia remarked. "You must allow me to make a donation to the shelter. God knows our city needs more vigilant people like you."

Smiling, Molly sipped at her coffee, not noticing the glare she was receiving from a few tables away.

Connor caught Marissa's daggers. He could see the jealousy permeate from every pore. She may have been something to look at, but underneath all the makeup and false bravado, she was ugly.

Marissa caught him staring and gave him a coy smile in return.

Turning his back on her, he wrapped an arm around Molly's shoulders as the first of the auctions were about to take place.

Eleanor took to the stage, the spotlight brightly shining down on her. This was the shit she lived for — being the center of attention.

"Well, I certainly hope you enjoyed that delicious meal, because we have some rather splendid things in store for you all," she gushed into the microphone. An applause erupted, and she nodded, absorbing the adulation, whether it was genuine or not. "We all know how important this cause is for our family, more so, my dear father-in-law, John Senior. We tirelessly try our best to raise awareness and funds to continue in the hope that one day we can eradicate illnesses that blight so many of us. So from me, and the entire Ellison foundation, thank you." Another round of applause erupted, then it was down to business. "So, for the first auction, we have had the pleasure of a lovely donation by the fabulous Vanderbilt family. For a week-long stay at their family ranch in Colorado, you get a personal cowboy — yes, I said cowboy — training from one of the best rodeo experts today, Ray Holborn. This is a once-in-a-lifetime chance to unwind, get back to the basics and learn how to run a ranch. Bidding starts at ten thousand dollars."

This was the part of the event that got ears pricked, mouths salivating and money dripping as they fought arduously for the best prizes going.

"Things will get nuts," Connor whispered into Molly's ear.

"I can only imagine."

The evening went by in a haze. So much money was being thrown at offers that no one could stand the chance of another outbidding them. Eleanor beamed as they reached their target of three million dollars in less than two hours. Which was a record.

The band played good music as everyone danced, celebrated, rejoiced in their shared love of all things grand and expensive.

Connor swayed from side to side with Molly in his arms. They didn't have to say a thing to each other. Their closeness was proof of how much in love they were.

"Guess what?" Molly whispered into his ear.

Rubbing his lips against her cheek, Connor asked. "What?"

"I'm not wearing any panties."

Connor was both surprised and aroused. The mere words alone were the sexiest thing she'd said all evening. He wanted her. He needed her. He craved her touch and there was only one thing for it.

Connor grabbed Molly by the hand and they slipped out of a little side door, no one noticing their hasty exit. They were like two lovesick teenagers in the throes of a new relationship.

Connor pulled Molly into the ladies' restroom, taking a sneaky glance to make sure it was empty, and just their luck, it was.

Closing the cubicle door behind them, Connor pulled at the hem of her dress, lifting it as their kiss intensified. Hot, wild and hungry. Running his hands over her bare buttocks, he couldn't hide his need for her a moment longer.

Molly slipped her hands down, unzipping his trousers. Reaching inside, she released his erection, gently stroking him.

Connor groaned before he kissed her again. Sliding his hands down over her breasts, down her sides, over her hips and in between her legs, he touched the place he wanted. As he circled around her clit, Molly let out a gasp into his mouth.

Pushing his trousers down with urgency, Molly lifted one leg, wrapping it behind him. Pressing himself against her, he lifted her as he pushed himself inside her. She was incredibly hot and wet as he began to move in and out of her. Her sweet breath brushed against his ear as he began fucking her.

Molly let out a series of moans, each one getting louder with Connor's hard thrusts, his movement hitting the very spot that left her gasping as the orgasm began to burn.

A breathless "I'm gonna come" was all it took from Molly to drive Connor to the point where he growled into her neck.

"Fuck!" he moaned as the tingling began in his balls. "Oh fuck!"

Together they moved, watching each other as their orgasms ripped through them, making their legs weak, their hearts pound and a satisfied grin spread across their faces.

Molly's hot breath danced lightly over Connor's face as he throbbed inside her. "You are a bad girl," he whispered as he kissed her forehead.

"Maybe," she replied, running her fingers through his hair. "But you love it."

"I love you!"

"I know."

Connor looked at her, loving the little deviant he'd just fucked. "Is that all I get?"

Giggling, Molly wrapped her arms around his neck. Kissed him hard, ignoring the smarting of her lip.

"I love you too," she whispered as she pulled her face away.

That was all he needed to hear. That was the thing that now defined him. Molly and her love for him.

Chapter Twenty-Six

Molly cleaned herself before leaving the cubicle. Connor splashed a little water over his face. He caught her reflection as she walked out. She smiled at him. Molly blushed a little, which only added to her already flushed cheeks.

"I'll go out first, make sure the coast is clear," Molly said, winking at Connor as he fixed the belt on his trousers.

"Okay. I'll not be too much longer."

Molly reapplied her lipstick before fixing her hair then slipped out of the door, leaving Connor to follow along.

Walking back toward the foyer, Molly was on cloud nine. Her head spun from delirious happiness. The evening was going in a direction she had never expected. Gone was the apprehension and worry, replaced by a renewed confidence, and she loved it.

Molly slipped back into the ballroom, made her way to the table and sat down.

"Where did you sneak off to?" a curious Claudia asked as she took a seat beside Molly.

"Oh, I just needed a little air. It's so hot in here."

"You do look flushed. Are you okay?"

"Absolutely," Molly replied. She couldn't hide it. She tried, but it was too obvious.

"Where's that young suitor of yours?"

Looking back at the door, Molly didn't see any sign of Connor and shrugged. "I think he's still talking to one of his father's friends."

"Men," Claudia remarked. "They do love to talk, a load of nonsense the majority of the time, but still, they never know when to shut up."

Moments slipped by and there was still no sign of Connor.

"Oh, we must exchange numbers. I would love to get more involved with the work you do at the shelter. Maybe even set up my own foundation," Claudia said as she opened her purse, taking out her phone.

"Oh, that would be fabulous," Molly replied, reaching her hand onto the table – she'd forgotten her bag. "Oh crap, I've left it in the bathroom. I'll be right back."

Molly walked out of the ballroom and looked around the busy corridor. Still no sign of Connor.

"Where is he?" she mumbled to herself as she strolled back to the bathroom.

Pushing the door open, she looked down at her dress, not noticing anything, not until the door had closed behind her.

Connor was pressed against the wall, a woman on her knees, her head moving as she fumbled at his crotch. "Stop it!" he shouted, not seeing Molly standing there.

"I can smell her on you," the woman growled as she released his cock from his trousers, stroking it.

"Get the fuck off me, Marissa."

Tears began to burn Molly's eyes when she realized what she was seeing.

Connor looked up and saw Molly. His face said it all.

Connor pushed Marissa to the floor, closed his trousers, fastening his belt as he walked toward Molly.

"Don't you come near me," Molly said through tears. "Don't you fucking dare."

Marissa's laugh echoed in the restroom. Clapping her hands, she stood and furrowed her brow. "I can still smell your pussy on him."

"Shut the fuck up, Marissa," Connor roared.

Molly grabbed her purse from the stool, turned her back on them and fumbled for the door handle. Once she was free from the restroom, she lifted the hem of her dress, briskly walking toward the exit. All the while hot, steaming tears fell down her cheeks.

Outside, the noise of local traffic became discordant as she tried to get her bearings. Spinning in a circle, she looked up at the starry night sky, her heartbeat reverberating through her head. Her breathing was labored and echoed as she looked back down, the twinkling of the streetlights blurred through her tears.

"Molly," Connor called after her. "Molly, please wait."

Molly ran down the street, wanting to be anywhere but there. She thought she was going to vomit as her stomach refused to digest what she'd just seen. How could she have been so stupid? She'd let down her guard and now she was broken — again.

"Molly," Connor's voice echoed from behind.

Molly pretended she didn't hear him. She didn't want to. She just wanted to escape, go back home, wash the filth from her and rid herself of the façade. Anything was better than feeling used.

A hand touched her. Spinning around, Molly met Connor's face with a hard slap. "Don't touch me. Don't you fucking touch me again."

"Molly, you've got to believe me, I didn't do anything."

"Fuck you!"

Trying to move away from him, Molly tried hailing a cab.

"She came on to me. She knew we were in there."

"I don't want to hear it, Connor," she cried, holding her hands over her ears.

"Molly, please, I didn't want any of that." Tears began to bubble in his eyes.

"Yeah," she seethed. "Well, from where I stood, your cock seemed to be responding quite well."

"Jesus Christ," Connor shouted as he ran his hands over his face. "I didn't want any of it. She did her usual shit. Molly, you've got to believe me. I love you and only you."

Molly stood in silence for a few moments, trying to absorb what he was saying, but it was pointless. The image of Marissa holding Molly's man's genitals in her hands would never leave her mind. A disgusting representation of what was wrong with their world. Their dark, seedy, sordid little world and she didn't want to be a part of it.

"I don't care."

"Molly, don't do this. Not after everything." He touched her arm again, this time trying to take hold of her. Molly pulled her arm, pushing at him at the same time.

"I wish you had jumped."

Connor's hand slipped from her arm.

Molly stared at him hard, regretting what she'd just said, but she wanted to hurt him. Make him feel used and worthless, just as she was aching. She wanted to repay him the same inner anguish she was going through, and if that meant pushing the dagger in deeper, then so be it.

Not saying another word, Molly hailed a cab, got inside and went to the one place she knew she'd feel safe.

* * * *

The glass of wine cried to be drank. Teasing her, chanting to her, enticing her with its sweet, intoxicating aroma.

Molly sat there, staring into her glass, her tears dripping as her hands shook. She hated herself more at that moment than she ever had. In all the things to have happened, the moment had arrived when she could no longer resist.

Lifting the glass with both hands, she trembled as she opened her mouth and tasted the first sip of the claret. Not another moment was wasted as she downed the entire contents. Signaling for the bartender to refill.

"Keep them coming," she said, not once making eye contact. She hated herself. She hated what she had allowed Connor to do. She despised having let him in, but promised herself that it would never happen again.

Time became nonexistent. Not when she was drinking herself into an episode she'd sworn she'd never allow to happen again. She had now entered a mental obsession, which meant that she couldn't leave it alone. The taste was too much to resist. The sense of numbness, the place that meant nothing could touch her, nothing could get in – the vortex of doom where she spiraled into the terrible dark loneliness and terror of all her pain.

Through a haze, she barely heard the bartender as he helped her to her feet.

"Wha —" she incoherently mumbled.

"I think you've had enough, miss," he said as he closed the door behind her, leaving her on the street.

Nothing made sense to her. Her feet wouldn't do what she wanted them to. Struggling to walk, she fell against the cold wall, trying her best to figure out where she was.

"Cab," she slurred as her blurred vision stunted her efforts to hail a cab. Stumbling, she raised her arm, but with all her exertion, it was pointless. Her arms didn't respond either. Her body was pissing her off more than all the pain.

All she wanted to do was go home.

The noise was odd, a ringing sound that pulsed through her head. She didn't know it. She didn't have time to comprehend what was happening. But she felt the warmth rush through her, as if she were flying. A heat radiated through her, numbed the ache in her heart. This was new, something she'd never experienced before, and she didn't want to leave it. She was at peace.

Finally.

Chapter Twenty-Seven

Connor poured another shot of whiskey into his glass before he paced back and forth in his parents' lounge. He hadn't slept, hadn't been able to sit still. His head was a mess.

"Connor, you need to relax. Try to get some sleep," his father said as he watched his son tear himself apart.

"Are you fucking kidding me?" he roared. "That bitch destroyed everything."

Connor's hands shook as he held the glass. Through labored breaths, he gulped down the brown liquor. But the more he drank, the more enraged he became. Connor threw the crystal glass against the wall. It smashed into smithereens, sparkling like tiny diamonds over the wooden floor.

"She won't answer my calls," he shouted.

Falling onto the couch, Connor finally caved, sobbing. His father looked on with pity. Gone was the steel glare of the man who more often than not treated his son with contempt. Now standing by his son's side was a man watching his child break.

John rested a hand on Connor's back and sighed. "Give her time."

Wiping his eyes, Connor felt the bile in the back of his throat curdle. He couldn't hold it any longer. Retching, he ran toward the door but didn't make it to the bathroom in time. The vomit was uncontrollable. A sickness he hadn't experienced in a long time. And as he knelt on the floor, his mother stepped into view. Dressed as if she had somewhere to be, she grunted, before picking up her purse and heading for the front door.

"She's a cold bitch," he muttered.

Mark walked down the hallway from the kitchen, carrying a tray, and stopped when he saw his friend on his knees. He set the tray on a sideboard then walked up to Connor, tucking a hand under his arm as he helped him to his feet.

"You need to sleep this off, and that's an order," Mark said as he helped his drunken friend to his old room. "What good are you to anyone in this state?"

"But, Molly… She hates me."

"She doesn't hate you. She's just angry."

Through his drunken stupor, Connor tried his best to make sense, but it was becoming increasingly difficult. His head banged, his heart was heavy and an ache in his soul told him that there could be no future — not if Molly wasn't in it.

Mark closed the drapes, threw a blanket over him, and as Connor slipped off into his drunken sleep, the last words to echo in his head were Molly's. "I wish you'd jumped."

* * * *

It was late evening by the time Connor awoke. His head spun as intense confusion swarmed his brain. Connor was lying on his side and his eyes fluttered open then closed again a few times before he finally focused on the wardrobe. Anything to stop the spinning.

His mouth was dry. A disgusting taste of stale alcohol turned his stomach as his eyes ached from trying to focus. Reaching out to the side dresser, he turned the clock to face him. It was just after eight p.m. and the thought of Molly began to consume his mind.

Sitting up on the bed, he held his head in his hands as the memories of the night before filtered through. Horrible things that pushed him closer to the edge the more Marissa's face flashed before his eyes. He hated her, despised her to the point where he would gladly have run her over given the chance. How could she be so evil? Why would someone be so intent on destroying another's happiness? So many things flew through him, so many questions that he was sure, if he continued thinking, his head would explode.

He stood and almost lost his balance but fought through the grogginess, making his way to the bathroom. Turning on the shower, he let the steam build before stepping in. Needing the heat to ease the throbbing headache and the water to wash away the sin.

"God, I'm so stupid," he muttered as he stood under the burning heat.

No matter what he did or said, it didn't erase the fact that he had allowed himself to fall under Marissa's calculating spell. She had wormed her way into his head in mere seconds. He hadn't wanted her — he hated her — but how could he deny his arousal? Molly had seen it. She'd witnessed it, and now she hated him. How could he ever live with that? The look on her sweet face when she'd realized what was going on. Then the worst thought of all, what if Molly hadn't come in? What would he have allowed to happen?

His stomach turned, the knife twisting deep in his heart. He was his own worst enemy and there was no salvation for someone like him. How could there be? He was a nasty monster. A motherfucker who deserved nothing but the misery that had now found its way into his life.

"Connor, you okay?" Mark shouted in from the door.

Connor turned his head, the water dripping down his face. The ache pulsing in his temples. "Yeah. Give me five."

"I'll be downstairs."

He didn't respond. He didn't need to. He knew Mark wouldn't be leaving any time soon. Not unless Cassie went into labor, which wasn't likely, not yet.

It was odd being back in his old room. Not once in the last eight years had he spent a night in the house, yet his mother made sure he had clean clothes, if ever an occasion arose that meant he'd have to stay the night.

Putting on a clean pair of pants and shirt, he looked

at himself, hating everything that stared back at him. Swallowing two Tylenol, he ran a hand over his face before mustering the courage to face the small gathering downstairs.

As he entered the large lounge, he was met with looks of pity, and in among the many faces that stared at him, he saw someone he hadn't expected to see any time soon.

"Connor, can you sit down?" his father asked, directing him to a chair near the large bay window.

"What's going on?" he asked, raising his eyebrows. "Jenna?"

Jenna looked over at Connor, her own face ashen, sleep deprivation evident from the bags under her eyes. "It's Molly."

Connor's chest suddenly felt tight, as if he couldn't catch a breath. Connor's hands trembled, as his head spun. Sweating, he didn't know whether to stand or stay seated, and the sense of complete dread sucked away at his reality.

"Molly was in an accident, Connor," Jenna said.

The words – those God-awful words – they echoed in his head as he looked at Jenna's solemn face.

Oh God, she's dead, he thought to himself as the room seemed to grow smaller, the air tighter, the need to run overbearing him.

"Connor, do you hear her?" his father asked, his voice sounding slow and distorted.

Connor looked up. His father stared down at him, his mouth moving. But Connor heard nothing. The only thing that rang in his ears was his own pounding heartbeat, then like a smack in the face, reality hit him hard.

"What?" His throat burned as he fought through it. "Where is she? Is she dead?"

The words. Those words. God, no... *She can't be dead,* he thought as he looked at his father and Jenna.

"She's in ICU at St. Francis's, but she's in a bad way." Jenna looked at Connor, her lips trembling, fighting hard not to break down.

"I don't understand." His mind raced. "I have to go to her," Connor said as he stood, the adrenaline beginning to pump through him.

"Is that necessary?" his mother said as she took a drag on a cigarette, blowing out the smoke.

"Fuck you," he roared and pointed at her. Connor walked from the room, grabbed his keys and didn't waste a moment longer. Even Mark calling after him wasn't going to stop him. He had to see her, make sure she was all right.

"Connor," Mark shouted as he ran down the driveway. "At least let me drive."

Throwing the keys to Mark, Connor got in and sat in silence for the entire journey to the hospital.

Complete fear consumed him. Not knowing what to expect. Not knowing if he would be able to handle it. Mixed feelings — guilt, anger, frustration — a combination of things that would easily push him over the edge.

Mark rested a hand on Connor's shoulder and gave it a gentle squeeze, saying, "I'm with you, bro, okay? I'm not going anywhere."

The walk to the public safety office took forever. Connor was on edge as the attending officer made a call up to ICU, getting permission for them to make the visit.

"Are you immediate family?" he asked.

"Yes, I'm her partner," Connor said as his voice trembled.

The officer continued talking until finally he assigned them visiting badges and gave them directions up to the ward.

"Connor," Mark said. "Are you prepared for what you're about to see?"

"Why? What did Jenna say?"

"Molly was hit by a car. She hasn't regained consciousness."

Those words alone sent a series of sickening pulses running through his veins. Connor's heart broke as though it were falling down into an empty pit of darkness and the only salvation was Molly. His beautiful, sweet Molly. He just wanted to rewind the past twenty-four hours. Turn back the clock, not go to the gala. His sixth sense had warned him. That unease he'd had, that had been his subconscious telling him something bad was going to happen. But he had ignored it.

The door to the ward buzzed open and they were met by a nurse.

"Hi, guys, just sign in here and sanitize your hands over there," the nurse instructed.

Once they had completed their tasks, the nurse led them down the long corridor. The beeping sound of monitors, breathing apparatus and various machines made the whole situation seem surreal. That was until Regina came into view.

Eyes swollen and red, she held her handkerchief to her mouth as her hand trembled. "What did you do? You promised me you'd look after her."

"I don't know what happened... I don't know. I'm so sorry... I tried to stop her leaving, but she wouldn't listen to me." Connor choked on his words.

"Then you have a lot of praying to do because that girl in there is fighting for her life."

Connor's heart shattered into tiny pieces. His insides ached as he made his way to the door. The beeping of the monitor made what he was seeing seem almost dreamlike. But the sight of Molly attached to so many machines scared him in a way he had never thought possible.

A nurse was taking OBs, writing in her file. Looking at Connor, she gave him a gentle smile.

"How bad is she?" Connor asked.

"The doctor will be along shortly."

Nodding, Connor stepped over beside the bed and began absorbing everything he was seeing. Molly's beautiful face was swollen. A ventilator was breathing for her — the sound alone was something he'd never forget. Touching her soft hand, he rubbed her knuckles. The cuts were superficial, but the bruising was already beginning to discolor her skin.

"I'm so sorry," he whispered as tears fell. Just as he was

about to bend down to kiss her, the doctor came along, making his presence known.

Anxious, Connor looked at the middle-aged man. "Will she survive?" The words alone hurt to say.

"Molly sustained a serious injury to the head, causing a bleed. I performed an emergency procedure—a craniotomy—to reduce the pressure of the bleed. She is now in an induced coma, which will help reduce the strain of the injury on the brain, giving us time to treat her other injuries," the doctor said. "She has six broken ribs and a broken ankle. Those will heal, but our main concern is her head injury and keeping her as comfortable as possible."

"What happened?" Connor's voice quavered.

"Molly was hit by a cab. Her blood-alcohol concentration levels were point two hundred, which put her at a dangerous level. She is lucky to be alive."

"Wait a minute, she was drunk?" Connor asked.

"Yes, another drink would have put her life at risk."

Connor slipped back over to the bed, touched his beautiful Molly's hand and sobbed. "I won't leave your side. I swear it... Please... Please don't give up."

He'd done this. He had destroyed her.

Chapter Twenty-Eight

Three Weeks Later

It was odd.

Molly floated through an endless fog. The kind of haze where she couldn't find her bearings. But instead of the chill that normally came with fog, she was warm. A nice comforting heat that radiated through her, easing some of the crushing anxiety. Yet there was a dull ache, a pain she couldn't define. It was there, throbbing beneath the layers, but she couldn't pinpoint exactly what it was.

Voices. So many voices. She was sure she knew them. She did know them. They were people she knew, but she couldn't see them. Molly tried to speak, but her voice failed her.

Looking down on herself, she saw that she wasn't really there. Nobody, nothing. *What's going on?* she thought as she continued to float. Completely confused.

"Molly, honey, we're still here." A voice filtered through the air, sounding so distant, yet so close.

Panic set in. *Where are you?* she thought as her voice failed to make a sound. Something was stopping her from responding. Something was stuck in her throat.

Oh God, I can't breathe, she thought as she choked. *Help me!*

Warm hands. Bright light.

Molly's eyes fluttered open a few times as she slowly regained consciousness, weakly grabbing for the tubes scratching at her throat. Totally unaware of her surroundings, Molly gagged, as if she were about to vomit, yet choking at the same time.

"Molly, I am going to remove this tube. Just relax and let out a little cough," an unfamiliar voice said, her face slowly coming into view as Molly's eyes tried to focus on her through the cloud of fog.

A new kind of panic began to set in. Pain, mixed in with an inner anguish, caused tears to seep down her face, wetting the hair behind her neck. Wide-eyed and very aware of the now-burning itch in her throat, Molly coughed as the tube was extracted from her throat.

The nurse wiped her mouth, but it was of no use, Molly couldn't hold it in. The contents of her stomach emptied in quick succession. She cringed, but was relieved at the same time.

"Molly," she heard his voice.

Connor came to her side and touched her hand as the nurse took her blood pressure.

Closing her eyes, Molly ached from exhaustion. She wanted to drift back to the warm fog, rest some more. It was too much effort trying to figure it all out.

"Molly, I'm going to take some blood, so you may feel a little scratch," the nurse said. And as sure as hell, the needle stung as it pricked her skin. Molly's eyes flashed open and stared at the nurse. "It's okay, sweetie. I'm just doing the rounds."

"Is she going to be okay?" Connor asked.

"The doctor will be here soon." The nurse was direct, but her warm smile was reassuring.

As the nurse left the room, Connor sat beside her bed, holding her hand. Molly opened and closed her eyes, focusing her gaze on the handsome man who'd fallen so deeply in love with her. His unshaven face looked tired, his eyes were sad and the way his voice quavered as he spoke hurt her in a way she had never imagined.

"I've been out of my mind with worry," he said as he held her hand to his face, placing soft kisses along the knuckles.

"Aggie," Molly hoarsely said.

Connor looked at her, his eyes now shining from the

tears ready to burst the bank. Looking over at the woman approaching the other side of the bed, Regina touched her face as she battled her own grief.

"Oh, honey, let's just focus on you for now," Regina said as she bent, kissing Molly gently on the forehead.

Molly looked at Connor, her eyes observing him. Really focusing on his expressions. She could read him like a book. She could tell he was keeping something from her. "Where's…Aggie?"

Closing her eyes again, Aggie's face flashed before Molly's eyes in a memory she had long forgotten.

It was such a warm, beautiful day. Aggie had insisted on a day out of the city, a picnic and plenty of sun lotion to protect her pale skin from the burning rays. Regina popped on one of her huge straw sun hats and sat beside the woman she loved as they drove to the Golden Gate National Recreation Park, where they intended on spending some quality time together, reading, relaxing and listening to nature.

Molly witnessed firsthand the genuine and deep love the two women had for each other. One would finish the other's sentences, resulting in raucous laughter.

"You two are perfect," Molly said as she wrapped her arms around Aggie's shoulders.

The dark-haired woman looked up at the beautiful brunette whom she loved and cherished as though she were her own child. "We make do."

Regina laughed that infectious laugh of hers. She was so happy it was hard to imagine seeing her being anything other than full of the happiness and joy for life. It radiated from her. She was the sun in Aggie's eyes, and together, they embodied everything that was right with the world.

The memory soon began to fade into darkness. A gloomy day, a time when Molly's heart knew what loss and grief felt like. The wicker casket – so beautiful, so typical of Aggie – was laid into the hole in the ground. The sun had gone from Regina's face, in its place a sadness, a cloud of hurt that Molly found hard to bear witness to. Her heart broke as dirt was thrown down over the casket, the last moments to reflect on the short period of time she got to be with Aggie. The lasting memories, the love, the happiness – the second chance of life.

* * * *

Molly's eyes opened again. This time she could see the pain in Connor's eyes, the realization – the truth.

"I'm sorry, baby," he said, holding her hand, gently caressing her with his thumb.

"I'm so…lost."

"Hello, Molly," Doctor McGraw said as he approached the bed. "How are you feeling?"

"Tired."

"That's to be expected. You've had a bit of a tough time," the doctor said as he shined a light in her eyes. "Molly, what do you remember?"

Tears trickled down the side of her face. "I don't know… It's all so jumbled."

Sitting down on the side of the bed, Dr. McGraw rested his hands on his lap. He was a balding man in his late fifties. "Molly, this might be difficult to hear, but I'm a believer in being direct and honest," he said. "Do you understand?"

"Yes."

"Three weeks ago you were hit by a car, which resulted in some life-threatening injuries. You sustained a serious head injury, so I performed an operation called a craniotomy to relieve the pressure on your brain, and to allow the swelling to heal," he said, keeping his voice calm. "We kept you sedated, giving your body time to heal, and we began to wean you off the ventilator three days ago. You've been showing signs of coming round, and today you woke up. But I cannot stress the importance of rest. Your body and brain have been through a serious trauma and it will take a while to recover. You have a great team on your side, and these guys have been here, willing your survival."

Molly closed her eyes, digesting what he was saying.

Three weeks of her life had passed her by. She had no recollection of being hit by the car, she could make no sense of any of it, yet her head throbbed, her body ached, and there was something niggling away beneath the surface, but she couldn't get to it.

"I'll be in to check on you later, and we can discuss the right time to take you back into theater," he said as he got up from the bed.

"More surgery?" Molly asked.

"Yes, a small procedure to replace the bone flap." Dr. McGraw smiled and touched her hand, giving her a gentle squeeze. "You're in good hands. Don't worry. Just rest."

Dr. McGraw smiled at both Connor and Regina.

Molly watched them both, how they fidgeted nervously. Neither saying much to the other, their faces telling Molly enough. They were hiding something, keeping some kind of truth from her. She hated being lied to, and more so than anything, she hated being the last to know what was going on.

A few hours had passed. Molly slept on and off in those two hours. Regina had gone home to get her a few things. Stuff that Molly would want. Connor sat by her side, afraid to move, afraid to leave her, touching her hand, letting her know he loved her.

"Did we have a fight?" Molly asked.

The question came out of the blue. She took Connor by surprise and the look in his eyes said it all. "Yes."

"What happened?"

"Baby, I don't think the time is right, not now," he whispered.

"Why?" Molly's gravelly voice scratched as she tried her best not to cry.

"Because you need to concentrate on getting better."

"No one's been to the grave. Why has no one been to the grave? The flowers will have died," Molly began to mumble, not making sense.

Connor stepped over to the bed and sat down beside her.

"What grave?"

"Aggie's... Aggie needs to have fresh carnations every Monday... What day is it?"

"Molly, Regina has taken care of things. Don't panic."

Molly's head was so jumbled nothing was making sense to her. Everything was compressed in a tight box, bursting to get out, details merging with other details, all cluttered.

"Why didn't you jump?"

The words cut through Connor like shards of glass. Ripping at his soul. Reminding him of the last words she'd said to him.

"Because you saved me." His voice cracked as the words came out.

"No... No... No." Molly began crying.

The world began to seem like an ugly place and Molly wanted nothing more than to slip back to the haze. Everything there felt less stressful. At least there, the truth couldn't touch her. At least there, she wouldn't have to look into the cheating eyes of the man who had broken her heart.

Chapter Twenty-Nine

Connor wasn't stupid. He knew it the moment she began muttering. The details had begun to filter through and Molly's tearful face was enough proof for him to know that he'd broken her.

Molly pulled back her hand. "What did you do?"

Connor couldn't hold it in any longer. The guilt was eating him alive. The darkest sense of defeat began to consume him. He couldn't lie. He couldn't pretend to her that he hadn't destroyed everything they had created. How could he? She would remember — it was only a matter of time.

"Do you remember the gala?" he asked.

Molly searched hard. Connor could see she was doing her best to remember.

"The Ritz Carlton?" she muttered.

God, she remembers, he thought.

"Yes, we were at the Ritz," he agreed. The knot began twisting inside and he felt nauseated. He didn't want to have to say it. The details alone sickened him to the core. Hearing himself utter those words would have been like sticking the knife into her heart. "You were so beautiful."

"A blue dress?" she asked, her eyes reading his face, looking for answers.

"Yes, a gorgeous blue dress."

"Your mother is a cow."

Smiling, Connor nodded his head. "Yes, she's that and a few other choice words."

"But… I'm sensing something… It's so confusing." Molly closed her eyes and tried to focus.

The memory of the night that their life had been turned

upside down would come back. It was there, it just wasn't clear. It was just a matter of time. Swallowing hard, Connor touched her cheek, running his fingers gently down over the contours of her jaw line. "You know I love you, don't you?"

Molly looked at him, her eyes all sad. Connor couldn't stand it. He couldn't take it. He was a coward and hated himself the more he watched her search for answers.

"We did it in the restroom," she cried. Touching her head, she rubbed her temples. "It's just so fuzzy. I can't think straight."

"Then get some sleep. I'll be here when you wake up." Bending down over her, Connor kissed her, rubbing his nose against hers. The thought of losing her was beginning to weigh heavy on his heart.

"Okay..." Molly replied as she closed her eyes. Reaching out, she touched his hand, her fingers brushing against his skin. "I love you too."

Connor sat, resting his arms on his knees, thinking pensively until Regina came back, carrying a small bag.

"How is she?" she asked, making sure she kept her voice down.

"Asking questions."

"Hmm, that she is entitled to, and you know it."

Regina unpacked a nightgown, resting it on the foot of the bed, her jaw rigid as she gazed at the sweet girl sleeping.

"I want to be honest with her, Regina. I never meant to hurt her."

"We're not doing this here, Connor." Regina glared at him.

"I need some air."

"You do that."

Connor got up and left, not wanting to get into a confrontation with Regina. He knew that Regina had every right to be pissed with him, and in a way, he wanted her to judge him, rip him apart. Nothing could have made him feel any worse that he already did.

When Connor stepped outside, he paced the path a few times before taking a walk around the block. He needed to clear his head, get some perspective, figure out what he was going to say once Molly faced the cold, harsh truth — he had allowed Marissa to come on to him. He was a stupid fool.

His phone rang, pulling him from his self-deprecating thoughts. "Hello!"

"Connor, we need to talk." Bruce sounded desperate.

"I'm in the middle of something, can't it wait?"

"I've got some information about the leaked info, but we can't do this over the phone."

Connor's heart began to race. The timing was all wrong. How could he just run off to meetings about a deal that had destroyed his reputation in corporate finance? Molly was his main priority, but he also knew that salvaging his career and reputation was important.

"I'm not interested, Bruce. My life is a mess and that fucking merger is the last thing on my mind."

The phone went dead. Connor popped it back into his pocket and looked up at the bright June sky. Life had an awful knack of turning the tables when you least expected. It frustrated him, angered him, made him think he no longer had control. No matter what he did, had or loved, he couldn't hold on to any of it. It left him convinced that he was finally losing the plot and maybe Molly had been right after all — he should have jumped.

Shaking his head, he tried his best to throw the incessant depression to the far reaches of his mind. Anything was better than experiencing the dreaded pits of despair. That dark place so few came back from. He didn't need it — not then, not ever.

A coffee with a few extra sugars boosted his lulling mood, then it was back to Molly.

Molly was awake and drinking some water through a straw with the aid of Regina when Connor came back into the room. Glancing over at him, she waved, before closing her eyes briefly. She looked so unwell and trying her best to appear okay—just to make everyone feel better.

"How's my girl doing?" Connor asked as he walked over to the bed, kissing her on her forehead.

"Well, she feels tired," Regina replied as she brushed Molly's hair from her face. "But she wants to talk to you."

Connor's heart skipped a beat. *Oh God*, he thought, his anxiety on the verge of exploding.

"Sure," he said as he smiled at Regina.

"Regina was telling me how you've been here almost every day and night," Molly said, sounding wearier by the second.

Smiling, Connor sat on the bed, looked over at Regina and nodded. "That would be right."

"She also said that you are taking care of things—" she tried, then lost her breath.

Connor knew what she meant. "Like I told Regina, I look after my own. You needn't worry about those things."

"But... I don't want to be indebted to anyone."

"Molly, I love you... Aren't I allowed to help you?"

Molly glanced at him before her eyes moved toward the window. "What kind of day is it?"

"It's gorgeous. Do you want me to pull the blinds back?" Regina asked.

"Yes, please."

Regina moved to the window, drew the blinds open, letting the magnificent rays of light beam into the room. Molly smiled. There was something so beautiful in the way her eyes lit up whenever she saw the sun. A radiance overcame her and Connor couldn't help the tears welling in his eyes.

He'd done this to her. He'd taken her away from all that she loved. He was a selfish bastard and hated himself.

"How about I go and get myself a coffee?" Regina suggested, making it obvious that she wanted to give them some time together.

"Are you sure?" Connor asked in desperation.

"Absolutely." She met his gaze, giving him a stern look. A

look that warned him not to hurt Molly — again.

Regina closed the door as she left, leaving Connor alone with Molly, and the guilt swimming to the surface.

Smiling, Molly patted the bed beside her, gesturing for Connor to sit.

"How's the head?"

"Like the worst hangover, but times that by a million, and you'd be nowhere near close."

"Well, you did kinda hit your head hard, not to mention you've had surgery."

"You look like you haven't slept in ages," Molly remarked as she touched the back of his hand.

"I'm exhausted, not gonna lie," he replied as he wrapped his fingers around hers. "You took priority."

"Is that all?"

"Not entirely."

"I know... I had the weirdest dream. It was more like a nightmare," Molly said, not once taking her eyes off his hand.

"What kind of dream?"

"You...and someone else... I just can't make it out. It's so hazy that when I try to see, the focus is so blurred that I close the door. It repeats over and over and then I'm back home, in the small damp kitchen, and I'm watching my parents shoot up. The smell of smoke is so strong that it literally burns the back of my nose. I close the door, and when I turn around, it's you...again, with someone else."

Connor's stomach heaved. He knew what she was trying to figure out. He just didn't know how to tell her the truth.

"Who do you see me with?" he asked.

"A woman I've never seen before. But she's on her knees..." Molly's eyes filled with tears. "But it's not a dream, is it? It's real."

Nodding, Connor validated her suspicions. "No, it's not a dream."

"Oh God —" Molly cried. "I knew it... I didn't want to believe it, but I knew it."

Snapping her hand back, Molly covered her face and sobbed.

"Molly, I swear on my life it wasn't how it seemed," Connor pleaded with her. "You walked in, assumed the worst, and you were right in thinking it."

"She had your cock in her hand... You were aroused." Molly said the words with so much venom Connor closed his eyes, trying to stop the tears.

"She came on to me, tried to seduce me, knowing you and I had just made love... She got me at the right moment."

"And that makes it fine?"

"Of course it doesn't."

"So, what am I meant to do?"

"Forgive me, know that I would never do anything to hurt you. Jesus Christ, I'd die for you." Finally, he couldn't hold it in. The tears fell, an ache in his soul crushed him from the inside, and he swore he'd never be complete if she'd never forgive him.

"I can't... Not yet. I don't know."

"Molly, I love you. Isn't that enough?"

"Sometimes love is never enough."

Connor stood, looked out of the window, knowing that the woman he loved was rejecting him. Nothing could compare to the devastation that ran through his body. He thought she had died, only to have her survive and cut him off without a second chance.

"Just know that I am sorry. I never intentionally set out to cause you pain. I didn't mean for any of this to happen." Connor turned around and looked at her. His sweet, beautiful Molly.

"Connor —" she tried.

"It's okay, Molly. I understand. Just take care of yourself."

Connor bent, kissed her on the lips, and inside, he screamed knowing this was their goodbye.

Chapter Thirty

Two months had passed, and recovering from such an ordeal was hard. Molly never realized how tough it would be. Simple things like going to the bathroom without losing balance, to eating a meal without feeling nauseated, right down to coming to terms with the loss of Connor — so many things had changed, and fast. Then there were the mood swings, the depression that had wormed itself back into her life, causing many sleepless nights, and days spent gorging on ice cream and watching reruns of Jerry Springer.

No matter how much she thought, how much she wanted to call him, her pride stopped her.

She was insistent that she wasn't going to become one of those women who let a man get away with any kind of indiscretion. That wasn't who she was. Coming from such a toxic environment as a child made her more acutely aware of the dangers that lies and deceit brought. She couldn't live with that, and no matter how much her heart tried to talk her head into contacting him, she stubbornly refused.

"Will these dizzy spells ever stop?" she asked Dr. McGraw on a routine check-up. Sitting up from the small examination gurney, Molly's head spun.

"Molly, you are still recovering from a serious brain injury. You need to be patient," he said as he wrote in her notes. "How's the mood?"

"Peachy!"

"Molly!" Regina chided her. "She's like a difficult teenager." Regina gave Dr. McGraw a look that said she was at the end of her wits.

"Are you taking the medication prescribed?"

"The happy pills? Sure, they're working wonders. Everything is just dandy."

Molly felt exasperated. She was frustrated, pissed off and on the verge of saying to fuck with it all and leaving. Yeah, leaving would have been a choice if it hadn't been for the ridiculous check-up appointments, talking things over with the shrink — whom she was convinced was only there to ply her with drugs and send her on her merry way.

"Molly, if we need to up the dosage, it can be done." McGraw looked at her.

"Honestly, I was thinking of coming off them all. To be honest, I've forgotten to take them a few times. No big deal, right?"

Putting down his pen, Dr. McGraw rested his hands together on his desk. "Molly, I know that things are difficult right now. There is a lot going on. But the medication prescribed is to help you, not debilitate you any more than you are already. You need to cooperate with us, to get you back to your old self. Brain injuries can have lasting effects on you. There is no doubt about that." Sitting back on his chair, he raised his eyebrows. "What do you want out of life?"

"I no longer know. I once had it all planned out, but I fucked up, screwed up my life, and now I'm a walking, talking time bomb waiting to go off, and there's not a damn thing any of you can do about it. So if you'll excuse me, I've a date with my sofa, a gallon of cookies 'n' cream to devour and my main man, Springer."

Molly got up, rested her hand on the back of the chair, before walking out of the doctor's office.

Regina was busy apologizing to the doctor, who in turn seemed content in knowing that everything Molly presented with was natural, brushing it off.

"Give her time."

Time? Molly thought. *Fuck time.*

Regina didn't say a word as she drove them home. She looked angry. But Molly was oblivious to any of the stress she was causing. Maybe she was being selfish, but in her own little world, Molly was convinced that her actions were justified. What kind of favors had her existence done for her? She was constantly battling a war she was never going to win. Why bother anymore?

As they settled in their apartment, Molly switched on the television, giving Regina the silent treatment. She wasn't interested in being spoken to like a child. She wanted to be left alone, allowed to sink into herself, where she felt the safest.

A few hours passed, when a knock at the door made Regina jump. Molly, on the other hand, was glued to the TV. Her eyes glazed, completely immersed in the show.

Jenna walked over to the sofa and sat down next to her. Regina sighed as she picked up her bag and left.

"I don't need babysitting." Molly didn't once take her eyes off the screen. "So do me a solid and fuck off."

"It'll take a lot more than that to rattle my cage," Jenna said as she rested her feet on the small coffee table, taking the spoon from the tub of ice cream and helping herself to a huge mouthful.

"I hate you."

"So does my fifteen year old. I'll get over it."

"Fuck you!"

"Is that it? Is that all you're capable of?"

Throwing the ice cream at her, Molly got up from the sofa, almost stumbling as one of her dizzy spells washed over her. Balancing herself against the wall, she inhaled a few deep breaths before walking to her room and slamming the door behind her.

"Sleep well, kiddo, I'll still be here when you wake up!" Jenna shouted from the living room, enraging her even more.

Lying on the bed, Molly lifted her phone, looking through it, then came across some pictures of Connor. Her heart sank.

Why did it have to hurt so much? Why couldn't she just

have hated him, moved on and forgotten about him?

She couldn't. She loved him. Probably always would. But her pride stopped her from doing anything about it. Her stupid, selfish arrogance stood in the way of her happiness and she wasn't strong enough to push it out of the way and take control of the situation.

As Molly drifted off to sleep, tears lined her face, her heart ached.

* * * *

Days seem to merge into one for Molly as she slowly became a shadow of her former self. There was no getting through to her. Nothing. No one could make her see that she had something to live for. Instead, she was happy to wallow in her own little pity party, and she was the guest of honor.

Then, out of the blue, she made a decision.

"I'm leaving."

Regina was just finishing up making them eggs, when she stopped in her tracks and looked at Molly. "What do you mean?"

"I've decided that I need to move away from here. Away from everything that reminds me of my past."

Setting the plates on the small kitchen table, Regina couldn't hide her shock. "Where are you going to go?"

"I don't know... Somewhere that isn't here."

Molly chopped the egg in half with the side of her fork, before eating a small portion.

"Molly, that's a big decision," Regina said as she glared at Molly.

"I know, but I've been giving it a lot of thought. I need to leave."

"What about your follow-ups with Dr. McGraw? Your rehabilitation has only just begun."

Sighing, Molly sipped some of her juice, again taking another mouthful of egg.

"I can't lie, I'm worried about you," Regina admitted as she reached across the table. "I don't want you to make rash decisions because you're angry with the world."

"Gina, I'm not angry with the world, I'm pissed with my life," she shouted. "And only I can change it, right? Isn't that something Aggie instilled in me? That I am in charge of my own destiny?"

"Yes, but you hadn't had brain surgery back then. Things have changed."

"So what?" Molly spat. "A stupid bump on the head and what? I give up on life? If that's the case, I may as well hold a gun against it and blow my fucking brains out."

An awkward silence befell the room. Regina was hurt, and Molly's anger was beginning to bubble.

Rising from the table, Regina picked up her plate and threw the uneaten food into the sink before walking to the kitchen door. She looked back at Molly, saying, "I can't talk to you when you're like this." Then left the room.

"Fine, then go… Join all the rest who have left me. Go on, see if I care."

Molly's eyes filled with tears, regretting everything she'd said. She just couldn't control it. She couldn't stop the anger.

You stupid fuck! she thought as she looked at her half-eaten egg and cried.

It was then she realized that leaving was, in fact, the right thing to do.

Clean break, new start, no memories.

Chapter Thirty-One

The past few months had seen Connor shuffle in and out of corporate meetings, cleaning up the mess that had been made for him. Bruce had yet to share the little information about who was behind the leak. Every time Connor convinced him to tell him, Bruce backed off, afraid that he was getting in way over his head. Connor was not only frustrated but on the verge of walking away from it all. Leaving town and all the pain that reminded him of everything he'd lost.

"You still pining for that young girl?" his father asked as he walked into his office.

Looking up from his computer, Connor pretended otherwise. "Forgotten long ago."

John closed the door behind him, sat on the small leather couch and looked at his son. He wasn't a man for reassuring words—hell, he wasn't a man to give any kind of warm advice. But he must have noticed the change in his son.

"I've been watching you these past two months," he said as he crossed his legs. "I'm thinking a change of scenery would benefit you. Help you clear your mind, maybe replace some of the old rigor for life you once had."

Connor sat back on his chair, listening to his father, actually contemplating what the man had to say.

"Our headquarters in Hong Kong could use you, and you could be my eyes and ears over there," his father said, making the proposition sound more inviting by the second. "I have a selection of condos that you can choose from, no expense spared, all will be taken care off. I could have you over there as soon as next Wednesday. What do you say?"

"But what about the Lanscorp cleanup? I mean, what does Mom say about this?"

"Your mother will be fine," John said as he stood. "I think a break from California and everything that reminds you of the burdens these past few months have caused could do wonders for the mind and soul. The offer's open, but I'll let you sleep on it," he said as he walked to the door. "Join us for brunch on Saturday. We'll discuss it more then."

Closing the door behind him, John didn't give Connor a chance to express his own worries.

"Hong Kong," Connor muttered as he glanced out of the window, the cold realization dawning that everything had changed and there was now no going back.

* * * *

Thursday night drinks were something he looked forward to with Mark. It was his chance to unwind, complain and just be himself.

"Any day now," Mark said as he opened another bottle of beer, handing it to Connor. "Two false alarms in the last week. I'm scared shitless."

Connor listened to his friend. It made a change from him offloading. "This is it, man, you're gonna be a daddy."

"Who'd have thought it, eh? All those years ago, on campus, being complete whores," Mark said as he laughed. "I mean, everything changed when Cassie came along, but we were on good form back then."

"Speak for yourself."

Laughing, Mark took a swig of his cola. "Dream on, I remember quite a few ladies who had their hearts broken."

"Maybe a few, but, we were kids. It was our rite of passage." Connor finished off his beer, then sat forward. "My father wants me to take office in Hong Kong."

Mark raised his eyebrows and shook his head. "Since when?"

"This afternoon." Connor stood and stretched. "He thinks

I need the change, and my presence there could serve him well. He has it all worked out — the condo, the car, the office. I could be over there as soon as Wednesday."

"But that's insane."

"I know."

"If you go, you'll miss the baby." Mark sounded hurt.

"I don't know what to do. I don't want to let you down. Jesus, this is huge for you guys, I want to be here, but... I can't stay in this city. I just can't. There's too much bad blood. Too many memories. Marissa and my mother — it's all too much."

"Then do what's right for you," Mark said. "I mean, I'm not gonna lie, I'll be crushed if you go, but staying just for me and Cassie, that would be selfish of us. Besides, Hong Kong is only a flight away, easy commute for the likes of me," he said as he smiled.

Connor helped himself to another beer from the bar. "She hasn't even called once. Not once. I mean, who can be that cold?"

"She's hurting too. You know that."

"Fuck," Connor shouted. "She's wiped me from her life. I thought she'd have at least replied to my texts or calls, but nothing."

Connor knew he sounded like a whining pussy. But he had to get it off his chest.

"Then do something about it," Mark suggested.

"How can I do that?" he sounded more defeated than he had intended.

"If you want something bad enough, you have to fight for it."

Those were fighting words. Words delivered by a man who was about to become a father and the right kind of kick in the ass Connor needed.

* * * *

Friday afternoon came around and Connor headed to the

one person he knew would be up front with him. Even if her words cut him to the bone.

"Can you tell me at least if she's okay?" Connor asked Jenna.

Sighing, Jenna poured a little milk into her coffee as both she and Connor sat out on the deck. "She's doing good, just a little angry at the moment."

"Because of me?"

"She's angry with the world, her parents, Aggie...you. She's not the Molly we all know and love."

Connor sipped his coffee, his eyes gazing at the ground. "I can't help but blame myself for all of this."

"Well, I wouldn't go as far as saying that, but yes, the events that transpired that evening certainly didn't help."

"I fucking hate myself." Connor sat, staring into his cup. The guilt swarmed through him.

"But you didn't make her drink, you didn't push her in front of that car," Barry tried to reason with him.

"Maybe not, but that doesn't make me feel any less guilty."

"Can I be honest with you, Connor?" Jenna asked.

"Of course."

"Molly's head injury has changed her in a way none of us anticipated." Jenna tried to explain. "Her personality has shifted. She's this angry, foul-mouthed and, quite frankly, childish young woman at the moment."

"Oh!"

"She's giving Regina a hard time," Jenna said. "I mean, we're all doing what we can, but things are slow with the recovery. We are the only family she has."

"I didn't know."

"Regina wouldn't let me contact you. She didn't think it right—not where Molly is concerned."

Connor appreciated how much both Jenna and Regina cared and looked out for her. He felt relieved knowing that if he did, in fact, go to Hong Kong, at least she'd be safe. It was a small blessing to have such good people and support, but that didn't stop him wanting her.

"I've been asked to move to Hong Kong," Connor said. "My father wants me to head up the financial division in the Chinese headquarters. I am meant to leave on Monday to begin my post on Wednesday."

"Have you given a firm yes?" Jenna asked, raising her eyebrows.

"Not yet. I'm meeting my parents tomorrow. I'll have my answer then."

Jenna sat back, scratching her chin, looking at Connor, who was searching for any kind of answer that told him not to give up on Molly – not yet.

"Do you love her?"

"Yes…with every inch of my soul."

"Then you fight for her. But just be careful, because she will bite. Molly has no control over what comes out of that mouth of hers, and believe me, she'll try to hurt you."

Connor took Jenna's words of advice seriously. Yet, the challenge of breaking down her walls gave him a new lease of life. Molly wouldn't see it coming.

Chapter Thirty-Two

Molly stood by the grave, staring down at the inscription on the headstone, looking like a statue. Not moving, not fidgeting, not even talking. She just stared, read the lines over and over, trying to figure out why she had ever bothered with coming to the grave weekly. *What is the point?* It wasn't going to bring Aggie back. In fact, it pissed her off, knowing that she had promised to visit weekly, bringing the same damn flowers. *This is a job for Regina,* her inner monolog complained.

Taking her time, she bent down, running her fingers over the engraved words, and smiled.

"I'll never get out of this world alive." Aggie's favorite verse from her favorite song by Hank Williams. Molly could never understand the reasoning behind having a song lyric on the headstone, but she had gone with it.

"You were a fool saving me," she muttered as she lifted out the wilted flowers and replaced them with fresh carnations. "Why didn't you just leave me be, huh? Let me die? You made me trust you, then you left me. Who does something like that?"

The tears began falling, but instead of calming, Molly's anger ignited into an almighty rage. "I wish you had left me well alone, old woman, then I'd have been spared this fucking life. How does any of it make sense? Life doesn't make sense. Life is bullshit."

As Molly turned to walk away, she got the fright of her life.

"Hey, baby. We've been looking for you. Heard about that little accident of yours." Her mother stood there, blocking her path, looking sickly and ravaged by her addiction.

Molly tried her best to ignore her mother. But it was hard when she kept moving toward her. "Get out of my way."

"I know you got money," she said, her sunken eyes glaring at Molly as if she were a piece of meat. "Just give me a few hundred and I'll be gone. It'll be our little secret."

"Is he with you?" Molly asked as she scanned the cemetery.

"Why? You miss your daddy?"

"Fuck you." Molly pushed at her mother, only to feel the back of a hand across her face.

"Don't talk to your mother like that." Her father appeared from behind a headstone, his hand cracked hard against her, knocking her to the ground. "You have a bit of respect for your elders."

That was rich coming from him, considering he had robbed his parents blind and beat the shit out of a few older addicts in his time. He truly had no place to talk about respect.

Molly's face stung, but that was the least of her worries. It was the throbbing pain in her head, the ringing in her ears and the dizziness that began to make the world spin.

"Just...stop," she pleaded as she held her hands against her head, trying to steady the disorientating sensation swirling in her skull.

"Oh, is little Molly not doing so good?" he mocked her.

"Look at those shoes, I bet they feel nice to walk in," her mother said as she began unlacing her shoes.

Molly kicked out, but her head began to pound harder by the second. "Just leave me alone."

"Not until you've done your folks a solid," her father said as he dragged Molly to her feet. "Now, give me your ATM card and pin — kinda simple, isn't it, kiddo?"

Molly had to think quickly. She had to do something. She didn't want to give her money to them. She knew that they would shoot up at the next possible chance, robbing her blind in the process.

Standing barefoot as her mother held the shoes, Molly threw caution to the wind. "I'll drive you."

Her parents glared at each other trying to gage how serious she was. Her father, Kit, turned to face Molly, spitting on the ground as he walked up to her. Grabbing her by the shirt, he pulled her close to his face. "You fuck with me, I swear I'll do more than redden your ass."

Molly, a grown woman, being reduced to feeling like that half-starved, innocent child again, wanted to shrivel up and die. Yet, a spark of that same survival instinct that had been awakened by Eugene remained. If she wanted to get rid of them, she had to take control of the situation.

"Okay, but no funny business," Kit warned, his stale breath reeking of nicotine and booze.

"Okay," Molly said.

Sitting in behind her, Molly's mother, Anna, leaned forward, anxious, ready to pounce at any given moment. As Molly stuck the key into the ignition, she sat forward, sticking her hand into her pocket, desperately scrolling until she pressed the call button. With her phone on silent, her actions were unnoticed by her father who was busy looking out of his window, making sure no one saw them. His paranoia was on overdrive.

Barefoot, Molly pushed on the pedal and slowly drove from the cemetery. Little did her parents know that she shouldn't have been driving, and she kept that little bit of information to herself.

"You've done good, getting yourself all fixed up, steady job—even a boyfriend, huh!" Kit remarked as he reached over, rubbing his hand across the back of her head.

Molly winced from his touch. She hated him.

Saying nothing, she continued driving until they were clear of the cemetery. Everything about the situation was unbelievable. So unrealistic, Molly would have found it hard to believe that things like this happened.

Molly laughed and shook her head.

"What the fuck you laughing at?" her father bellowed.

"Nothing," Molly replied, trying her best not to lose too much control. "The irony."

Anna nipped the back of Molly's arm, leaving a deep red mark. "Don't try no foolishness or I swear your head won't be fixable this time."

Swallowing hard, Molly concentrated on driving. The city was only forty minutes away, she could keep up the pretense. It was what she was good at.

Molly remembered the last time she was coming back from the cemetery in San Rafael and her heart sank. The night she saw Connor on the bridge.

No, no, no, not now, Molly, she thought.

"I'll stop at Market Street. You can take all the cash, just leave me alone, okay?" Molly said.

"Take all the cash, just leave me alone," Kit mocked her. "We gave you life. We own you, you ungrateful little bitch."

"Dad… I've got nothing else to give."

"I remember a time when you were very giving, isn't that right, Mama-bear?"

"You dirty little slut, you loved it," Anna said, her voice grating on Molly. "Who would've thought my little baby Molly could be a cock sucker."

"Mom…" Molly's eyes hurt as she blinked through the tears. "Please… Just stop."

Kit and Anna loved getting a kick out of tormenting their child. They were the perfect example of why some people should never have been allowed to procreate.

"How much longer?" Kit asked as he scratched at his crotch. "I've a meeting with Benny Boy tonight, and I need my monies."

"Soon," Molly answered, then asked. "How…did you find me?"

Anna laughed, clapped her hands, then her voice began to sound weirder by the second. "We've been watching, listening and waiting. We knew it would happen, sooner or later… You would have to come and visit your dear old Aggie."

Aggie would be turning in her grave if she saw what they were doing. Molly had to be brave just a little longer. Surely someone would come to her aid. Someone out there would see how insane her parents were and would save her, and if not, Molly would not think twice about driving off the edge of a cliff.

Less than fifteen minutes later, Molly drove through traffic, the ache in her head beginning to pound, and finally, she saw the bank up ahead and looked for a place to pull over.

Please, please, please, she prayed in silence, hoping someone would have heard the whole thing.

She needed her savior now.

Chapter Thirty-Three

Connor drove like a lunatic.

There was no way in hell he was letting those two bastards weasel their way back into her life. Not now, not after everything she had been through. Having made a call to Barry and to his friend Eric, in the local precinct, he made sure that he'd have them taken care of.

If this was the challenge Mark had suggested, then Connor was about to fight to the end for the woman he loved. Even heeding Barry's warnings, he didn't care about Molly's changed personality. She had been let down so much in life, he had to give her a reason to want to live again, to be more than a survivor, to be someone who could be happy with life.

Turning onto Market Street, Connor looked out for the Bank of America, watching out for Molly's small blue Fiat. Taking it easy, he pulled his foot off the gas and concentrated, then he saw it, sitting in on the left. Three people inside.

"The motherfuckers," he muttered to himself.

He picked up his cell and called Barry. "Hey, they're here. They're still in the car… Yeah, I'll wait, but I can tell you now, they try anything, I'm not going to be able to control it."

Just as he was pulling over, a patrol car appeared. It sounded its siren as it pulled alongside Molly's car.

As Connor jumped out of his car, his vision became tunneled.

Connor raced across the street and tried to get to the car as two police officers approached the vehicle from the rear.

Connor could clearly see Molly hunched over the wheel, not moving.

Jesus Christ, he thought as he began to fear they'd already done something to her.

A long-haired man tried to run from the car, but Barry had his way blocked.

"Don't you fucking touch him," a woman roared as she appeared from the back seat. "Get your hands off him."

"Molly," Connor whispered as he opened the driver's side of the car, gently touching her, afraid that they'd hurt her.

Turning her head, she looked at him. Her face was streaked in tears, her nose red and her mouth bleeding. Closing her eyes, she let out a long breath, before lifting her head from the wheel, looking out at the chaos her parents were causing.

"Are you okay?" Connor whispered as he wiped the blood from her mouth.

"I don't know."

"Thank God you called. I don't know what I would have done—"

"Connor, just shut up for a minute. All the noise is giving me a headache." Molly closed her eyes again. "I can't hear myself think."

Connor was instantly taken aback by her. But he had to remember that her accident had caused damage. "I just want to make sure you are okay, nothing else. I don't expect anything from this," he lied.

"Okay," Molly replied as she looked at him.

Kit and Anna were on the ground, handcuffs being attached, as their rights were read. Molly smiled when she saw the look on her father's face. Complete satisfaction.

Molly got out of the car, a bit unsteady as she stepped onto the curb, barefoot. "How does it feel, you sick motherfuckers?" Spitting on them, she turned around, looking at Connor, then at Barry. "The bitch stole my shoes. They were going to rob me, take every penny I've saved…

I hope they die."

Connor couldn't believe the tone in her voice. She sounded mean and emotionless. Not at all like the woman who had saved him from the bridge. Barry gave Connor a sympathetic look, shook his head and approached the weary Molly.

"I think we should get you home," he said as he touched her shoulder, Molly flinching from the touch.

"Don't dare come near me." Her eyes blazed with so much anger Barry drew back his hand, not wanting to cause a scene.

"Molly," Connor said as he stepped up to her. Holding out his hand, he offered it for her to take. "There was a time when you stepped into my life, saving me from myself. Please let me do that for you."

"I don't need saving," she spat, trying not to cry.

"Then at least let me take you away from this."

Glancing down at his hand, Molly stood still. "If I let you do this...it doesn't mean anything."

"No strings, I promise," Connor replied, desperate for her to allow him to do this one thing for her.

"Okay." Molly took hold of his hand, not making eye contact with him, but still touching him.

Connor's heart raced from the touch of her skin against his. He knew he wasn't to get his hopes built up, but damn it, it was so hard when she was there, next to him, looking and smelling like the woman he loved.

Barefoot, Molly crossed the street, refusing to touch her shoes that her mother had so cruelly taken.

"I'd rather not, thank you," she said as she got into Connor's car.

"Okay, I'll leave these right here," Connor replied as he set them next to a trash can.

It was hard for Connor not to stare at her. To not reach out and touch her, grab her into his arms and kiss her. Simple things that had felt so natural not so long ago, and now — now he was afraid, even to say her name.

Pulling out, Connor drove slowly, not wanting to give Molly another reason to get out, or, worse, berate him. There were so many things he wanted to say, yet he couldn't find the right moment—if there would ever be a right moment again.

"Thank you," Molly said out of the blue, staring straight ahead, not once looking in his direction.

"No problem," Connor replied as his stomach did a flip. "I would gladly help you if I can."

"A real gentleman, huh?"

"I'm not sure about that, but I do have my moments." Connor glanced over at her, wanting to step back in time and stop any of the hurt he'd caused.

"I remember your good moments," she said. "You're a good person, Connor."

"So are you, Molly."

"I should have known they were cooking up some stupid-assed plan," she said as she rubbed her temples. "It was due."

"How do you mean?"

Molly let out a long breath and glanced over at Connor, her sad eyes observing him. "This is what they do. Disappear for a few months, maybe a year at the most, then show up, blackmailing me. The last time they showed up at the shelter. They made such a scene that I almost lost my job."

"I'm so sorry you have to deal with that."

"Yeah, me too." Molly sounded miserable.

Connor turned onto Molly's block, taking his time, before pulling over, getting ready to watch her walk back out of his life again.

"Listen, I know I've made a mess of things, but how about we get out of the city for the night? Go to the villa, relax—and I promise, no funny business." There, he had said it, he propositioned her, but in a way he hadn't actually planned.

Molly stared at him for a few moments, then scowled. "You're un-fucking-believable. Seriously? Like, are you out of your mind?" she roared. "Get a fucking grip, Connor.

I mean, how in God's name am I meant to sit with the guy who broke my heart for near two hours, let alone be together under the same roof? I know I'm the one with the head injury, but, boy, you're stupid crazy."

Connor was completely taken aback. He looked at her, observing how her face twisted when she got angry, but then he saw it, the glimmer of something in her eyes. A small hint of something, but it was enough to convince him that she still loved him, even if she refused to admit it.

"I am stupid crazy in love with you, is that not enough?"

"It was once."

Connor's heart sank.

Looking down at her hands, he could hear her breathing change. "I thought we would be together forever. I was so stupid to ever think that." Opening the car door, Molly got out, avoiding having to look at Connor at all costs.

"Molly," Connor called after her. "I didn't mean to upset you. I only wanted to spend some time with you, that's all."

Molly stopped, not moving, looking down at her bare feet—her hair hanging over her face. "If I do this, promise me one thing."

"Anything."

"I don't want to feel like you are doing this out of pity. I don't want your pity."

"I would never do anything to upset you, you should know that."

"Whatever," Molly chided, then bit her bottom lip. "Give me ten minutes, I'll go grab a few things."

"Okay," Connor replied as his heart began pounding. He wasn't sure if it was anxiety beginning to get the better of him or excitement, but whatever it was, he had to lose it fast. He couldn't risk Molly thinking he had ulterior motives.

Controlling his breathing, he waited patiently for Molly to come back and just as he suspected, Regina came thundering behind her.

Opening the trunk, Molly threw in her small overnight bag, ignoring Regina.

"Molly, this is not a good idea," Regina said.

Molly opened the door, got in and glanced over at Connor.

The way her eyes met his was electric. Still full of the same passion they had had before their world went nuts. Connor was sure that if they were to give each other a chance, they'd surely rekindle the love and wash away all the pain. Their kind of love was worth the effort, he owed it to her and to himself.

If something was worth fighting for, then you'd die trying.

Chapter Thirty-Four

"This is a bad idea," Regina said as she held open the door, looking across at Connor.

"Gina, isn't the decision mine?" Molly asked as she glared at her.

"Yes, you can make your own decisions, but I am offering you some sage advice. This is wrong." She made eye contact with Connor. "Connor, this is crazy. What if something happens? Are you willing to risk her health in some crazy attempt at rekindling your romance?"

"Gina, go back inside, I've got this," Molly said. "I promise the moment I don't feel well, I'll call you and Dr. McGraw."

Molly knew from the way Regina stood that she was uneasy, and the deep frown she wore made her look more wicked than she actually was. "Connor, if anything happens—"

Connor cut her off before she could deliver the warning. "It won't. I'll have her back here before noon."

Regina closed the door, folded her arms and watched as Connor drove away, taking him and Molly back to the one place Molly adored—Capitola.

* * * *

Sitting in silence for almost an hour, Molly rummaged through her bag, pulling out a small bottle of pills. Popping one in her mouth, she helped herself to Connor's water before swallowing.

Connor looked over at her. "Are you okay?"

"Just a headache brewing. I'll be fine once I eat."

"Oh, if you're hungry we can pull over somewhere, get something to eat."

"Stop fussing, Connor. I'll survive," she replied as she rested her head back and closed her eyes. "You have no idea how stir crazy Regina and Jenna were making me."

Connor smiled as he listened to her.

"Seriously, the two of them have driven me nuts," she said as she turned her head and looked at him. "You know, I took my car without getting the green light from McGraw." Her eyes glistened when she said it.

Connor glanced at her and frowned. "Wait, you weren't meant to be driving?"

"Nope," Molly replied. "I just had to get out of there, go pay Aggie a visit, then those two fucktards showed up and... Well, you know the rest."

"Fucktards?" Connor asked surprised. "Since when did you use that terminology?"

"No idea, but it suits them, right?" Molly laughed, then her tone began to sound more serious. "I don't know... I think the bang in the head has fucked me up in a way. Everything gets so jumbled sometimes. Like, I want to say something one way, but it comes out all wrong, or, worse, I cut those who care for me with some pretty nasty things."

Connor slowed down as he pulled up outside the gates of the beach house. Molly smiled when she saw the palm trees and the small water feature as they drove up the driveway. There was something about being at the beach house that brought a sense of calm over her. She could never pinpoint what it was, but it was almost like coming home.

"I love the smell of the air," Molly said as she closed her eyes, inhaling deeply. "I sound stupid, don't I?"

Connor lifted their bags from the trunk, observing her the whole time. "No, not at all. One day I'll leave city life behind me and settle here for good."

Molly turned to look at him, really taking in everything he'd just said. She'd never heard him talk about settling down before, not here or in the city.

"I didn't know you had those kinds of plans."

"I'm a dreamer." He beamed and Molly's heart did that involuntary flutter that made her cheeks blush and her palms sweaty.

"Sometimes dreams are all we have."

Walking into the house, Connor took Molly to the guest bedroom on the other side of the hallway. "I hope you'll be comfortable in here. There's a nice view of the beach and the balcony is all yours if you feel like listening to the waves if you can't sleep."

An awkward silence cut through the air. Neither of them knew what to say next.

"I think I'll take a shower, then maybe we can eat," she said as she slipped off her shoes, more or less gesturing for him to leave the room.

"Oh yeah, sure, take your time," Connor said as he moved toward the door. "Maybe we can order in. I'm not in the mood to cook. Would that be okay with you?"

"Yup!"

Molly closed the door and her heart sank. She knew deep down inside that being so close to him was killing her in a way she had never expected. All the anger, the hurt, the disappointment was gone. She no longer dwelled on his indiscretion with Marissa. Yes, it had hurt her, but she knew that if she was ever to move on, she had to let go of the resentment.

Looking in the bathroom mirror, she rubbed her hair from her face, fairly conscious of the small patch of hair that was no more than tiny sprouts. "This was a bad idea," she said as she looked at herself. "Big mistake."

Turning on the water, she stepped in, letting the sting of the cool water prick her senses, letting her know this was, in fact, real. She was there, again, and didn't have a clue what she was thinking.

As the water touched her skin, she washed away her father's touch, the disgusting stain he'd left on her. Closing her eyes, Molly tried to find a happy place to focus on, the one place where she felt safe, and in all the mixed-up confusion, she smiled as she rested her head against the tiles.

Molly brushed her hair and tied it up on the top of her head, trying to conceal the patch that made her feel ugly, then slipped on her shorts and tee. She wanted to be comfortable, but knew it was going to be hard being around Connor.

Gulping, she bit her bottom lip before walking down the stairs, and saw Connor sitting out on the deck, his feet resting on another chair, just watching the setting sun glow in the horizon.

Inside, her nerves were so close to bursting her seams. She was sure she wasn't going to cope with being near Connor.

"Hey," Molly said as she awkwardly made her appearance, trying her best not to be overly confident, but also not wanting to give away too much.

Glancing up at her, he patted the cushion next to him. "Come chill. I love this part of the day."

Molly slipped down beside him, crossing her legs as she looked at the beauty before her. "Me too. Kinda gives me hope. Sounds silly, right?"

"No," Connor replied as he smiled. "I think hope is the one thing that connects us all. Without hope, we'd all have given up a long time ago."

Molly listened to him. Wondering if he had lost all hope that night. "So that night, on the bridge…what changed?"

"You… You gave me hope."

"Connor, I—" she tried to find the right words.

"Let's order. I'm starving," Connor interrupted her. She knew it was a ploy to avoid having to face reality, the severity of their 'break-up'—he didn't want to have to deal with it.

Nodding, Molly followed him to the kitchen as he set out a few menus. "You choose, but I can totally recommend this place," he said, holding up a Thai menu. "Their salmon panang is real good."

Molly read through a few of the menus, not knowing what she wanted. Then decided on Connor's recommendation.

"So, how's work?" she asked as they sat on opposite sides of the kitchen island, one as awkward as the other.

"Work's been interesting."

"Really? I thought there was the whole huge fallout because of that failed deal thingy," Molly said as she folded the side of the menu, giving her hands something to do.

"There is, so right now it's a case of cleaning things up. Trying to salvage my reputation, and of course find the leak."

"How do you mean?" Molly asked as she made eye contact with him, her cheeks burning a little as his gorgeous green eyes devoured her as he watched her.

"Someone gave their shareholders some information. Pertinent info that only my department had access to."

"Ooooh," Molly replied. "So basically, you could be working with someone who is essentially an enemy. Someone who doesn't really give a shit about you or Ellison Enterprises."

"Yup, more or less," Connor said as he smiled at her. "So my job is damage control."

Molly held her breath as Connor got up from the stool and walked to the refrigerator. Finally exhaling when she realized he wasn't coming anywhere near her. *Good*, she thought. She didn't want to have to deal with trying not to want him. Because the fact remained—she did want him. She did love him.

The doorbell chimed and Connor practically ran to pay for the food.

Connor set out the plates as Molly unpacked the food. "This smells so good," she said as her stomach decided that the food was a good option after all.

"Just wait until you eat it." Connor's face beamed.

There it was again, the gorgeous smile that made her insides go all mushy. How she'd survive the night was scaring her by the second, yet the more they interacted, talked, enjoyed each other's company, the more she realized how she couldn't live without him.

Sometimes, fate had a peculiar way of stepping in.

Chapter Thirty-Five

It felt good to be able to hear the musical lilt of her voice again. It calmed him, bringing him a sense of happiness that he'd almost forgotten, yet the fear that there was no going back to that perfect place they had scared him. Connor was, at times, his own worst enemy. He could never pinpoint it, but there was this air of darkness that seemed to absorb all the joy, suck it dry and leave him gasping for some kind of escape. A release, a place where he could just close his eyes and all the bad would be gone. The emptiness of not being close to Molly cut him in a way he thought not possible. The guilt being his biggest enemy.

"Sometimes, I get this whole sense of déjà vu, like, I've done this all before. It's so weird that it stops me dead in my tracks and I try to make sense of everything," Molly said as she finished her meal. "I sound nuts, don't I?"

Connor lifted her plate and set it in the dishwasher. Turning around, he rested his hands on the counter and smiled. "No, not at all. I think we all experience that at some point in our lives. Sometimes many times over."

"Maybe," Molly replied, shrugging "I don't know why I keep doing this to myself."

"Doing what?"

"This, letting myself believe that there is still something here, something worth salvaging."

Connor was surprised by what he was hearing. Out of the blue, just like that, she began addressing them — as a couple.

"I mean, I get it, the whole attraction thing. I feel the connection every time we are near each other," she said as she rubbed her forehead. "I just don't know if I'm ready for romance or love… Maybe I'm just destined to be alone forever."

Connor's heart sank to a new depth. Her words cut through him, deep and bloody. He wanted nothing more than to take a bottle of Scotch and drink himself into oblivion, but that would have defeated all purposes of winning her back. Of ever rekindling that blossoming love they'd once had.

"Molly, I didn't invite you here to try to win you back," he lied. His voice almost broke as the words left his mouth. "I just wanted to spend some time with you. That's all. And given what happened today, I think you being away from the toxic environment of the city is exactly what you need."

"Maybe," Molly muttered, trying not to look at him. "But the fact remains, when I'm with you, like this, it hurts me."

Connor could feel the sweat beginning to do its thing at the back of his neck. The anxiety beginning to present itself. Not great timing, but it never was. Gripping the counter, Connor closed his eyes, trying to control the little vortex of vision that now hovered in front of him. He could see Molly looking at him from his peripheral, her eyes questioning his silence.

Not now, he thought as his chest began to contract, a tightness ripping through him.

"Connor, are you okay?" Molly jumped off her stool.

Finally giving in, he fell to his knees as he began struggling for breath. Molly knelt by his side, resting her hand on his back.

"Try to take some deep breaths," she advised as she reached for the phone.

Shaking his head, he pushed her hand away from the phone. He didn't need medical assistance, he just needed the attack to pass.

Closing his eyes, Connor focused on his breathing, very conscious that he looked like a fool in front of Molly. No matter how hard he tried, the spinning wouldn't stop. The continuous pull of the attack wouldn't subside. It was relentless. A monster that wanted to crush him.

Finally, after several minutes he opened his eyes, his body covered in perspiration. Molly was still beside him, rubbing his back.

"I thought the panic attacks were a thing of the past," Connor muttered. He was embarrassed about looking like a loser in front of her and refused to make eye contact.

"I didn't know."

Connor wiped his nose and rested on his knees before standing. "Nothing like witnessing a grown man crumble, huh?"

God, he was embarrassed, completely mortified. He wanted the ground to open up, swallow him and release him from the shackles he'd placed around his own feet.

"I wouldn't say that," she replied as she got up, filled a glass of water and handed it to him. "Here, this will help."

Connor took the water, gulping it down, his head still pounding — the after effects of his anxiety.

"I'm sorry you had to witness that."

"Don't be silly," Molly said as she sat on the ground next to him. "You're only human, it happens to the best of us."

Resting his head against the cupboard door, Connor looked over at Molly. "I think I'm my own worst enemy at times."

"What makes you say that?"

"I don't know," he said, scratching the top of his head. "Maybe I've unresolved parental issues. I've never been good at standing up for myself. Always taking the easy route. Being a total dumbass in the process."

"I don't think you're a dumbass at all, but I think you need help. Those attacks need addressing. You and I both know that."

"They've been happening for as long as I remember. This one time, I was about eight or nine and we had swimming lessons at school. I was so nervous, I'd vomited before leaving the changing rooms. I had a complete meltdown at the side of the pool and pissed myself. Can you imagine trying to live that down? Of course, Mommy Dearest made up this whole thing to cover her own embarrassment, saying that I had a UTI and had no control over what happened."

Molly took Connor's hand, rubbing her fingers lightly over his. "I think your mother is a prize bitch. Maybe even a fucktard."

Connor smiled then said, "I don't think I'll ever get used to you saying that word, but right now, I think it's a perfect tag for my mother."

"Wanna know a secret?"

"Sure."

"I think I had Tourette's in a past life." Molly winked at him, earning herself a smile in return.

"Molly?" Connor asked as she looked down at her hand touching his.

"Yes."

"Would it be wrong of me to tell you that I love you?"

Molly looked at him and his heart raced knowing that her response would either make or break him.

"No, it wouldn't," she whispered.

"I know timing is everything, I'm not stupid," Connor said as he glanced at her, her beautiful azure eyes staring back at him. "I can't imagine my life without you. It's impossible for me to even think that I can go on without you. I know I hurt you, and God knows I've tried to put things right, but you're everything to me, Molly. You complete me."

They sat in silence for a few moments. Neither talking, each of them afraid of what to say next.

Connor felt he had overstepped the mark. Putting pressure on her when she didn't need it.

Molly gripped his hand tight, her shoulders moving, and he knew she was crying. "Shhh, please don't. I didn't mean to upset you," he said as he wrapped his arm around her. Her body fitted into his like a glove. "I'm sorry."

Connor's own tears bubbled beneath the surface. Swallowing hard, he resisted the urge to break down. He had to be the man. The one to be strong.

"You haven't upset me," Molly mumbled as she wiped her eyes. "I just feel bad because I don't know if I can be the woman you want."

"I love you, Molly. Doesn't that tell you something?"

"No, Connor. It just tells me that you're in love with the idea of being in love."

She'd done it. She delivered the one thing he didn't want to hear. Complete rejection. "Wow, you know how to kick a guy when he's down." Letting her go, Connor stood and walked to the patio doors. "Regina was right. This was a bad idea."

Standing, looking out at the moonlight shimmering on the surface of the water, Connor felt his heart shatter into tiny pieces, knowing there was no chance in hell of ever finding his happiness with her.

"I think I should go," Molly said.

Connor turned his head to the side and his shoulders slumped in defeat. "No, it's okay. You stay. I can arrange for a car to pick you up tomorrow. Take all the time you need. I won't bother you again."

Before Molly had the chance to stop him, Connor fled the house, driving far away from Molly and his broken dreams.

Sometimes there really was no hope, and at that precise moment in time, Hong Kong seemed like the better end of a bitter deal.

Chapter Thirty-Six

Molly never slept a wink. She twisted and turned the whole night, her guilt being the driving force behind the ache in her heart. She felt bad that she'd driven him from his home. Even more so, she was terribly on edge, knowing she'd pushed him away.

Stupid bitch, she thought to herself as she finished cleaning the counter, putting the dry dishes back in the cupboard. Occupying herself until the car came.

"I should never have come," she muttered as she picked up her phone, scrolling through it until she found the number she wanted.

Sitting, Molly dialed the number and waited for an answer.

"Hey, Jenna, I think I've screwed up."

Tears fell, streaking her pale cheeks.

"What's wrong?" Jenna asked.

"Everything," she cried. "I thought I was over this. I was so sure that all those feelings were dead, but they weren't and now I've hurt him and I know there's no coming back from this."

"Molly, slow down," Jenna said, her calm voice and controlled. "Where are you?"

"In Capitola, at Connor's place."

"Do you want me to come get you?"

"No, Connor's arranged for a car... That's not the problem."

"What is?"

"I love him and I've pushed him away. Who does something like that?" Molly couldn't hold it in. The anger, the pain, the heartache and the guilt—a whole cluster of emotions she'd kept locked away, hidden from everyone, including herself.

"Molly, you've not been yourself, you've had a hard time, and recovering from the accident has been hard, but you know what? You're a tough cookie, don't ever question that," Jenna said. "Here's the thing—you push everyone away, you've done it for as long as I can remember. It's part of who you are. The whole trust thing. It's an issue. So my advice to you is if you want Connor, if you truly love him, then you've got to let the guy in. Stop beating yourself up over the past. Forget it, move on and live for now, because life will pass you by and you will have so many regrets they'll eat you alive on your deathbed."

Molly knew Jenna was right. She was always honest and blunt, but it was what she needed. She didn't need anyone pussy footing around her. She needed cold, hard facts, and though they hurt, it was the bitter truth.

"I don't know how to fix this."

"Don't dwell on that now. Just wait until you get back to the apartment. I'll stop by and we can figure this out together. Okay?"

"Deal!" Molly said, ending the call, mindlessly staring out at the mellow sea.

Molly had never been this hung up over a guy before. Connor had her in a mindless state of despair. A restless energy that had her biting her nails, pacing the floors, thinking, chastising herself for how she had treated him. She didn't even know where he lived or where he would be. All she could think of was that she had to tell him her true feelings and try to salvage what they had before it was too late.

* * * *

The ride back to the city was the longest ever. Molly sat in the back of the Mercedes, thinking, and too much thinking led to a headache that had her eyes blinded by the light when they finally pulled up outside her apartment block. The driver got out, opened the door and held it as Molly got out.

"Thank you," she said as she lifted her bag and walked inside, knowing Regina would be waiting for her.

Molly took her time and was in no rush to hear the 'I told you so' or the 'What were you thinking?' speech. She didn't need it. In fact, she was sure she'd have a pretty good response to anything Regina intended saying. She wasn't a child and didn't need the lecture. She knew it had been a bad idea, she just needed to make things right.

Opening the door, she could hear Regina from the bedroom. Throwing her bag, she walked into Regina and Aggie's room and saw Regina on her knees, putting some of Aggie's belongings inside.

"What are you doing?"

"I think it's about time I sorted through this clutter," Regina replied as she folded some clothes, setting them inside.

"But... It's too soon," Molly muttered as she sat on the end of the bed.

"No, it's been nearly a year. I think Aggie would rest better if she thought some poor soul out there got some use out of her things."

"Maybe," Molly replied, lifting one of Aggie's silk scarves, smelling it as her tears began to slip down.

Regina looked up at Molly, her own eyes full of grief. "This was never going to be easy, but it's the right time."

Nodding, Molly knelt beside Regina and began folding a small pile of clothes. Everything smelled of Aggie's sweet musk perfume. Everything brought her grief to the surface. So much guilt, so much anger — regret.

"How was last night?" Regina asked as she sealed a box with some tape.

"It was...a disaster."

"How so?"

"I don't need the sermon," Molly said, completely jumping the gun.

"I wasn't going to give one. But since you mentioned it, what happened?" Regina asked as she stopped what she was doing, looking at Molly, waiting for answers.

"Nothing happened, that's the thing. I totally rejected him. I made him feel like the world's biggest loser."

"I told you that it was a bad idea. There's too much that went wrong between you. The timing isn't right," Regina said as she stood, holding out her hand to Molly. "How about some cocoa?"

Molly's eyes were full of tears, her nose was red raw. She glanced at Regina's hand and took it. "Okay."

Stirring the milky contents, Molly stared out of the window, her mind blank, not wanting to think any longer.

"Molly, you're like a daughter to me, so anything you do, or say, will always cause me to have an opinion," Regina said as she touched Molly's arm. "Your accident, whether you don't want to admit it, was a result of what happened between you and Connor. He may not have made you drink or walk out in front of that car, but the fact remains, if things hadn't transpired the way they did, then none of this would have happened."

Molly looked at her. "I know."

"I don't want to be a killjoy. Hell, I know what it's like to love, but Connor, regardless of his good intentions, may not be the one after all."

"But how can I get over him when he's all I want?" Molly cried. "There's this little part of me that blames him for everything, then the other part of me that wants to run into his arms, get lost in him and just be his. Is that so wrong?"

"Baby girl," Regina said as she held Molly's hand. "Of course it's not wrong. But can you get past the wedge that's been created? Can you, hand on your heart, say that you won't throw things in his face when times get tough, because, honey, no relationship, no matter how in love you are, runs smoothly. Are you able to leave the past where it belongs and move forward with your life? Because if you can't, then I'm afraid the relationship would be doomed from day one."

Molly sat staring into space, completely deflated, and the only thing that pressed on her mind was Connor. Was she throwing the chance of a lifetime away based on pride and stubbornness?

The doorbell rang.

Molly sat upright, her posture rigid. Days like that were the kind that drained her mentally and physically.

"Come right in, Jenna, we're in the kitchen," Regina's voice echoed from the hallway.

Jenna's footsteps were loud on the wooden floor. When she popped her head in the doorway, her broad smile beamed as she waved to Molly. "Now why so glum?"

"She's lovesick," Regina said as she walked past her, lifting her cup. "And it seems that our little lamb is lost."

"Then we'd better point her in the right direction, hmm?"

Jenna sat down on a chair beside Molly, folding her arms across her chest. She was clearly waiting for her to say something.

"What?" Molly asked.

"If you want this man, then you are going to have to cut out this whole bullshit of sitting here, wallowing. No one likes pity parties and we both know how those end so buckle up, and do what you want to do." Jenna was pretty direct when she spoke. "Where's the girl with the fire in her heart?"

"Burning." Molly sighed.

"See, this is what it's like," Regina complained. "If you love this man, regardless of his indiscretion, then you and only you need to let him know."

"Gina's right and you know it," Jenna was quick to back her up.

"I broke his heart last night. He told me he loved me and I rejected him. Who does something like that? A cold-hearted bitch, that's who. Maybe I'm like my folks after all."

"Want some cake to go with all the woe?" Jenna asked, not giving in to her self-deprecation.

"Fuck off," Molly said in defense.

"Hey, less of that," Regina piped in. "Aggie would have given you a good slap for that."

Regina was right. If there was one thing Aggie hated more than marshmallows, it was bad language. The two left a nasty taste in her mouth and she didn't allow either in the apartment.

"Sorry," Molly muttered as she held her cup of cocoa in her hands.

"Molls, you need to chase your dreams. If you want him, then go get him." Jenna again was straight to the point.

"Yeah, about that," Molly said, raising her eyebrows, "do you happen to know where he lives, or, erm, maybe, where Ellison Enterprises is? Maybe Barry can do a little digging for me?"

Both Regina and Jenna looked at each other, sighing and shaking their heads.

"Only you, Molly, only you!" Regina said.

Chapter Thirty-Seven

"Here, have some more bacon," Eleanor said as she handed the platter to Connor, who sat across from her.

"The flight will leave tomorrow," John said as he ate a mouthful of sausage.

"I thought Monday?" Connor inquired.

"Yes, but we had some changes to make. Liao Minsheng wishes to meet you in person, introduce you to some of the directors before he leaves for Europe on Tuesday. Edward will be going with you. I've promoted him and he's a good asset to the Hong Kong branch." John sipped at his coffee, observing Connor the whole time.

"I see," Connor muttered. His appetite wasn't great. He struggled to eat as his mother continued to ply him with food.

"Liao is more than happy to shadow you once he's back from his trip. He's keen to show you the ropes and I am sure you will get on with him," John said as he sat back, looking very pleased with himself.

"How was your trip to the beach house last night?" Eleanor asked, raising an eyebrow.

Connor knew nothing was ever sacred. He could never have a private life, not when he was here, under their snooping eyes. Maybe Hong Kong would serve as a great way to do what he wanted. Maybe he'd never come back.

Just as they were finishing up, heels clicked on the terrace. "Apologies for being late, I got held up at the spa," Marissa said as she sat down beside Connor.

Connor spurned her advances. The sheer thought of her touching him sickened him to the pit of his stomach. He despised her. Everything about her was poisonous and evil. He didn't want her in his life.

"I thought this morning was all about family?"

Eleanor smirked as she stirred sugar into her tea. "Of course it is. Marissa is a huge part of this family."

"You can never leave it alone, can you, Mother?" Connor's jaw clenched as his eyes bore into his mother's. "Forever sticking your nose in where it's not wanted."

"Oh, stop causing a scene, Connor. It truly doesn't become you. I blame that God-awful girl. She's influenced you in a way that truly doesn't suit you. The sooner you forget about her, the sooner you will begin to focus on the things that matter." Eleanor smirked as she sipped at her tea.

Between Marissa and his mother, he couldn't decide who he hated the most.

"Oh yes, I remember her. The skinny little thing that thought she could fill shoes that were evidently two sizes too big," Marissa gave her two cents' worth. "Silly how some of these fools think they can come along and take what's not theirs."

Reaching over, she tried to touch Connor's hand, only to have him push her away. "Get your fucking hands off me."

"Connor!" his mother gasped.

"I think you ought to leave, Marissa," John said as he stood.

"What? Why? I'm here to support Connor."

"The hell you are. You are no better than her," he shouted, pointing to his wife. "Always sticking your nose in where it's not wanted. Guess what, Marissa, the world doesn't revolve around you and your fake tits." That earned him a slap across the face. "Oh, and furthermore, I can categorically say that you give the worst head going. You might do well to get in a bit more practice if you fancy yourself marrying a millionaire. And for the record, Molly is in a league of her own. Your dirty money could never buy that kind of class. Now if you'll excuse me, I have things to do that do not concern you…"

Looking at his father, he smirked before walking away.

Sometimes, Connor surprised himself. Just every once in a while he had the balls to stand up for something he believed in, and right at that precise moment, he stood up for Molly and rebelled against everything his world stood for. Money or not, manners were something that didn't cost a dime, and Marissa proved she had neither class nor manners.

Before Connor got into his car, his father had followed him onto the driveway. "Listen, Connor, I know that things have been strained."

"You reckon?"

"Your mother gets a little ahead of herself," he said, running his hand through his thinning hair. "Marissa has been your mother's preferred choice from day one. I, on the other hand... I don't believe in controlling that aspect of your life."

"No? So, it's just my working life you want to control?"

"That's not fair, Connor, and you know it."

Leaning against the side of the car, the two looked at the ground. John slid his hands into his pocket. "If I can't count on you to keep things ticking over for me, then who can I count on? When I die, all this goes to you. Your brother, I love him, but he's not cut out for this industry, but you are."

"Dad, I... How am I meant to run things like you and Carl?"

"You've been doing well up until the merger. What happened?"

Connor looked up at the bright blue sky, his heart heavy, and his head full of so many things he just wanted to escape. "I don't know. I just can't figure out why someone would screw us over. Bruce is convinced he knows who the leak is, but he isn't confident about being so forthcoming."

"Interesting," John replied. "Maybe with you going to Hong Kong he might cave from a little pressure — which relieves you from any suspicion."

"What?"

"The board of directors has aired their concerns, considering your brush with the...you know."

"You can say it, Dad, I'm not that bloody sensitive." Connor's eyebrows narrowed as his father danced around the delicate subject of attempted suicide.

"I suppose it's a well-known fact now," John replied, glancing over at his son. "We'll get past all this. It will just take time."

"Time seems to fuck me over."

"You're only young. You have a whole life ahead of you."

Sighing, Connor rubbed his face. "And no one to share it with."

"How is Molly?"

"She blew me off. I had my chance, but that bitch in there destroyed it all, and there's not a thing I can do." Connor was angry. "Dad... I don't think I can ever be happy. Not truly. I feel like I am destined only to exist."

"That breaks my heart," John said as he looked over at his son. "I know I've been hard on you. That doesn't mean that I've never cared."

"It's okay, Dad, you don't need to explain yourself to me."

"I think I do."

The two men stood together, united for the first time. Being father and son, no interruptions from Eleanor, no condescending remarks, just genuine warmth between them.

"Take a walk with me," John said. "Your mother was quite a woman back in the day, she still is now, but, people change over time. Her once gentle nature became corrupted by the prominent world we live in. She became a woman of means, and that came with a small price to pay." John looked solemn as he spoke. "I've always been driven, something your grandfather drilled into me from a young age, but your mother made it her business to make sure I became head once my father retired. There were never any doubts about it. And twenty years later, here we are, a family that has become estranged, convoluted and at war with itself."

Connor understood everything his father was saying. He had lived within the confines of the empire all his life. He had seen firsthand the lengths his mother went to, to remain top dog. He'd witnessed the cruel world where money made everything okay and no one had a conscience.

"Why can't she just let me do my own thing and be happy for me?"

"Because, in her mind, there is a natural order, a process, and when that's fucked with, all hell breaks loose," John said as they strolled through the hilltop garden. "She doesn't even realize what she's saying half the time. It's like she goes into autopilot mode and does what she was bred to do."

"She ripped Molly apart the night of the gala," Connor said as they stopped near the pool. "I'm sure she put Marissa up to following us."

"Marissa is the kind of woman who, when she sets her sights on something or someone, she won't let go," John remarked as they looked out over the pool. Their world was in sharp contrast a place of sanctuary away from the struggles of daily life, the worries of not knowing where the next meal was coming from, the fear of not being able to survive. Connor knew he had it good, he wasn't naive enough to think otherwise, but he also knew how seedy and corrupt his kind were, and that was something he found hard to comprehend.

"She screwed my chances with Molly. She took that away from me."

"I know." John was sympathetic. "But maybe some distance, some time apart, away from all temptation of falling back into old habits and things that drag up unsavory memories is exactly what you need."

"Nothing is ever simple... Women, eh?" Connor sighed.

"Women are creatures of habit, or so is the case with your mother," John stated. "Sometimes a clean slate is the only solution. If it's meant to be, then it will happen when the time's right. You can't force something to happen. It goes against nature."

"You're right," Connor finally admitted, accepting that Hong Kong was to be his new beginning. "This is exactly what I need in my life right now — clear direction. Thanks, Dad."

A beginning away from all the heartache of California was the path he had to go. If he was to be happy, he had to cut his losses and take a chance on something new, no matter the pain.

Chapter Thirty-Eight

Molly helped Regina pack the remaining boxes into the back of her car, taking her time, trying to avoid an impromptu dizzy spell. Sundays were always her day of respite. A day for books, chocolate and sleep, but restlessness crept through her. She knew what she wanted to do, but she didn't know if she had the guts to go through with it.

Regina, her proverbial conscience, was the one to drop the little bombshell. "I got a call from Luke late last night."

Molly looked at her and asked, "What did he say?"

"Eugene wants to press charges against you."

Molly went silent as the words rang through her head. She couldn't believe it. The man who had beat and tried to rape her wanted her charged. It was ridiculous.

"Why?"

Sighing, Regina rested her hand on the car, as her other hand fixed Molly's hair away from her face. "Because he's a dumbass fool."

"Will he have a case against me?"

"Nope. Barry has already begun his own case against him."

"Oh… I forget sometimes what Barry does for a living," Molly said, sounding deflated.

"Honey, the man tried to rape you," Regina said. "We were there. We saw what that monster did to you."

"But I hit him!"

"In self-defense."

Molly's head ached from all the information filtering through. The memory of that day, the way he had made her feel. The vision of him jerking off as he pinned her against the wall made her dry heave. "Why can't these assholes just go and die."

"Because the world doesn't work that way," Regina remarked as she locked the car. "Come on, let's take a walk. Grab a coffee on the way." Her warm smile was enough to convince Molly that a little walk would help.

The two women linked arms, walking down the street as Sunday morning traffic buzzed by.

"What about my folks?" Molly asked, knowing that Regina would be honest with her.

"They were released without charge."

Molly's heart sank to another level.

"They're never going to leave me alone, are they?" Molly asked. "They're always going to be there, sneaking, watching me, knowing my every move."

"Most likely. Either that or they'll take one hit too many and die in the gutter," Regina said as she held on tight to Molly.

"Would it be bad of me to wish they'd just die?"

"We never wish death on those who've hurt us. Always remember that." Regina had a way with words, a way of making Molly listen, and even though things were jumbled in her head, Molly knew Regina was right. Wishing death on them would have made her exactly like them and she didn't want to stoop to that level, no matter the hurt she was feeling. "Both Aggie and I, we came up against a lot of bad people in our time, but our one saving grace was that we never once wished ill on those who hurt, or tried to hurt, us. We placed all our faith in God and our beliefs. Because if there's one thing, the man upstairs does right by those who've been wronged."

Molly sat down outside a small bistro. She quietly sipped her coffee, listening to the laughs from the people who surrounded her. It felt as if it had been a lifetime since she had laughed heartedly. She wanted that joy back in her life.

"I need to make things right with Connor," she said as she

glanced over at Regina. "I know you're going to try to talk me out of it, but, what if this is it, my one chance? I can't let that go."

"Then chase your dream. Just come home if things don't go the way you want." Regina reached across the table and held Molly's hand. "I can see the passion, the love, the determination in your eyes. If he can make you happy, then you have my blessing." Her eyes filled with tears. "I just don't want you hurt again."

"I love you, Gina, even though I've been a bitch lately," Molly said, her voice almost a whisper. "I'm working hard to keep that tongue of mine in check."

Laughing, Regina fanned her face with her hand and said, "Good thing my skin's made of leather."

Molly shook her head before finishing off her coffee. "Mind if I go? Are you all right with taking the boxes over to Goodwill yourself?"

"You go do what has to be done. Just be mindful of yourself and that little head of yours. It's taken quite the beating lately, and well, we both know the things that can go wrong."

"Yes, I know... I promise, you will be my first point of contact if I get all weird and shit."

Molly stood, planting a kiss on Regina's cheek before going about her business. If there was one thing Molly had learned through everything that had happened, it was that if she truly wanted something bad enough, she had to go get it herself. Her happiness was in her hands and it was up to her to secure her future. She just didn't know exactly how she was going to do that.

Molly took her phone out of her back pocket and called Jenna.

"Hey, did Barry happen to get that address I was looking for?"

"I'm good, thanks for asking." Jenna's sarcasm was obvious. "Yes, of course he did."

"So...?"

"So… Are you sure this is something you want to do? Do you want me to come with you?" Jenna asked.

"Seriously? C'mon, Jenna, I need to do this alone."

"Well, how about I drive over to his place? I'll just sit outside. I promise, I won't cramp your style."

Molly thought for a few moments, biting down on her lip. "I don't know."

"What harm can it do?"

"Okay," Molly conceded. "I'm on Sacramento. Just by the park."

"Give me five minutes. I'm not too far away. Just dropping Arianna off at a friend's."

"No worries."

Molly knew that between both Regina and Jenna, she was never going to do this alone. They had her back and while at times it made her feel like she couldn't breathe, she was pretty damned happy at the prospect of having someone to go to if things went wrong.

Jenna pulled up and honked the horn, making Molly jump. Waving, she made her way to the car. Her stomach sank as nerves began to get the better of her.

"You ready to do this?" Jenna asked, raising her eyebrows.

Nodding, Molly closed her eyes, envisioning Connor in her mind. "Yes."

As they drove off toward her destiny, Molly found herself thinking, reassessing everything that had happened since May. The bridge, the way Connor had been so broken when she'd helped him, to how he had come along and whisked her away after her escape from Eugene. Right down to the night of the accident, the reality hitting her hard. So many little pieces of the jigsaw finally fitted together.

Wounded and hurt, she accepted that the time had come to move past all the suffering.

In just under ten minutes, they pulled up outside the apartment block on Mission Street. A knot of unease made itself known to Molly as she looked up at the building, her heart hanging by a thread.

"Apartment three-zero-ten," Jenna said as she looked at Molly.

"Oh God, I feel ill." Molly couldn't hide the nerves. The anxiety was becoming too much.

"No, you don't. Not when you've got this far. Go in there, say what you have to. I'll be here regardless," Jenna said, reaching over to open the door. "You said it yourself yesterday, you're the only person who can make this right."

Molly looked at her, the palms of her hands sweaty, as her heart pounded. "I can do this, right?"

"Absolutely."

Molly got out of the car, her head dizzy from the anticipation. *God*, she thought, *I'd better be doing the right thing.* Standing still as she mustered up all the courage she'd ever need, she inhaled deeply before stepping through the entrance of the building.

The air conditioning billowed around her as she walked inside the main foyer of the building. Getting her bearings, she eyed the front desk. A well-built man sat behind it.

Lifting her head, she walked with confidence toward the desk, smiling at the man as she approached.

"How may I help you, miss?" he asked.

"Apartment three-zero-ten, Connor Ellison," Molly said as she kept eye contact.

"I'm afraid Mr. Ellison has left for the airport." The concierge smiled as he delivered the devastating news. Unbeknown to him, Molly's heart stopped beating.

The air suddenly got tight. "What? What do you mean?"

"Mr. Ellison was picked up fifteen minutes ago."

Molly's world suddenly came crashing down around her. It was too late.

She had fucked up.

She had screwed whatever chance she'd had. Panic began setting in.

"Where's he going?"

Unsure of whether to deliver the information, the man could see the desperation in her face. "He's bound for Hong

Kong."

"Oh God!" she gasped.

"Miss, are you okay?"

With tear-filled eyes, Molly ran from the apartment block, out to the car where Jenna stood, waiting.

"He's gone! He's left for the airport," she cried. "I'm too late."

"What?"

"Hong Kong," she muttered as her head spun. "I've lost him."

"No, you haven't. Get in."

"What?"

"Get in the damn car," Jenna stormed. "We can still make it."

Not wasting another minute, Jenna made it her mission to help Molly salvage something she was sure she'd never have again.

Chasing the dream, the one person who completed her, Molly's mind raced. Losing him now wasn't a prospect she could face. If she'd lost him for good, then she'd spend the rest of her life in deep regret.

Chapter Thirty-Nine

Connor stood in line, waiting to check in. His heart was heavy, but he had become very adept at switching on his business head. Locking all his emotions in the back of his mind, refusing to address them ever again, he'd decided that he'd never revisit the past. Falling in love meant being vulnerable, and that exposure meant weakness — no more.

Moving up the line, he looked back at Edward, his travel companion. "I should have taken my father up on the charter." He was exasperated at the many people who stood in front of him.

"Why didn't you?" Edward asked as he got his passport and ticket ready.

"Because I won't give my mother the satisfaction."

"Sometimes you should just take the perks that come with being an Ellison." Edward winked at him.

Connor knew Edward was right, but no matter what, he still couldn't stomach the thought of his mother having one up on him.

"Patience, just a little patience, and this part will be over." Connor tried to convince them both.

Standing there, Connor switched off his mind to the lot. Hong Kong was now his priority. The company and his career. Everything his father wanted was now the one thing he knew he could achieve. Romance, love and all the hijinks that came with it would have to take second place.

Finally, after a good twenty-minute wait, he stepped up to the check-in desk, handing over his passport and ticket.

"Good afternoon, sir, how are you?" the blonde asked him.

Connor smiled, scanning the red lipstick on the mouth that pouted at him. "I'm very well, thank you."

Looking up from his passport, the flight attendant gazed at him. "And have you packed your luggage yourself?"

Connor was a man women found attractive and it helped him at times, especially when he was pissed or wanted to get away from something fast. He couldn't deny the buzz it gave him, but still, women and all their weird mind games were something he didn't want or need.

"Yes." He was cool as he answered.

"No sharp objects?"

"No."

"Has anyone else had access to your luggage?"

"Nope."

"Very well, sir." She smiled at him as she handed him his passport and boarding pass. "Here's your gate, and the flight will board thirty minutes prior to departure. Have a nice journey."

Connor nodded at her, smiled then turned his back, walking away from the desk. He stood patiently waiting for Edward to go through the same process.

"Again, another reason to have taken advantage of your father's private jet," Edward said as he stuffed his passport and boarding pass into the inside pocket of his jacket.

"Wanna grab a beer before we hit security?" Connor asked out of the blue.

"We can do that from the other side."

"I'm real thirsty."

"Let's get through security, then we'll have all the beer we want."

Edward was a stickler for protocol, and being Connor's right-hand man when it came to traveling, he knew how and when to reel in Connor.

Agreeing, Connor nodded and proceeded to the long line ahead. His insides twisted. *For fuck's sake,* he thought. Connor never did have patience and his private school, bad boy attitude was getting a little too close to the surface.

"Next time I suggest flying commercial, shoot me," he complained.

"Absolutely."

Edward grinned as he stood beside Connor, trying his best not to gaze at the ass of the redhead in front of them. Connor noticed it, cringing at the way Edward bounced back on his heels, practically salivating.

"Stop it before you get yourself arrested," Connor whispered.

"Just taking in the sights."

Shaking his head, Connor ran a hand through his hair, looking off in the opposite direction, not wanting to be seen as a pervert. Completely unaware of the commotion coming from the back of the line.

Murmurs from disgruntled passengers raised voices and security guards making their way got Edward's curiosity. "Uh-oh, they're coming for me," he joked.

Connor laughed, patting Edward on the back. "I'll be sure to tell Liao you send your apologies."

Then he heard it.

"Connor!"

Connor spun around, his heart pounding hard. It didn't make sense. It was as if his brain had broken down and needed resetting. Everything became vague, a tangent, a series of little explosions in his mind, trying to decipher what was happening.

"How could you...you coward," Molly shouted as she pushed toward him.

People moved aside, letting her get within inches of him. Security headed straight her way.

"You tell me you love— Then this?"

"Molly... I..." He couldn't find the words.

"Don't you dare." Tears slipped down her cheeks. "Don't you even think about telling me more bullshit."

Just as he was about to say something, two security men were on either side of her. "Miss, can you step aside, please?"

Molly shrugged them off.

"It wasn't enough that I nearly died, no, but you had to go and break my heart, not once, but twice," she cried. "What kind of a man does that?"

Edward shot her a look, as though she were nuts. Connor stepped up to the retractable belt barrier. "Molly, you don't understand."

The security men each took one of Molly's arms. "Let go of me," she stormed as she fought them.

"Please, let her go," Connor pleaded.

The men eased their grip on Molly, who gave them a series of bad looks. Jenna ran over to where she stood, trying to get her to back away, but Molly pushed her, not wanting her near.

Quite the crowd had gathered. The commotion was enough to pique people's interests.

"You told me how you felt the other night, that was proof it was over," Connor said in defense.

"But Hong Kong? Why?"

"Distance and new beginnings." His words were cold.

Molly's face paled. She raised a hand to her chest as she listened to the words. Her cheeks were wet from tears. "And this is your new beginning? Never mind the mess you're leaving behind."

"I didn't do this... You know that." Connor gritted his teeth, clenching his jaw, trying not to say the words that would have broken her in two. "I tried with you. I really did, but... You're not the Molly I fell in love with. We both know that."

Rejection was easier than having to live with the constant reminder of what he'd done to her. In his mind, this was the best way, even if it meant tearing his soul apart.

"You...don't mean that. I know you. I've been with you. You're not this stone-cold, heartless bastard."

"Am I not?" Connor asked.

Molly stepped up to the barrier, looking up into his face. "No."

"So why did you make me feel like the world's biggest asshole?" His voice broke.

"Because I lost sense of what it all meant," Molly whispered. "But you left...and it was then that I knew I couldn't be without you."

"Molly." Connor's heart thumped hard, making his head spin. Breathing through the building anxiety, he glanced at her, seeing the pain on her face. "I'm sorry. I think we both need to go our separate ways."

Jenna was soon by her side, her hands resting on her shoulders. Molly tried to brush her off, but she wasn't going anywhere.

"You don't mean that." Molly's eyes refused to leave his. "Please don't make me beg."

Connor turned his face away from her in shame. He hated himself more at that point than at any time before. He could see the wound he was inflicting on her. Shaking his head, he swallowed the same lump in his throat over and over again, finding it hard to stomach the emotions running through him.

"Molly... Just go."

"No..." she shouted. "Not until you say it."

Connor knew exactly what she was asking of him. He didn't want to say it. He didn't want to deliver the words that would shatter both their worlds.

Reaching out toward him, Molly tried to touch him, only for Connor to spurn her advances. "Don't..."

"Listen, sweetheart," Edward piped in. "He doesn't want you. So move along and stop causing a scene." Patting Connor on the back, he gestured for them to move forward along the line.

Jenna's eyes blazed. "Molly, come on, this was a bad idea," she said, grabbing Molly's hand.

"No!" she shouted. "Not until he says it."

Connor turned back to look at her and felt sick. The guilt, the instant remorse, the hell he was now in. The words slipped from his tongue before he had the chance to stop them. "I don't love you."

Gasps from the crowd echoed in his head as he watched Molly's reaction. Her beautiful face was crippled in the pain he was mirroring inside. He saw the damage he was doing.

Letting go of them, of who they were, was a hard decision to make, yet, at the back of his mind, he'd convinced himself it was the right thing to do. But at that point in time, he despised himself.

A world without Molly was certainly a dreary prospect, and he had only himself to blame.

Chapter Forty

Pressing the heels of her hands into her face, Molly saw nothing but a blanket of darkness. Jenna tried to help her sit, but she stumbled and fell onto the ground, trembling as her head spun.

The security men walked away, satisfied that she wouldn't make another scene. None of it made sense to her. How could he have suddenly fallen out of love with her? All in a split second everything she wanted, hoped to have, dreamed of, was gone, snatched away, and all by the hands of the man she loved.

Jenna knelt on the ground beside her, consoling her. Wrapping her arms around her, trying her best to ease some of the pain, but it was pointless. Molly was now allowing the despair to consume her and there wasn't a thing anyone could do.

"Come on," Jenna said, helping Molly to her feet. "Let's get you home." Molly didn't even fight it. There was nothing left within her to muster the strength to run back inside. It was over and she had to learn to live with that.

Traveling back to the apartment was a blur. Molly had no recollection of the journey. Regina was waiting for them when they walked in, but Molly was too far through even to talk about it. She was mentally exhausted and just wanted to switch off, and escape. Two Xanax later, Molly was out for the count. Her body needed the rest, and her mind needed to rid itself of all the thoughts, the memories — the newfound pain that meant recovery was on a whole new level of impossible.

* * * *

Groggy and feeling more hungover than refreshed, Molly sat up, glancing over at her clock. It was well past noon, and for a split second, she'd almost forgotten about the previous day's events. Then reality came crashing down around her and she cried.

Connor's words rang through her head. It was as though he had cut out her heart and broken it in front of her eyes, for all the world to see. Life wasn't doing her any favors. In fact, life kept kicking her hard. And getting up each time was now feeling as if she were climbing a mountain, never destined to reach the top.

It was all too easy for Molly to sink back into old habits. The thirst was hovering over her like a dark cloud, refusing to leave, teasing her. The longing for just one drink lingered, almost impossible to ignore. It had been the first time since the accident — that God-awful night she vaguely remembered — that she really wanted to drown her sorrows. Somewhere in the back of her mind she'd convinced herself she had been cured of her demons, but that was just wishful thinking.

Walking into the bathroom, Molly opened the cupboard, eyeing her colorful display of medications. Lifting out a small container of Campral, she took two, anything that meant she wouldn't have to face the temptation too much longer.

Molly closed her eyes and refused to stare at her pitiful reflection. Having to look at herself meant facing the harrowing reality of what her future meant, and that was hard to stomach.

A quick shower, a fresh pair of pajamas and a broken heart, Molly knew she couldn't hide from Regina any longer.

Molly walked into the kitchen. Regina was sat at the kitchen table, writing a list. Peering over her glasses, she took one look at Molly, stood and held out her arms.

It didn't take Molly any coaxing. She ran into Regina's embrace, breaking down into an uncontrollable sob.

"Shhh," Regina consoled her, gently brushing her hair with her hand. "It's better out than bottling it all up."

Molly couldn't control it. A whole ocean of pain had taken over her small body. So much anguish, anger, hurt, complete confusion. Nothing made sense, yet at the same time, she knew it...or so she thought.

"He was so...cold," she sobbed as she broke the embrace. Wiping her eyes, she sat on one of the chairs. Bending a leg, she lifted it up onto the chair and rested her chin on her knee. "He said he...he didn't love me." The words alone felt like glass in her throat as she said them. "How could he?"

Molly searched Regina's face for an answer. But Regina had nothing for her, only words of comfort.

"Oh, honey, I'm sorry," she said as she sat beside Molly, touching her arm. "He is a fool for losing you."

Shaking her head, Molly rubbed her forehead, trying to think. No matter how many times she revisited it, the same throbbing ache pulsed in her head. The sickening sensation of utter doom. "I...just can't get my head around it."

"Sweetie," Regina said. "Sometimes, no matter how much we hurt, there is always something to be learned from the experience."

Molly shot her a look. "What? So, having my heart broken serves as one of life's many fucking lessons?" she shouted. "Well, I'm sick of learning all these valuable lessons. I just wish I had never met him. I wish I'd never stopped on that bridge."

"You don't mean that."

"Oh, don't I?" Molly stood, the anger now on the verge of exploding. "Wanna know something else? I am done with this place. So fucking done with all the shit that's been served to me lately. Eugene, my parents... Connor – they can all go to hell. Fuck them all."

In a rage, Molly stormed back to her room, pulled a bag

out from her closet and began packing.

Regina stood at the doorway, her arms folded across her chest. Molly could feel her watchful eyes on her.

"Where are you going to go?"

"Anywhere that's not here."

Molly threw clothes, books and a picture frame inside. Slipping on a pair of jeans and a sweater, she then put on her sneakers, determined that life away from San Francisco was the only way of recovering.

"What about your job? Jenna? Your meetings?" Regina asked as Molly packed away her meds, filling her toiletries bag with necessities.

"Fuck it all, Gina," she said, shrugging. "I need this for me."

"Then why not just take a short break, but come back home," Regina suggested.

Scoffing at the idea, Molly raised a hand into the air. "No... Not this time. I can't bear to spend another moment here. This room. That bed... Everything reminds me. I have to go."

"Okay," Regina said, her face completely unreadable. "If leaving will help, then do what you have to."

Molly stopped in her tracks, waiting for the ultimatum, but it didn't come. Not like how she expected it. "I'm not doing this to hurt you."

"I know, which is why I know that I have to let you go."

Molly suddenly came to the conclusion that any happiness that she thought she was once entitled to was all, in fact, a pretense. None of it had been real, not in the sense that she could have forged a future from their brief liaison. And since she had kept her heart alive by hope and sheer will, her delicate qualities and intangible emotions had been jeopardized. She no longer felt the surge of optimism. It was gone, and so was her silver lining.

Molly sniffed as her eyes filled with tears. She zipped her case closed. "Have I let you down?"

"Oh, honey," Regina said as she walked up to Molly.

"I've never been prouder. You've come through so much, and you're still here, fighting—albeit a little wounded—but you are no quitter."

"I feel like the world's biggest loser." Molly broke down again.

"Molly, what was the one thing Aggie always told you?"

"To follow my heart."

Regina took Molly's hands in hers, squeezing them gently. A reassuring touch to let her know that she wouldn't be judged for leaving. "There'll always be a home for you here, no matter where you go. This will always be your home."

Molly hugged Regina tight. Frightened and unsure of where she was going, but leaving was the only thing she felt she had control of.

"I need this. I need to find myself," she whispered as she rested her head on Regina's shoulder.

"I know, baby, but before you go, at least let me cook for you," Regina said, touching the side of Molly's face.

"The last meal, very poignant. I'm not Jesus and about to be crucified," Molly tried her hand at a joke.

"That's blasphemy." Regina hit her playfully on the arm. "Sorry!"

Molly followed Regina back to the kitchen where she made them an omelet and spicy couscous. The two women ate, talked and were the most relaxed they'd been in recent times.

In the back of her mind, Molly replayed Connor's words over and over again. Trying to ignore the inner echo, she indulged in lighthearted conversation with Regina. Anything that meant she didn't have to stomach the words.

"So now that you are sure you want to go, where will you go?"

Molly knew the question would be asked again. There was no avoiding it. "Montana."

"Montana?" Regina replied in shock. "Why Montana?"

"Remember Jenna's mother, Adelaide? She has said that I am more than welcome to visit any time, so I think I'll take her up on the offer. A break from all of this… It's the right kind of medicine."

Sighing, Regina swallowed hard before she spoke. "I guess we'd better get you sorted with travel arrangements. I think we ought to let Jenna know."

Nodding, Molly stood and kissed Regina on the cheek. "Thank you."

Molly walked back to her room. The weight of the world bore down heavy on her shoulders. Her head ached from all the thinking, the unwanted memories, the bad taste that it all left in her mouth.

Once inside her room, Molly paid a little more attention to what she packed. She made sure she had the necessities, a few trinkets that reminded her of home, but, more importantly, the album she and Aggie had put together shortly before her death.

With a heavy heart, Molly tied up her hair, applying a little makeup to cover the heartache she wore on her face. If she wore a mask, then no one would know or suspect that everything she had ever wanted was now gone.

The sound of the door knocking pulled her out of her pensive thoughts.

Jenna.

"So Montana, huh?" she said as she leaned against her bedroom door.

"Yup." She avoided having to look at her. Instead, she pulled on her light denim jacket.

"Mom will be glad of the female company. The farm could use an extra pair of hands."

"She always said any time I needed the break, I'd be welcome, and I figure no better time than the present."

Molly checked her room one last time, making sure she hadn't forgotten a thing. She lifted her bag from the bed and turned off her lamp. Walking to the door, Jenna held her hand out to her. "Let me take that for you."

"Sure."

Following her up the hallway, she could hear Regina

putter about the kitchen, keeping herself busy.

"I made a few calls, you can catch the six-twenty," Regina said as she filled up three cups of coffee.

"Okay, that sounds fine to me. I need to stop at the bank, sort out some cash," Molly replied as she lifted the hot cup into her hands. "Are you able to find out what services are available to me, you know, AA wise?" she asked Jenna.

"You know I will, and besides, with Mom being a teetotaler, you've no worries about temptation there," Jenna said, trying her best to keep the mood as light as possible.

"Excellent," Molly muttered.

As she sipped at the coffee, she looked over the cup at both Regina's and Jenna's faces. They were evidently distraught, how could they not have been? The girl they had helped restore from the broken and pitiful state she had once been in was now fleeing the nest. Molly's false smile hid a thousand wounds, some so deep she had convinced herself she'd never recover from them.

Now the awkward conversation was forced, each one of them trying to fill the void. The insecurity of having to let go and say goodbye.

Molly hated goodbyes, but new beginnings meant a second chance, something she needed. Time to heal, time to learn to forgive and time to find her true path in life.

Chapter Forty-One

One Year Later

To hate oneself was a horrid disease. One Connor was learning to live with fast. He found himself slipping into a world fueled by alcohol and pointless dates with women who meant nothing to him. He felt dead inside. He existed simply to run his father's company. Whatever came after that was jaded and clouded with drunken outburst and blackouts.

Hong Kong lived up to his brother's stories. Women who loved Western men with money, and men who loved showering their little conquests with lavish gifts, all to keep their silence.

Edward walked into the office, looking at his watch. "My flight leaves in a few hours, you sure about staying here? Running things solo for a few weeks?"

"Absolutely, Liao will be back on Monday and I've a ton of work to catch up on," Connor answered as he rubbed his eyes.

"You look tired. Maybe lay off the juice for a few days."

Connor scoffed at his friend's advice. "No can do, I've a dinner date in an hour. I need something to make it through."

"Then why bother even going out if she's that bad?" Edward asked.

"Because anything is better than spending a night on my own."

Connor had slipped into bad habits. A ritual of bad decision making and countless hours spent hating himself.

It was how he saw his future. If he didn't wind up dead by the age of forty, he'd be surprised.

"Enjoy the pity party," Edward said as he walked to the door. "But before you pull the trigger, maybe you should count your blessings. You have a great job, a secure future, you are a king compared to some. You dumped that girl. So what? Those kinds of wounds heal, but, man, this shit, it's going to destroy you, and I can't stand back and watch you do this, not while your name is attached to the sign on the top of this building."

"I can always count on you being blunt," Connor replied, sighing as he looked out over the breathtaking city. Standing, he popped his hands into his pockets and stared at the symphony of lights twinkling.

Connor was a million miles away from everything he'd left behind. No matter how hard he tried to find himself, or something worth living for, nothing compared to what he had thrown away. It was slowly destroying him one day at a time.

"Well, you know me. I say it like it is," Edward replied. "Anyway, I'll see you in a few weeks. Just, you know... Look after yourself."

Connor did not once make eye contact with his friend. Instead, his mind was off somewhere else. A familiar place he wanted to return to – Molly.

God, he hated who he was becoming. He couldn't stomach the pretense, the façade, the mockery he was making of his own heart. A never-ending undercurrent of regret and sadness that no amount of medication could fix.

The evening went by in a blur.

Ning chatted over dinner, her words drowned by the wine Connor drank. But the busty girl didn't seem to mind. Connor had tried to avoid calling her, considering their disastrous first date, but she was an easy distraction and he needed his mind on something other than the past. "You wanna get out of here?" Connor asked as he tried to focus on her face.

"Yes, okay. I don't mind."

Throwing down his card, he drunkenly raised his hand and called the waiter over to the table.

"Check!"

Once they were in the back of the car, Ning giggled as Connor ran his hand up the insides of her thighs. Connor slid a finger in through the side of her panties, teasing Ning, as he kissed the back of her neck.

Gasping, Ning trembled as he slipped a finger inside her, twirling it around, opening her a little more, so he could stick in another.

"We should stop…" she moaned.

"Why?" Connor bit on her ear, his tongue touching the flesh of her lobe.

"Driver…watching."

"So what?" Connor grinned. "Give him a show."

Before Ning could respond, Connor was kissing her hard, their tongues dancing together as Ning trembled from the building orgasm.

"Come for me," he whispered in her ear.

As he rubbed her clit, Ning held on to the seat, her warm breath brushing against Connor's cheek. Sighing and moaning, she threw her head back against the headrest. "I'm coming," she moaned out.

Connor didn't stop. He stared at her face, watching it scrunch up as the wave of pleasure took over. Her hot wetness seeped over his fingers, dripping down in between the cheeks of her buttocks. Warm musky moisture that left a scent in the air.

Giggling, Ning looked at the driver. His eyes stared back at her from the rearview mirror. But there was no surprise. Little did Ning know that this was something he'd become used to.

"Good girl," Connor said as he wiped his hands on his handkerchief. "Where do you want to be dropped off?"

A look of horror spread across her face. "Pardon me?"

"We are done for the evening. Where would you like my

driver to take you?"

Ning was lost for words. Connor was sure she thought a night of passion was on the cards for them, but no, Connor had no intention of allowing her near him, not in that way. He didn't want that kind of intimacy. He was more than happy to give a little, have some control, but sex was never on his agenda.

"You can let me off here," Connor directed to his driver. "I will walk back. Please take Ning home."

The driver nodded, slowing the car. Connor opened the door, then looked back at an angry Ning. "I'll call you."

Before she had the chance to shout at him Connor closed the door. He inhaled the night as he walked to his apartment complex, completely disgusted with himself and ready for a heavy night of booze and regret.

* * * *

The phone woke him shortly after nine a.m. Groggy, and worse for wear, Connor reached over, knocking an empty bottle of whiskey onto the floor.

"Hello!" he sleepily said, not once lifting his head off the pillow. "Mark, it's Saturday."

"So, did you forget?"

"What?"

"Ollie's first birthday?" Mark sounded pissed.

"Ah shit..." Connor said as he sat up, holding the back of his head as the headache made the room spin. "Fuck!"

"You're his godfather, you know how these things work."

"I didn't know you wanted me there as in, fly back."

Connor stumbled out of bed naked, walked to the kitchen to grab a bottle of water and chugged down half the contents before belching.

"You could still make it," Mark insisted.

"I'll feel terrible if I miss it...but, man, I'm..."

"Hungover?"

"Yes."

Connor walked to the large windows. The hazy sun shone in on his face, the unshaven shadow a mess.

"Cassie and I understand the whole issue with coming back, but you're family, it won't feel right without you." Mark was sincere.

"I'll see what I can do."

"Thanks, man."

Once Connor hung up, he rested his hands behind his head. His self-destructing behavior was now in overdrive. It had manifested into something he never knew he was capable of. He'd used Ning, made her feel like a cheap whore and he sickened himself to the core because of that.

"Fuck!" he roared.

Simpering down, he showered, washing away the effects of the booze from the night before, knowing he'd have to make the journey back home, and to the place that brought too many memories to the surface.

Once he was freshly dressed, he tidied up his condo. The whole while the thought of Molly flashed through his head. He still found it hard to believe that a year had passed, and he missed her more with each new day. Yet the more he missed her, the more he abused himself, never allowing himself a chance to recover.

Knowing all it would take was one phone call, he made contact with his father, who was surprised to hear from him.

"What can I do for you?" John asked.

"How are you fixed for flying me home in time for Ollie's birthday?" Connor asked, swallowing his pride.

"I can have a plane ready for you in a few hours."

"Thanks, Dad."

"Connor?"

"Yes."

"You know Marissa will be there?"

"She kinda comes with the territory."

"Okay, just as long as you know. I'll arrange a car to pick you up," John said.

"I guess I'll see you tomorrow."

"Safe travels."

Connor hung up, this time rushing to his room, packing a bag and putting his passport inside his jacket. Nerves nearly got the better of him. He wasn't in the right frame of mind, but damn it, family had to count for something, and if he let down those who'd been there for him during his darkest days, then he was no more than a coward.

There were some things in life that never made sense, and going home, right back to where it all began, was in fact a car crash waiting to happen. But who was he to stand in the way of fate?

Chapter Forty-Two

Adelaide had just made a fresh pot of soup when Molly returned from town, carrying a bag of groceries, her face the picture of health. Life in Montana had done a world of good for her. Gone were the dizzy spells, impromptu language, and she'd learned to control some of the bad moods.

"I thought I'd never get away from Mrs. Bradshaw. That woman loves to talk." Molly laughed as she took out the contents of the bag, then put the eggs in the refrigerator.

Adelaide was a seventy-six year old who had more energy than people thirty years her junior. She still ran the farm, keeping the books in order, and knew how to order her staff around, but she also knew her limitations and was happy to leave those things to Molly.

"Jenna called earlier," Adelaide said as she stirred the soup.

"Is everything okay?" Molly's insides twisted. She hated the thought of something happening and being completely out of the loop, but it came with the territory of not being back in San Francisco.

"Oh yes, honey, don't be going all worrisome over a phone call."

Letting out a sigh of relief, Molly buttered some rolls and set the table. "Is it the hearing?"

"Yes, Barry's going to call you after supper," Adelaide said as she ladled out two bowls of soup and set them on the table. "Now eat up. How are you going to get yourself a man if you've no meat on those bones?" Adelaide winked at Molly as the two of them ate, enjoying the warm broth.

Molly had taken to country life very well. She'd found

herself capable of so many things, and the fact that city life seemed so far away made her feel secure. There was no way her parents would ever track her there. She was safe and that helped her sleep at night.

After they finished, Molly cleared the table, leaving Adelaide time to read the paper and have a nap. Taking out the rest of the soup in flasks, she went to the barn and gave them to Matt and William.

"Here, this'll warm you up." Molly handed them the soup.

"Thanks, Molls," William said.

"How was town?" Matt asked.

Molly laughed. "Your mother is an interesting woman."

This made William laugh too.

Through the heavy facial hair on his face, Matt went red, only for Molly to pat him on the arm. "Don't worry, she had only good things to say about you."

"She never shuts up. I swear she wants to marry me off to anything that moves," Matt complained.

"She's probably sick of cleaning up after your sorry ass every day," William joked.

Molly observed them. William was the elder of the pair and Jenna's older brother. He still lived with Adelaide, but his life had been a struggle, and from what Molly understood, alcoholism ran in the family. Or so she had been told by town gossips. The farm proved therapeutic to William and he'd been clean eight years.

"Okay, I've books to check and a call from Barry in a few hours. I'll see you guys later," Molly said, smiling at the men, then she went back to the house.

Filling up a fresh cup of coffee, Molly opened the ledger and began totaling figures. Checking over Adelaide's calculations, she sipped at her drink every few minutes.

A year had passed since she'd found herself alone and broken. There were times when she often slipped back to that day at the airport, remembering Connor's cold eyes and his words. Then she'd pull herself back from the memory, not allowing herself to give it any life.

There were days when she'd awaken in a sweat, her heart pounding, her sheets soaking from the dreams. They were few and far between, but no matter how much she placed all the hurt in the far off reaches of her mind, it was in her sleep that it sometimes crept in.

On days like those, it would have been easy to slip off into one of the bars in town and drink herself stupid. But after overcoming so many hurdles, she knew that to go down that road again would have been like dancing with the devil, and she didn't fancy burning in hell any time soon.

The phone rang, making her jump.

"Hello," she said.

"Hey, how's the little farmer?" Barry asked, his voice the same as always — happy.

"She's doing really well," Molly replied. "So, it's happening?"

"Yes, but you knew it was coming. We've been over this."

"Do I really need to be there?" she asked, having almost convinced herself that it would all happen and be done without her being there.

"Molly, we've discussed this. Your evidence will put him away."

"Damn it," Molly cursed. "I thought I wouldn't have to be there."

"The defense will cross-examine you, Molly."

Shock eased itself inside Molly. "But I'm not ready."

"Of course you're ready. We've been over the cross-examination, the kind of questions they may ask. You can do this."

"I guess I'll have to," Molly said, sounding defeated already. "When?"

"Wednesday morning."

"Jesus, Barry, that's in four days," she complained.

"I know, and I'm sorry. I tried calling last night, but Adelaide mentioned that you and she went out for dinner."

"Yeah, I treated her to a steak and ice cream." Molly

smiled.

"That woman does love her T-bones." Barry laughed, then his voice got serious. "Listen, we need you to fly down tomorrow. I've got a flight booked and I'll pick you up, okay?"

Molly's head spun as she tried to make sense of all the details. Her heart skipped a beat when she realized she'd be going over the events of the day and that's when she felt as if someone were squeezing her neck.

"Molly... Are you still there?"

"Yeah." Molly choked back the tears. "What time do I need to be at the airport?"

"About two-thirty. Your flight's at three-fifty-five p.m. I'll have William drop you off. You'll get in just before eight, and I'll be there to get you, okay?"

"What about my ticket?" Molly's head raced.

"Have you got a pen handy?"

"Yes."

"Here's your confirmation number, just hand it in at the kiosk."

Molly wrote down the number as the nerves began to swarm inside her. She had known the hearing would be coming soon, but she hadn't anticipated having to be in the same room as Eugene. That thought alone made her skin crawl. No matter how much she tried to be brave, having to revisit that day was going to cause some serious problems.

"Just breathe," she whispered to herself.

Molly checked in on Adelaide before she went up to her room. She packed her case and got ready for what was going to be something she would never want to talk about again.

* * * *

Flying was something Molly hated. The confined space, the close contact of strangers, the thought of crashing, and not to mention the thought of having a panic attack in front of a bunch of strangers.

The entire four-hour flight was uncomfortable. The guy beside her made idle conversation, talking about his wife and four kids, how he still had a two-hour drive ahead of him after landing. The stench of stale alcohol fermented through the air as he spoke to her.

"Man, it's been a long week. I hate working these long weeks, but I guess I have a few days off, so I get to make it up to the little ones," the man said as he opened a pack of pretzels.

Molly didn't want to be rude, but damn, she felt like asking him if he wanted a mint, maybe even a hammer to knock himself out. She was already too wound up and the poor man's attempts at banter made the journey all the more unbearable.

Finally they landed, and it took a lot of composure for Molly not to clap for joy. Disembarking the aircraft was her main priority — and hand sanitizer.

The gent waved goodbye to her as she made her way to the bathroom. She washed her hands a good few times before applying some sanitizer. If there was one thing Molly couldn't stand, it was the thought of germs, which also happened to be a newfound dislike, given her past of working in the shelter.

As she walked toward baggage claim, Molly looked at her phone, checking for missed calls — nothing. Standing in the line around the turnstile, she absentmindedly began people watching. Observing an elderly couple who were warm and affectionate with each other, Molly smiled. Even the grumpiest of fools would have found it hard not to.

The turnstile buzzed and began moving. This was the part she agonized over. Having to bend down and try to remove her case without falling over and looking like an ass in the process.

Determined to remain standing, she stepped up close, and eyed the bags as they began moving past her, then low and behold, she saw hers. *Come on*, she thought to herself.

Let me get the hell out of here.

Grabbing her case, she pulled up the handle to make maneuvering through the crowd easier. Molly walked toward arrivals, her phone vibrated in her hand, and as she looked down she bumped into someone, nearly falling over from the impact.

A hand shot out, grabbing her arm, steadying her before she landed on the ground.

"I'm so sorry," the man said as he lifted her case upright.

As Molly glanced up, her eyes nearly popped out of her head. Molly brushed the hair back from her face, her cheeks blushed, and so did his.

"Molly!" Connor muttered in shock.

"Oh my God... I've... I've got to go." Molly didn't waste a second longer. She all but ran from him, looking back at the man she had loved, the one who had let her go.

If this was fate's way of playing games with her, she certainly didn't appreciate it.

Chapter Forty-Three

Connor's heart all but stopped beating. Out of all the people to meet, he had never once thought it would be her. How their stars had aligned and they were both in the airport at the same time was unbelievable. It had to mean something. There had to be some reasoning other than stupid facts. They were destined to be together, he could feel it in his bones.

The ache in his heart was now pressing into his throat as he called after her. "Molly!"

Molly kept running, not once looking back at him, and who could have blamed her? He certainly didn't, not after how he had spoken to her the last time they had seen each other.

A whole new feeling came over him. The fight he'd thought he'd lost was suddenly restored. Everything reversing itself, and with it came the sudden realization that this was the moment he'd been waiting for, and by God he wasn't allowing it to pass him by.

Connor ran after her, out into the arrivals lounge, searching for her. So many different faces, people moving to and fro, greeting loved ones, businessmen, not to mention the face of his father's trusted chauffeur, Martin.

Then he saw her again, looking back toward the crowd as she walked out of the building, Barry by her side.

Connor knew she was glancing back to see him. He could tell. There was something in the way she gazed at him when they'd walked into each other. He'd seen that look in her eyes before and knew that he'd never get another chance.

Connor ran out of the door after them, calling her. "Molly,

please wait."

Barry turned around, getting in between the two of them. Connor put up his hands. His jaw tightened as his fists clenched into tight balls.

"Connor, I think you need to leave her alone," Barry warned.

"I just want to talk to her."

Molly stepped back, sneaking a look in his direction before averting her gaze.

Barry's fist had made contact with Connor's face before he had the chance to plead. Connor's eyes watered as the taste of blood filled his mouth. Spitting out a mouthful on the sidewalk, Connor wiped his mouth. His head spun in a daze as he said, "Okay, I deserve that."

"Connor, just go about your business. She doesn't need you fucking with her head," Barry snapped. His eyes were wild with anger.

"I want to hear that from her, not you," Connor demanded as blood dripped down his chin. "Tell me now, and I swear I won't ever annoy you again."

"Fuck you!" Molly shouted as she turned her back on them both and walked away, then she stopped, spun around and glared him. "What gives you the right to come to me, expecting me to forgive you for breaking my heart? Are you on something? Because you are out of your mind."

"Molly, please, just listen to me."

"Why?"

"Because I've never stopped loving you. All that shit I said, it was just that — shit. I said what I thought you wanted to hear. Those words cut me to the bone. I thought I was doing you a favor."

"By breaking me? By destroying me? By taking everything I had given you and ripping my heart out? I was in pieces because you didn't want me. You were over us and you stood there, in front of everyone, telling me you didn't love me... Do you even know what that did to me? Have you any idea of how much I loved you, even after all the crap with that bitch?"

Barry tried to intervene, but Molly wasn't having any of it.

"For over a year I've been rebuilding my life, getting over you, recovering from the accident, and suddenly this… You telling me you love me." Tears burned her eyes. "What am I meant to say? What do you want from me?"

"I want you," Connor said as he stepped close to her. "It's always been you. I was such a fool to let you go."

"No!" Molly stormed. "You can't just expect me to accept this."

"Then what do I have to do?" Connor held his hands against his chest. His eyes ached. His heart pounded as he silently willed her to forgive him.

"Nothing, Connor. Absolutely nothing."

Molly gripped the handle of her case and stormed off. Barry followed her, looking back at Connor, his glare serving as a warning.

Connor stood still, watching Molly as she walked away. This time there was something in her voice that told him that things weren't over, not by a mile, but he knew she was hurting.

Giving her a little time and space was acceptable, he knew that. He was a reasonable guy, and now that this new turn of events had presented itself, he wasn't letting her go—just yet.

* * * *

It was shortly after ten by the time he got back to his apartment. He had made sure that things had been kept clean and tidy in his absence, having all mail forwarded to his address in Hong Kong. But there was no denying it, it felt good to be home.

A small hamper sat on the kitchen counter full of cheese, crackers, wine, chocolate and a small note. *Love, Mom.*

Unimpressed by his mother's attempts at welcoming him

home, Connor opened the wine, drinking straight from the bottle, not giving her a second thought.

Turning on the TV, he flipped through the channels then decided a shower was needed. His body ached and he craved a hot shower. He still hadn't got over the hangover from Friday night's bender and wanted nothing more than the soothing sensation of water.

The water was like heaven as it washed over him, easing his sore body. His jaw ached from the impact of Barry's fist. There was no denying it, the man knew how to throw a punch. Not bothering to shave his stubble, he dried off as his hunger pangs made their presence known. He wrapped the towel around his waist and went to the kitchen. He rummaged through the basket, taking out the cheese and crackers, and swigged from the bottle.

As he ate, he didn't pay any attention to the TV. He scoffed down the crackers, drank his wine and looked out at the San Francisco skyline, feeling weird considering it had been a year since he last enjoyed the view. He'd never thought he'd come back. He had been getting pretty comfortable being a train wreck and doing it all away from the prying eyes of his parents.

Screwing up his face at the aftertaste of the wine, he dumped the rest of it down the drain and brushed his teeth. His mother's tastes weren't his own. *Fucking typical,* he thought as the doorbell rang.

"Who the fuck?" he mumbled as he looked at the clock.

It was well after midnight and he wasn't in the mood for a late-night booty call from Marissa. *God,* he thought, *that's all I need.*

Taking his time, he swallowed hard before opening the door.

Molly stood, gazing at him. He couldn't believe she was actually there, at his door, looking sexy as hell and angry.

A hard slap across the face left his ears ringing. The heat from the force stung like hell. Just as he was about to say something, Molly pushed him inside, resting her hand on his bare chest, reaching up. Her lips brushed against his, then she pulled back.

Once she was clear of the doorway, she closed the door behind her.

Was he dreaming this?

Surprise and delight filled him as he looked down at her. Her gorgeous blue eyes glistened as they looked up into his.

Connor didn't need any coaxing. Pushing her back against the door, he kissed her. He didn't care about how sore his jaw was, he just needed to taste her and drink her in. Running his hands down her back, he pulled up the hem of her skirt and pushed her panties over her knees, letting them fall to the floor.

Molly ran her fingers through his hair as their breath danced together. Connor slid a finger down over her clit. Molly let out a moan as Connor teasingly rubbed her, before slipping a finger inside, drawing her onto her toes.

Gasping, Molly's mouth searched for his. Their kiss, long, passionate and hungry. A world away from anything he'd experienced before.

His arousal was visible from under the towel. Letting it fall to the floor, Connor grasped her bottom, lifted her up, wrapping her legs around his waist and smoothly walking them to his bedroom.

Laying Molly down on his bed, Connor had no control over his desire. He tugged at her dress. Molly raised her arms, letting him remove it. He unhooked her bra, dropping it to the floor, leaving her firm, round breasts begging for his touch. Connor leaned over her, rolling his tongue teasingly across her nipples, licking, kissing and massaging them. He savored the scent of her sweet aroma as his lips traced little kisses on her chest.

Molly moaned, arching her back to his mouth as little electrifying currents tingled through her body. Groaning against her flesh, Connor kissed down over her abdomen. There wasn't a part of her body he left untouched.

Lightly sliding his tongue down over her wetness, he drank her creamy moisture. His fingers found their way to her lips, pulling them apart as he ran his tongue up, finding her swollen core, flicking his tongue against it, making Molly moan. Connor glanced up at Molly, seeing the want and need in her eyes. It immediately made him lay his mouth on her clitoris, sucking hungrily, twisting his tongue on it as Molly bucked her hips against his mouth.

Connor slipped a finger inside her soaking wetness. The feeling of her tightness grasping at his finger hungrily made his hardness throb. Not able to take any more, he pulled away from her, keeping his fingers deep within her, pressing against the little spot that began to drive her wild. Kneeling, he used his other hand as he rubbed her clit, working it in circles while moving his fingers in and out of her with more urgency.

Molly's body tensed as the orgasm began to grip her from deep inside. Her walls tightened around his fingers. Her cries of pleasure filled the air as wave after wave of intense tingles shot through her body.

He kissed and licked his way up her body, pressing his lips down on hers, needing to feel her against him with ravenous desire.

Breaking the kiss, Connor looked down at her, rubbing his nose against her. "God, I love you."

"I love you too," she replied as she trailed her nails up his back.

Connor, wild with lust, smiled before grabbing her hips, quickly turning her over, forcing her face down on the bed.

Kneeling behind her, Connor massaged her ass before pulling her cheeks apart with his fingers, resting the tip of his cock against her. Molly pushed against him, enticing him to fuck her.

Connor pulled her back onto him and thrust deep inside her, filling her to the hilt. The feeling of the hot tension surrounding his cock, her insides contracting around him left him moaning, needing more... Craving more.

God, she felt so good. The way her body molded against his — she was the perfect fit. A fine sculpture and she was his.

Molly gasped every time he slammed into her, his cock hitting all the right spots. Her little moans drove Connor into a wild hunger. Pulling out completely, only to thrust inside her again, this time harder.

Reaching up, Connor entwined his fingers through her hair and pulled back gently, making Molly gasp in a mixture of pain and pleasure. An urgency took over once he heard the giggle that accompanied the moan, and he began ramming into her, his balls slapping against her ass as his thrusts became harder.

The warmth of pleasure seemed to begin in her stomach. Connor could feel the pressure. The need to fuck her, to have her climax, to have that complete sensation of being one with her.

Connor dug his nails into her hips, unable to hold back a second longer. The tightness in his balls became an all-consuming pleasure and when he began to moan, Molly let out a series of guttural whimpers as her orgasm swept through her.

With one last thrust, Connor exploded deep inside her, his seed intensifying her climax. The mixture of his bodily juice with hers made the sensation the most intense feeling he'd ever experienced. The two of them were breathless as their hearts pounded.

Connor couldn't believe it. After everything they'd been through. The year-long silence, the pain, the anguish, the acceptance that they were done and this happened.

Holding her in his arms, Connor vowed never to risk losing her again. They had been destined to be together, and after all the heartache, they'd found each other again.

"Molly?" he asked.

"Yes?"

The sound of her voice made his heart pump a bit faster as her warm face rested in the crook of his arm.

"Marry me?"

The words were out before he knew what he was saying, but as he said them, nothing had ever felt more right.

Chapter Forty-Four

"Marry me." The words echoed in her head. "Marry me." *Oh my God*, Molly thought. *Is this happening?*

"Are you serious?" Molly asked as she sat up, pulling the sheet around her.

This was not what she had expected. None of it was. She hadn't even known where she was going when she had decided on a late-night drive. Somehow she ended up here, and well, there was no going back.

"Yes, I am very serious," Connor said as he rested back on the bed. "If I've learned anything over the past year, it's that the heart certainly does grow fonder. I've missed you, missed seeing your beautiful face and regretted the day I told you I didn't love you." Sitting up, he took her hand in his. "I can't live without you... Not a day goes by when I don't think of you and if I could go back to that day, I'd have run after you. I'd never have said the things I did."

Molly's mind was working overtime. Gazing into his face, seeing the sincerity behind the proposal was enough to convince her that he was serious. But so much information was trying to filter through. She wanted nothing more than to say yes, to fall into his arms and be his, but a brick wall full of fear stepped in.

"I..." She tried to find the words.

"I know this is a sudden request, but you're my future," Connor said, cupping her face. "You're my eternity."

Molly couldn't hold it in any longer. The tears fell as the lump swelled in her throat.

"Yes." She cried.

Connor pulled her into his arms, kissing her softly. The

love they both felt at that exact moment was the promise of hope. A future where the splendor of their love would blossom and grow. A mutual understanding of their burning desire, the craving, the need, the completeness.

The future was theirs.

Lying down, they slept entwined in each other's arms, the happiest either of them had been in a long while.

Molly felt as if she had finally come home and her heart was at peace.

* * * *

Molly filled a glass of juice and sipped at it as she looked out over the beautiful view from Connor's balcony. She giggled to herself, shaking her head as the same amusing feeling overcame her.

Crazy, that was one thought, yet it all made perfect sense. Loving him was easy, letting him love her was the thing that made her feel alive. The way he loved her erased so much of the pain that it was easy to fall back into his arms. She wanted this. It was owed to her and nothing was going to step in her way again. She'd grabbed the chance of happiness with both hands, her mind made up.

"What's going through that pretty little head of yours?" Connor asked as he wrapped his arms around her waist.

Molly rested her head back against his chest, smiling. "You. Me... Us."

"Us, yes, we are pretty damn hot."

Playfully hitting his arm, Molly couldn't hide the euphoria. "So, when do we announce things to our families?"

Lifting her left hand, Connor ran his thumb over her ring finger. "When we get some bling on this finger."

Molly's heart danced. Everything was suddenly becoming so real her head raced, her insides were ready to burst. It was far from anything she thought would happen to her and now that it was, there was no coming down from the high.

"Then we let them all know?"

"Absolutely, I want to show you off to the world," Connor declared as he kissed her on the side of the face.

"Are we nuts?"

"Yes, but the best kind," Connor joked, making her laugh.

"You're such a dork." Molly turned around to face him. "I think I can get used to this."

"Good, because there is no stopping me now."

Connor's face was a picture of happiness. It radiated from him, mirroring Molly's own feelings. She couldn't stop smiling, and who'd have blamed her? She was now destined to spend the rest of her life with the gorgeous man in front of her, and he was besotted with her.

"Okay, I've got to go," Molly said as she pulled away from him, not wanting to, but knowing she had to make the meeting with Barry. "I don't want to be a killjoy, but the court case on Wednesday… I have to take the stand."

"Oh God, I didn't have any idea."

"You weren't to know. I only found out on Saturday, so I flew in."

"Flew in from where?" Connor asked as he followed her back to the bedroom, watching her get dressed.

"Billings."

"Montana?" Connor sounded more surprised than he wanted to.

"Yup, I've been living there," Molly replied as she slipped on her shoes. "I left Cali. This is the second time I've been back in a year."

"Wow," Connor said, running a hand through his hair. "I guess I wasn't the only one who ran away."

"Nope," Molly said. "But I guess we were destined to be together, because no one could ever make up what happened at the airport."

Molly glanced over at the man she loved, smiling, taking delight in his unshaven face and messy hair. His strong arms were made for holding her, and if there was one thing she had learned, it was never to question a second chance at love.

"That was crazy, right?" Connor said as he pulled on a pair of jeans. "But I'd take the fist in the face again if it meant I got to see you."

"You are so romantic in a totally unconventional way." Molly giggled.

"That's me, Mr. Unconventional, totally in love with Molly Rice, who has made me the happiest man alive."

Molly all but bounced up into his arms, wrapping her arms around his neck, kissing him hard, lost in the moment of bliss.

"Okay, lover boy, but I really have to go," Molly said as she broke their embrace.

"What are you doing later?" Connor asked as he leaned against the door to his bedroom, unable to take his eyes off his woman.

"Umm, other than my meeting, nothing. I'm free after three."

"Good, because I want you to accompany me to a little thing happening this afternoon."

"What kind of thing?"

Molly felt a small pang of nerves. She wasn't sure she could take any hostility from his mother, yet knew it had to happen sooner, rather than later.

"My godson's first birthday bash."

Molly was surprised. "You've got a godson?"

"Yup, little Ollie."

Molly really had missed so much in the past year. So much had happened, so much growth. A world of change in both their lives, yet they'd never lost that spark that lived on within them, even though they had tried to move on.

"Okay, but the moment your mother pisses me off, I'll sock her one," Molly warned as she smiled. "And I can't wait to meet little Ollie."

"Aww, man, you're going to bust my balls, aren't you?"

Molly laughed. "Well, it all depends on what I want to do with them." She stopped to peck him on the cheek as she walked through his apartment, Connor following her. "So, pick me up around three?"

"You bet," he said as he pulled her in for one last kiss. "You've made me a very happy man."

Resting her head against his, Molly ran her hands up and down his arms. Not wanting to leave, she forced herself to walk to the door. "I love you," she said as her hand rested on the door.

"And that there is a good reason to smile," Connor replied. "I love you more."

Molly opened the door and left the apartment, knowing that that day was the first day of the rest of her life. She now had to think about the hearing, focus on the questions she would be asked. It was then the nerves kicked in.

* * * *

Barry set the file on his desk, looking all businesslike. His face was serious, but he was a professional, and knew that Molly needed a little reassurance.

"Molls, it will be fine, I promise."

Molly sighed. Her palms were wet from nerves. She couldn't help it. The whole point about the meeting was to go over the details, answer the kind of questions the defense would ask, and therein lay the problem. Molly was afraid of addressing the assault. Of addressing her past. Because she knew they would bring that up. Anything to smear her case.

"Will they bring up my past?" she asked.

"I very much doubt it. That has nothing to do with the assault. They will do all kinds of things to unnerve you, discredit you. Which is why you have to be strong, okay?"

Nodding, Molly tried to show him she was ready, but deep down inside she felt sick and wanted to run away. But there was no running from this.

"Okay then, let's start."

The three hours passed by in a haze of questions, answers,

being told not to fidget or lose composure, and Molly was sure she wouldn't make it through the hearing.

Sometimes the tests that life threw her way made her feel as if she was never going to overcome the bad beginnings, but her fight was now stronger. Her will to be happy was the ambition. *Fuck Eugene and his lies,* she thought, because there was no way in hell anything was going to stop her from living her life free from all the pain, bad memories and experiences.

Aggie certainly would have been proud of the fire burning deep in Molly's soul.

Chapter Forty-Five

Connor stood looking at the rings. So many choices, so many stunning shiny diamonds, but he wanted something that was perfect for Molly. He knew she wasn't big on the whole bling thing, and decided that something understated, elegant and beautiful was the way to go.

"These are some of our best for our more elite clients," the attendant said.

"Money isn't a question here," Connor said, sounding more obnoxious than he had planned.

But when he thought about, he did look a little rough around the edges. His five o'clock shadow from Saturday was fast turning into a stubbly mess, which, to be fair, was earning him a few looks of admiration from some of the ladies in the jeweler's.

"Can I see this?" He pointed to a gorgeous platinum solitaire.

"Certainly," the jeweler replied. "This is a classic Cartier design."

"It's gorgeous," Connor replied as he examined the ring. He knew this was the one. It was just perfect. "I'll take this one."

"A wise choice, sir."

Picking out the right ring size was easy for Connor. He was well educated on things like this. Smiling, he waited as the ring was boxed. The excitement was almost hard to contain. He couldn't wait to slip it on her finger, confirming his love for her.

Connor walked away from the shop and couldn't hide his joy. It was evident from the way he grinned. Who would have thought that his trip back home would have led to an unlikely reunion, one that was now leading to marriage?

Knocking at the door, Connor couldn't wait to see her.

Regina opened it, her eyes scanning him. Her reception was frosty. "I guess you'd better come in."

As he stepped inside, Connor felt the awkward atmosphere. It was hostile, but Regina wouldn't give him the satisfaction of being the one to address anything. She was more than happy to make him squirm.

"I'll be right out," Molly called from down the hall.

"Okay, no problem," he replied.

Regina sauntered past him, into the living room, refusing to talk to him. It was up to him to break the silence.

"You know I never meant to hurt her," he said as he sat on the chair across from her.

She shot him a look from over her glasses. It was full of contempt.

"We've worked things out."

"So she told me," Regina said, sounding colder by the second.

"I'm not going to hurt her."

"I vaguely remember you uttering those words once before."

"Regina, give me a break here. I'm trying," he said, feeling as if there was never any way of her trusting him again.

"I'll give you a break when you prove yourself. Molly deserves more than nice words, fancy trips—she needs someone to depend on. Someone who loves her, flaws and all."

Ouch! Her words were mean and cold, but it was true. Molly needed all those things, and Connor was more than willing to do everything in his power to deliver them.

"Then I guess I'll spend the rest of my life proving that to you," he responded.

"Oh, it's not me you need to prove anything to, it's that girl in there. And let me tell you something, sunshine, if as much as a hair on her head is hurt this time, I promise you,

you will never get another chance."

Connor swallowed Regina's warning, understanding firmly where he stood with her.

Molly bounced into the room, looking gorgeous in a blue and white dress, her hair slightly pinned back on one side. A picture of radiance.

"Okay, let's do this," she said holding her hand out to him. "I'm not sure I'll be home tonight, Gina, but I'll give you a call."

"No problem, just have a good time," Regina replied, her eyes glaring at Connor.

"Bye, Regina," he said, breathing a sigh of relief once they left the building.

"Are you okay, you look pale?" Molly asked as he opened the car door for her.

"I think Regina just cut my balls in half and fed them to me."

"Ouch, the third degree?"

Getting into the car, Connor looked over at Molly and smiled. "Basically."

"I knew it." She scowled. "But to be fair, she does have a right."

"So you're gonna bust my balls now?"

"Nope, I'll leave that to later." Molly winked at him.

God, she was everything to him. The way she looked at him was enough to make him mere putty in her hands. She had a profound effect on him and she didn't realize how much he needed her.

"Speaking of later, I've got a surprise for you. He winked at her.

"Oh, God, I hate surprises," Molly complained. "You know that... What is it? Can I have it now?" Her face beamed.

"Nope, I want to give it to you at the right time."

"Ah," Molly said, smiling at him. "You do know that what you think are cryptic clues are actually very easily worked out?" Molly poked fun at him. "I mean, I can pretend that I haven't got a clue, if that makes you happy."

This was exactly what he loved about her. "Damn it, you want it now, right here, in the car, out the front of your home?"

"Yes, give it to me." She giggled. "That sounded like the corniest come-on ever."

"I'll give it to you later all right, but right now," he said as he pulled a small box from the inside pocket of his jacket, "I think your hand is missing something."

Connor grinned when he held the small velvet box in front of Molly. His heart raced as he opened the box.

"Oh, Connor, it's too much," she gasped.

"Nonsense," he said as he lifted the ring out, taking her hand in his. "This is just a small token of my love for you," he said as he slid the ring onto her finger. "Not entirely how I planned on doing this, but… I love you, Molly Rice, and I'm forever yours."

Molly's eyes glistened with tears as she looked down at her hand. "I don't know what to say. It's gorgeous… It's perfect, thank you."

Molly reached over and kissed him, her tongue gently brushing against his, the taste of her mouth igniting the simpering flame in his core. If they had been alone, and not in the car, he'd have shown her exactly how he was feeling.

"I love you too," she whispered, then sat back, admiring her ring. Connor couldn't have been happier.

Smiling, Connor pulled off, knowing that at the end of the evening, he'd get to show her over and over again just how much he loved and craved her.

* * * *

The door to the house opened and Mark gave Connor a huge manly embrace. "About time you showed your sorry ass around here."

"Yeah, yeah. I've someone I'd like you to meet," he replied as he stepped aside and held out his hand to Molly, who looked more nervous than she needed to. "Mark, this is Molly," he introduced her.

"Welcome to the madhouse, Molly, come on in," Mark greeted her, the two of them shaking hands.

"Nice to meet you too," Molly responded.

Connor was happy to see his best friend, and even more happy because he'd accepted Molly into his home.

A beaming Cassie walked down the long hallway toward them, holding the little birthday boy himself.

"Well, look at you, kiddo," Connor said, holding his hands out to the little boy. "What are you feeding him?" he joked as he took the child into his arms.

"Ha ha ha, yeah, this little man loves his food and his mother's specialty," Mark joked.

"Oh, shut up, you idiot." Cassie playfully shot her husband a glare. "Molly, it's so lovely to finally meet you," Cassie said as she embraced Molly, who was beginning to relax in their company.

"He's such a gorgeous little guy," Molly said as she looked at Ollie.

"Thank you, he's a little angel, and completely spoiled," Cassie said as she caught sight of the ring on her hand, and her smile seemed to take on another life.

Leading them through to the garden where other family members and friends had gathered, Cassie didn't waste any time introducing Molly. Everyone was warm and genuine, and more than interested in getting to know the woman who had claimed the heart of Connor.

"She's gorgeous," Mark said to Connor as they stood watching Molly engage with Connor's parents, laughing and being a delight. "And that ring... Someone is serious."

"I've never been more serious in my life. She completes me."

"Well, buddy, if she makes you happy, then we are happy." Mark patted his back. "I just can't wait until your mother hears about this."

Connor laughed, knowing exactly the tsunami that would

come with that, but he didn't care. This was his life and her opinions no longer counted.

"What, she's not here?"

"Nope, something came up," Mark said, rubbing his chin.

"I'm sure she'll be delighted, regardless." Connor laughed.

It was odd. Odd in the sense that never in his wildest dreams did he think that he'd be there, with Molly, at his godson's party. It felt like the most natural thing in the world to him. Molly had gained a confidence that made her so easy to be around, everyone loved her, approved of her, and, more importantly, they had welcomed her into their world with open arms.

"They are so lovely," Molly said as they held hands, walking through the garden.

"Yes, I have to admit that they're not a bad bunch."

Nudging him in the ribs, Molly laughed. "What have I let myself in for?"

"Hmm, a life with me, something you'll not get anywhere else."

"You're such a dork." She grinned.

"Yup, call me El Dorko. I don't mind, I won't take offense."

It was true. She could have called him anything she wanted and he didn't care. Her being there with him, wearing that ring, confirming their relationship was all he needed. It was everything he'd ever wanted.

Chapter Forty-Six

"I feel sick," Molly said as she buttoned her jacket.

"You'll be fine. We'll all be there," Connor replied, trying his best to ease the burden.

"Oh, God, I can't believe I have to face him."

Hands trembling, Molly knew she'd be coming face to face with the man who had beat her in an attempt at raping her. Nothing could take the ill ease away.

"If there was any other way, believe me, I wouldn't be letting that bastard lay his eyes on you again." Connor couldn't help it. He was pissed.

"Regardless of feelings," Barry interrupted, "we need today to proceed without a hitch. If we want justice, then we need a verdict that will put him away."

Molly swallowed hard. Her head pounded, and for the first time in a long while, she courted the temptation of wanting a drink.

"Okay." She sighed. "I can do this."

"Yes, you can," Regina said as she touched her hand. "We will all be there."

"Molly," Jenna said. "We are all here, supporting you because we love you. Don't allow that asshole to unnerve you, okay?"

Molly hugged Jenna. "Thank you."

Connor wrapped his arms around her neck, whispering in her ear, "Be brave, baby."

Molly gave them a wry smile then was escorted to a room where she sat with Barry's assistant, Lenora.

Barry came in one last time, just to make sure she was okay, then he was gone. It was the longest few hours of her life, giving her so much time to overthink, going over the details in her head. A horrid sensation spun in her stomach as she thought about the attack.

The door opened. It was show time.

* * * *

Molly was called into the courtroom, where she was sworn in and took a seat on the stand. Her nerves presented themselves in a sweat patch in the palms of her hands, her stomach churning the whole time.

"Ma'am, would you state your name for the court, please?" Barry asked.

"Molly Rice."

"And how old are you?"

"Twenty-nine," Molly replied, her voice shaking.

"I'm going to direct your attention to the afternoon of Monday, May twenty-second of last year. Were you working at The Sanctuary?"

"Yes."

"And do you recall what time your shift was that day?"

"Yes, I was working the three p.m. to eleven p.m. shift."

"Can you recall who was working with you that day?"

"Yes, I was doing inventory with Regina Burbank. Ashley Slater and Cheryl Saunders were both on site."

"At what point did the accused, Eugene Salter, make an appearance?"

"It was shortly before five p.m. He came to the window of the office, looking for bleach."

At that point, Molly's mind went blank and she found herself back in the basement, unlocking the store, lifting out the bottles of bleach.

"Can you take us through the events that followed Mr. Salter requesting the bleach?"

"I grabbed my keys and went to the basement. We keep all products in locked storage in the basement for inventory purposes. I recalled walking past him, expecting him to stay at the office —" Her voice broke a little. "When I was in the basement, I was just closing the storeroom door when I turned around... Eugene was in front of me. I was initially spooked, not expecting him to be there, but then I became aware that he was masturbating."

The memory turned her stomach.

"Can you describe the events that took place after?"

"I dropped the bleach, trying to make a run for it, but he grabbed me by my hair and hit me..." Her voice broke.

Molly went into great detail, recalling the attack. At times she felt the tears burn her eyes, the need to cry, to vomit. She even wanted to run. Glancing into the crowd, she saw Connor's eyes. They, too, were filled with tears. He placed his hand against his mouth and gave her a reassuring nod. Not once did he flinch. He didn't let her down.

"Can you tell us if the accused is in the court?"

"Yes," Molly replied, then pointed to Eugene, who sat beside his attorney, looking every inch the decrepit human being he was.

When the cross-examination from the defense got well underway, Molly found herself repeating answers over and over. Then Eugene's attorney threw it at her.

"Is it true that you gave my client the come-on?"

"Absolutely not." Molly spat the words.

"Mr. Salter believes that you hinted at meeting him in the basement."

"That's not true."

"Is it also true that you have had a very colorful past?"

"Objection, Your Honor," Barry stormed.

That did it. Molly could feel the anger burn in her stomach. "Being sexually abused as a child does not make a person promiscuous."

The trial lasted longer than she'd expected, having been cross-examined and ripped apart by the defense. As she walked away from the courtroom, she broke down.

She was sick, tired, angry — so many emotions — and there wasn't a thing she could do about it.

Connor held out his arms to her when she saw him. Not wasting a moment, she ran into them, holding on to him for dear life.

"That was horrible," she cried.

"I know, baby," he said, consoling her. "But you did brilliantly."

Barry came out of the court, his face unreadable.

"So?" Connor asked.

"We wait for a verdict," he replied. "Molly, you did well in there. I know it was hard, but I'm proud of you."

Molly didn't know what to say or think, all she knew was that she needed to get as far away as possible from the memory.

It didn't take long before they were called back into the courtroom.

"Is this bad?" Molly whispered to Barry.

Shaking his head, Barry said, "No, this could be in our favor."

The words from the juror made Molly's head dizzy. She couldn't believe it. The past year, everything she had gone through, the entire process had left her mentally exhausted and was finally over.

Barry's face was a picture of relief. Eugene's was one that told her he was pissed as hell and as he was walked out of the court, handcuffed, Molly sat down.

Guilty, she thought over and over, her head fuzzy. "Can I go?" she asked, not wanting to be there any longer.

"Yes, absolutely," Barry replied.

Molly tried her best to smile but couldn't hide the strain the trial had put on her. "Thanks."

Regina was busy wiping her eyes, and Molly could see the pain. "Hey, Gina, I need to get away from this place. Are you okay with that?"

"Oh no, you two do your thing. I've got to drop by the shelter. It's that time of the week again," Regina said, ushering Molly to leave.

"Jenna, thank you so much for being here, as always,"

Molly said as she held Jenna's hand.

Nodding, Jenna hugged her. "That's what family does. Now go on, go be somewhere other than here."

Molly didn't need any convincing, she wanted out of that place.

Once she was inside the safety of Connor's car, she rested her head back, closing her eyes.

"I'm so proud of you," Connor said as he touched the side of her face.

"Connor?"

"Yes."

"Let's not speak of him anymore, not unless we have to, please," Molly whispered.

"If that's what you want, then I can do that for you."

"Thank you."

"Now, where should we go?"

"Maybe it's time you reintroduce me to the in-laws?" She couldn't believe she had suggested it, but there seemed no better time than the present, considering everything she had just gone through.

"Well, that's...unexpected."

"I know. Maybe I'm insane after all," she tried her hand at a joke.

"If you're serious, they'll be at the club," Connor replied, sounding nearly as nervous as she.

"Let's do this."

Connor didn't ask twice, and Molly didn't change her mind.

* * * *

Molly took off her jacket. Taking her hair down, she let it fall loosely around her shoulders. Applying a little gloss, she then pinched her cheeks, much to the amusement of Connor.

"Women!"

"What?" she asked.

"You're gorgeous regardless of the gloss or rosy cheeks," he said, gazing at her.

"That's easy for you to say."

"How so?"

"You're a dude, you have no idea."

"I'm also thankful I've no idea because I think I'd fail miserably as a woman."

"You idiot." Molly laughed.

Molly looked out at the building in front of her and her stomach did a nervous somersault.

Connor pulled up outside the entrance, the passenger door was opened for her, and as she got out, a valet took the keys from Connor, handing him a ticket in return.

"Thank you," Connor said.

"You're welcome, Mr. Ellison."

Molly giggled. It was a mixture of nerves and amusement. "Mr. Ellison, huh?"

Connor wrapped an arm around Molly's waist and pulled her in close to him, kissing the top of her head. "Don't be cheeky."

Walking up the steps and inside the grand doors, Molly couldn't get over the opulence of the main foyer. A waiter, dressed like something out of a period drama, nodded at Connor as he walked them down some steps and out into a vestibule that led to a huge conservatory.

Molly felt as if she were walking into an alien environment. "So this is how the other half lives?" she whispered as Connor led the way to a table, occupied by his parents.

"It's how they pretend the world is perfect and their bank balances remain untouched in some tax haven," Connor joked. "Now, don't be alarmed, but they have company."

Molly had already seen exactly what Connor was referring to, and for a brief moment she wanted to pounce like a wild animal, ready for the kill. But instead, she smiled, remaining demure.

"Mom, Dad," Connor said. "Room for two more?"

John smiled when he saw Molly, immediately standing.

"Of course."

Connor and Molly sat at the table, each one almost as nervous as the other, but holding their ground quite perfectly.

"How nice of you to bring your friend for afternoon tea," Marissa said as she lifted her teacup to her lips, glaring at Molly the whole time.

"Well, actually, we came to share some news," Connor said, looking at Molly with loving eyes.

"How was little Ollie's party?" Eleanor interrupted him. Ignoring Molly's presence. "The little dear is such a sweetie. I was sorry that I couldn't make it, but I had an appointment that couldn't wait."

"Connor proposed and I accepted," Molly blurted out, holding her ring high enough for them all to get a good glimpse of the diamond.

Marissa nearly choked on her tea, coughing as liquid slipped out of her nose. Molly sniggered at her discomfort and took great pleasure in the announcement.

"Well, this is a surprise," John said. "Congratulations. I guess there's only one thing to say — Welcome to the family, Molly."

Molly had never thought she had such determination, but there was a force within her, a glimmer of something that made her stand out from the crowd, and there was no stopping her now. She had come into her own, and, boy, had she grown.

Chapter Forty-Seven

"Isn't this all rather sudden?" Eleanor asked, unable to hide her discomfort. Her hands trembled as she set down her cup.

Eleanor glared at Molly and it was hard for Connor to remain composed. He didn't appreciate the way her eyes ridiculed the woman who was to be his wife.

"Not at all, Mother, it was always going to happen. It just took a little time," Connor replied, wrapping an arm around Molly's shoulders, making sure both Eleanor and Marissa got the message, loud and clear.

"It's ridiculous," Marissa aired her feelings. "Who is she?" she raised her voice. "She doesn't belong here. We are not her people."

Connor reveled in Marissa's contempt for Molly. It proved to him exactly the kind of woman she was. She was loathsome, a user, a sorry excuse for a woman, and he was well and truly done with her and his mother's dire attempts at matchmaking.

"Oh, shut up, you stupid fool," Connor said. "Molly is something you will never be. She has more class than you've ever had, so why don't you do us all a favor and go torment some other sad fucker with your whiny, needy, manipulating ways, because quite frankly, you bore us, and I know you bore the shit out of my father."

Open-mouthed and in shock, Marissa tried to think of a comeback, but it was pointless. She had been put well and truly in her box, and no one was coming to her aid.

"Enjoy her while you can, because from what I hear, she loves nothing better than a good drink. How's the head, darling?" She directed the question to Molly. "Not thirsty, are you?"

"Nope, can't say I am," Molly replied, smiling the whole time. "Connor tends to my thirst these days."

Marissa's face screwed up. Her fingers scraped along the top of the tablecloth, looking more feral by the second.

"Marissa, I think you should leave," John said.

Both Eleanor and Marissa gave him a steely glare. Each one as horrified as the other. Eleanor was about to say something, only to be cut off by John.

"Pipe down, dear, this is our son's life, not ours."

Smiling, Connor reached over and patted his father on the back. "Thanks, Dad."

"You know what?" Marissa shouted. "I thought you'd learned your lesson. But oh no, you go running to an alcoholic gold digger." She glared at Molly as she stood. "You were meant to come to me. I went to so much trouble getting those files into Miller's hands, and for what? Nothing! You make me sick, Connor Ellison. You are nothing but a coward."

The truth finally came out, leaving both Connor and his father stunned. Even Eleanor looked at Marissa in horror.

"It was you?" Connor couldn't believe the revelation, but it all suddenly made sense.

Marissa laughed and threw back her head. "You have no idea the kind of things I can do," she said. "And now you will never have the chance to redeem yourself. You're stained, you let that thing touch you, dig her nails in— you are filth and I will make it my business to ruin you." Marissa walked around the table to where Molly sat, and spat at her.

"You bitch," Connor roared as he stood. "You are everything that is wrong with the world."

"Oh, honey, there are two kinds of people in the world— go-getters," she said, pointing to herself, "or little brain-dead fuckers like her." She pointed at Molly.

Molly wiped Marissa's spittle with a napkin, scraped her

chair back and stood. Marissa slapped her hard across the face, but Molly was on fine form and had made contact with Marissa's face before Connor had the chance to determine what she was doing.

Marissa fell back, stunned and unsteady. "I'll sue you for that."

"Go right ahead, honey, because I've been itching to do that for a while," Molly replied as she sat back down, staring at the faces of the other club members.

"Did anyone see what just happened?" John asked the other patrons.

Many shook their heads, while others went about their business.

Marissa pounced forward, grabbing Molly by the hair, pulling her off the chair and onto the floor. Molly didn't waste a moment as she hit back into Marissa's face, pushing her off her. The two women fought until Connor and a waiter separated them.

"Marissa, I think you need some rest," John said. "I will also be in touch with your father," he warned her. "Kevin?" he called one of the security men. "Can you please escort Ms. Rivers from the building?"

Nodding, the security guard took hold of Marissa's arm and led her away, shouting and cursing, revealing her true colors.

"You will pay for this, Connor Ellison. You'll wish you were dead," Marissa screamed, looking insane in the process. "You and your whore will pay for this."

There were some things in life that could never be explained. Connor's father was one of those things. Yet, through all the darkness, the trepidation, the many months of feeling unwell, his father had stepped up, shown that he could be dependable.

John sat back down and called over one of the waiters. "I think we need some coffee and a sweets menu." Looking over at Molly, he smiled and shook his head. "Where did you learn to hit like that?"

Molly laughed. "I've no idea but she had it coming to her."

At ease, relaxed and over the worst, Connor touched Molly's face, much to the scorn of his mother. But Connor didn't care. It was something she'd have to learn to live with because Molly wasn't going anywhere.

"Now, dear," John said to Molly, "what would you like?"

Connor's smile spread across his face as he watched Molly engage with his father. She was funny, articulate, smart and beautiful. She was the perfect package.

"Have you set a date?" Eleanor asked.

"No, not yet," Molly replied. "We wanted to involve you in the arrangements. Isn't that right, Connor?"

Clearing his throat, Connor was surprised by Molly's attempts at building bridges. "Yes."

"You impressed me with the way you organized and ran the gala, and I suppose there is no better woman," Molly said, smiling the entire time.

Eleanor's face lit up. "Well, yes, I have organized many events in my time. Nothing would give me greater pleasure."

Connor wasn't sure if that was a good or bad thing, but with Molly taking the lead, and controlling things, he was pretty confident that both the women in his life would find a way to compromise.

"Now, how about you show me that ring of yours?" Eleanor beamed. "I hope no expense has been spared." She gave Connor a look, and smiled once she saw the solitaire. "Only the best for an Ellison."

That was it, those were the words that confirmed Molly's acceptance into their empire. It was quite the U-turn, but it was something both Connor and Molly needed.

The remainder of the evening went by successfully, despite Marissa's outburst. Molly fitted in well. Eleanor was on her best behavior, doing her best not to rock the boat, and John was more than happy to indulge in his son's happiness.

Once they were outside, Eleanor and John bade their goodbyes.

"How about dinner on Sunday?" Eleanor asked as she lit a cigarette.

"That would be lovely," Molly replied, smiling as Connor slipped his arm around her waist.

"We'll see you both then," John replied. "Take the rest of the week off. We can discuss things on Sunday."

"Cheers, Dad," Connor replied, and the two men shook hands.

"It was a pleasure, Molly," John said as he kissed her cheek. "See you over the weekend."

Connor and Molly watched as his parents were driven away.

"That was…interesting." Molly laughed.

"You are a feisty little thing, aren't you?" Connor said as he wrapped his arms around her, kissing her lightly as the car pulled up.

"You could say that." Molly giggled as she got into the car.

As they drove away, Molly touched his hand. The stranger who had saved his life. The woman who had opened up his heart and mind to the possibilities. The beautiful girl who'd healed his wounds, helped him discover his true self. Their love was a testament that anything was possible, and together they could overcome the many tribulations that came with life. They were united.

"I think we're going to be happy," she said.

"I agree," he replied as he took her hand, kissing the back of it. "Let's go home."

Connor held on to her hand as they drove away from the country club, away from San Francisco, and to the one place they both felt at peace. Their little haven away from everything, their little piece of heaven.

Epilogue

They stood on the bridge of the boat. Connor steered straight ahead. The warm breeze caressed his skin as though it were leaving soft kisses against his face. The heat from the sun, the glimmer of the stretch of sea — everything that made it their little piece of heaven.

Their love was the irresistible kind. It was a union of endless promises, where a tender look became a daily habit. A kiss on the lips became a ritual. The touch of their flesh uniting their souls for many lifetimes over. Their love made their spirits crawl out from the darkness of their pasts, replacing all the hurt and pain with something that completed them.

Molly came up from below deck, carrying a plate of sandwiches. Molly stood next to Connor and grinned as she rested her head against his arm.

"Let's stay out here forever," she said.

Wrapping an arm around her shoulder, Connor kissed the side of her head. "I would love nothing more than that."

Molly giggled, glancing up at him.

"Then how about we extend this trip by a few days?"

"I think that could be arranged."

They stood together, saying nothing. Just embracing the beauty of being free and enjoying the gift that life had given them.

Molly let out a little gasp then took Connor's hand, resting it on her swollen abdomen. The little flutter of movement swarmed through her womb, little bubbles popping.

"Someone is happy," Molly said as she held Connor's hand against her.

"Who'd blame him?"

"Her!" Molly giggled.

"It's a boy, I can feel it in my bones," Connor said, grinning as if he'd won the jackpot.

"Excuse me, but you have no more say in the sex of the baby than I do. So pipe down." Molly laughed, trying to be serious.

Kissing her, Connor ran his hand up, tracing the outline of her breasts, giving them a playful squeeze. "I still say boy." Connor chuckled and held on to Molly as he steered the boat, the horizon of the hazy blue water welcoming them.

Who would have thought a bad day, a hasty decision, a chance encounter would result in two people coming together, creating a little life of their own.

Happiness comes in many forms, and for Connor and Molly Ellison, it was a life where their joy became a deep-rooted realization that everything would be okay. It was the kind of freedom where they would go through life without the weight of the burdens that once controlled their every waking moment.

They were free.

They were happy.

They were one.

They were complete.

About the Author

Julieanne Lynch

Julieanne Lynch is an author of YA and Adult genre urban fantasy, crime and contemporary romance books. Julieanne was born in Northern Ireland, but spent much of her early life in London, United Kingdom, until her family relocated back to their roots.

Julieanne lives in Northern Ireland, with her husband and five children, where she is a full-time author. She studied English Literature and Creative Writing at The Open University and considered journalism as a career path. Julieanne has several projects optioned for film.

You can take a look at Julieanne's Website, read her Blog and follow her on Facebook and Twitter.

Julieanne Lynch loves to hear from readers. You can find contact information, website details and an author profile page at https://www.totallybound.com/

Home of Erotic Romance